THE RAINBOW TROOPS

(Laskar Pelangi)

The Rainbow Troops

Andrea Hirata

TRANSLATED FROM THE INDONESIAN
BY ANGIE KILBANE

HARPERCOLLINS PUBLISHERS LTD

The Rainbow Troops
Copyright © 2005 by Andrea Hirata
Translation copyright © 2009 by Andrea Hirata
All rights reserved.

Published by HarperCollins Publishers Ltd, by arrangement with Farrar, Straus, and Giroux, LLC

Originally published in Indonesian in 2005 by Bentang Pustaka, Indonesia, as *Laskar Pelangi*. English translation originally published, in slightly different form, in 2009 by Bentang Pustaka, Indonesia. First published in the United States in 2013 by Sarah Crichton Books / Farrar, Straus and Giroux. First published in Canada by HarperCollins Publishers Ltd in this original trade paperback edition: 2013.

First Canadian edition

No part of this book may be used or reproduced in any manner whatsoever without the prior written permission of the publisher, except in the case of brief quotations embodied in reviews.

HarperCollins books may be purchased for educational, business, or sales promotional use through our Special Markets Department.

HarperCollins Publishers Ltd
2 Bloor Street East, 20th Floor
Toronto, Ontario, Canada
M4W 1A8

www.harpercollins.ca

Library and Archives Canada Cataloguing in Publication information
Hirata, Andrea
The rainbow troops / Andrea Hirata.
Translation of: Laskar pelangi.

ISBN 978-1-44341-575-0

I. Title.
PL5089.H57L3713 2013   899'.22133   C2012-906104-2

Designed by Abby Kagan
Printed and bound in the United States
RRD 10 9 8 7 6 5 4 3 2 1

To my mother, N. A. Masturah Seman,

and my father, Seman Said Harun;

to my teachers, Ibu Muslimah Hafsari and

Bapak Harfan Effendy Noor, and my

ten childhood best friends, the members of

Laskar Pelangi—the Rainbow Troops

THE RAINBOW TROOPS

1 ✿ TEN NEW STUDENTS

That morning, when I was just a boy, I sat on a long bench outside a school. The branch of an old filicium tree shaded me. My father sat beside me, hugging my shoulders as he nodded and smiled to each parent and child sitting on the bench in front of us. It was an important day: the first day of elementary school.

At the end of those long benches was an open door, and inside was an empty classroom. The doorframe was crooked. The entire school, in fact, leaned as if it would collapse at any moment. In the doorway stood two teachers, like hosts welcoming guests to a party. There was an old man with a patient face, Bapak K. A. Harfan Effendy Noor, or Pak Harfan—the school principal—and a young woman wearing a *jilbab*, or headscarf, Ibu N. A. Muslimah Hafsari, or Bu Mus for short. Like my father, they were smiling.

Yet Bu Mus's smile was a forced smile: she was apprehensive. Her face was tense and twitching nervously. She kept counting the number of children sitting on the long benches, so worried that she didn't even care about the sweat pouring down onto her eyelids. The sweat smudged her powder makeup, streaking her face and making her look like the queen's servant in *Dul Muluk*, an ancient play in our village.

"Nine people, just nine, Pamanda Guru, still short one," she said anxiously to the principal. Pak Harfan stared at her with an empty look in his eyes.

I, too, felt anxious. Anxious because of the restless Bu Mus, and because of the sensation of my father's burden spreading over my entire body. Although he seemed at ease this morning, his rough arm hanging around my neck gave away his quick heartbeat. It wasn't easy for a forty-seven-year-old miner with a lot of children and a small salary to send his son to school. It would have been much easier to send me to work as a helper for a Chinese grocery stall at the market, or to the coast to work as a coolie to help ease the family's financial burdens. Sending a child to school meant tying oneself to years of costs, and for our family that was no easy matter.

My poor father.

I didn't have the heart to look him in the eye.

My father wasn't the only one trembling. The faces of the other parents showed that their thoughts, like my father's, were drifting off to the morning market as they imagined their sons better off as workers. These parents weren't convinced that their children's education, which they could afford only up to junior high, would brighten their families' futures. This morning they were forced to be at this school, either to avoid reproach from government officials for not sending their children to school, or to submit to modern demands to free their children from illiteracy.

I knew all of the parents and children sitting in front of me—except for one small dirty boy with curly red hair, trying to wriggle free from his father's grasp. His father wasn't wearing shoes and had on cheap cotton pants.

The rest of them were my good friends. Like Trapani sitting

on his mother's lap, or Kucai sitting next to his father, or Sahara, who earlier had gotten very angry at her mother because she wanted to go into the classroom quickly, or Syahdan, who wasn't accompanied by anyone. We were neighbors, Belitong-Malays from the poorest community on the island. As for this school, Muhammadiyah Elementary, it, too, was the poorest, the poorest village school in Belitong. There were only three reasons why parents enrolled their children here. First, Muhammadiyah Elementary didn't require any fees, and parents could contribute whatever they could afford whenever they could do so. Second, parents feared that their children had weak character and could easily be led astray by the devil, so they wanted them to have strong Islamic guidance from a young age. Third, their children weren't accepted at any other school.

Bu Mus, who was growing increasingly fretful, stared at the main road, hoping there would still be another new student. Seeing her empty hope scared us. The South Sumatra Department of Education and Culture had issued a warning: If Muhammadiyah Elementary School had fewer than ten new students, then it, the oldest school in Belitong, would be shut down. Therefore Bu Mus and Pak Harfan were worried about being shut down, the parents were worried about expenses, and we—the nine small children caught in the middle—were worried we may not get to go to school at all.

Last year Muhammadiyah Elementary had only eleven students. Pak Harfan was pessimistic this year. He had secretly prepared a school-closing speech.

"We will wait until eleven o'clock," Pak Harfan said to Bu Mus and the already hopeless parents. We were silent. Bu Mus's face was puffy from holding back tears. Today was her first day as a teacher, a moment she had been dreaming of for a very long time. She had just graduated from Sekolah Kepandaian Putri

(Vocational Girls' School), a junior high school in the capital of the regency, Tanjong Pandan. She was only fifteen. She stood like a statue under the bell, staring out at the wide schoolyard and the main road. No one appeared. The sun rose higher to meet the middle of the day. Waiting for one more student was like trying to catch the wind.

The other children and I felt heartbroken. Our heads hung low.

At five till eleven, Bu Mus could no longer hide her dejection. Her big dreams for this poor school were about to fall apart before they could even take off, and thirty-two faithful years of Pak Harfan's unrewarded service were about to come to a close.

"Just nine people, Pamanda Guru," Bu Mus said. She wasn't thinking clearly, repeating the same thing everyone already knew.

Finally, time was up. It was already five after eleven and the total number of students still did not equal ten. I took my father's arm off of my shoulders. Sahara sobbed in her mother's embrace. She wore socks and shoes, a *jilbab*, a blouse, and she also had books, a water bottle, and a backpack—all were new.

Pak Harfan went up to the parents and greeted them one by one. It was devastating. The parents patted him on the back to console him, and Bu Mus's eyes glistened as they filled with tears. Pak Harfan prepared to give his final speech. When he went to utter his first words, *"Assalamu alaikum.* Peace be upon you," Trapani yelled and pointed to the edge of the schoolyard, startling everyone.

"Harun!"

We turned to look. Off in the distance was a tall, skinny boy, clumsily headed our way. His clothes and hairstyle were very neat. He wore a long-sleeved white shirt tucked into his shorts. His knees knocked together when he moved, forming an X as his body wobbled along. A plump middle-aged woman was trying with great difficulty to hold on to him. That boy was Harun, a funny boy and a good friend of ours. He was already fifteen years old, the same age as Bu Mus, but a bit behind mentally. He was extremely happy and half running, as if he couldn't wait to get to us. His mother stumbled after him, trying to hold on to his hand.

They were both nearly out of breath when they arrived in front of Pak Harfan.

"Bapak Guru," said his mother, gasping for breath. "Please accept Harun. The special-needs school is all the way on Bangka Island. We don't have the money to send him there. And more importantly, it's better that he's here at this school rather than at home, where he just chases my chicks around."

Harun smiled widely, showing his long yellow teeth.

Pak Harfan was smiling, too. He looked over to Bu Mus and shrugged. "It makes ten," he said.

Harun had saved us! We clapped and cheered. Sahara, who couldn't sit any longer, stood up straight to fix the folds on her *jilbab* and firmly threw on her backpack. Bu Mus blushed. Her tears subsided, and she wiped the sweat from her powder-smudged face.

2 ❁ THE PINE-TREE MAN

Bu Mus looked like a budding giant Himalayan lily—her veil had a lily's soft white color, and her clothes even gave off the flower's vanilla aroma. She went up to each parent seated on the long benches, striking up friendly conversations before taking roll call. Everyone had already entered the classroom and gotten their deskmates, except for me and that small dirty boy with the curly red hair whom I didn't know. He could not sit still, and he smelled like burned rubber.

"Pak Cik, your son will share a desk with Lintang," Bu Mus said to my father.

Oh, so that was his name, Lintang. What a strange name.

Hearing the decision, Lintang wriggled free, pulling away from his father's grasp, then jumped up and rushed into the class to find his seat on his own. He was like a little kid sitting on a pony—delighted, not wanting to get down. He had just leapt over fate and grabbed education by the horns.

Bu Mus approached Lintang's father. He resembled a pine tree struck by lightning: black, withered, thin, and stiff. He was a fisherman, but his face was like that of a kind shepherd, showing he was a gentle, good-hearted, and hopeful man. Unlike other fishermen, he spoke softly. However, like most Indonesians, he wasn't aware that education was a basic human right.

Lintang's family was from Tanjong Kelumpang, a village not far from the edge of the sea. In order to get there, you had to pass through four thatch palm areas, swampy places that were hair-raising for people from our village. In those spooky palm areas, it wasn't uncommon to encounter a crocodile as large as a coconut tree crossing the road. Lintang's coastal village was in the easternmost part of Sumatra and could be said to be the most isolated and impoverished part of Belitong Island. For Lintang, the city district of our school was like a metropolitan city, and to get there he had to begin his bicycle journey at Subuh, the early-morning prayer, around four a.m.

Without a doubt, all previous generations of men from his family were unable to lift themselves from poverty, inevitably becoming fishermen in the Malay community. These fishermen were unable to work for themselves—not for lack of sea but for lack of boats. This year Lintang's father wanted to break that cycle. His eldest son, Lintang, would not become a fisherman like himself. Instead, Lintang would sit beside the other small boy with curly hair—me—and would ride a bike to and from school every day. If his true calling was to be a fisherman, then the forty-kilometer journey over a red gravel road would break his determination. That burned smell I noticed earlier was actually the smell of his *cunghai* sandals, made from car tires. They were worn down because Lintang had pedaled his bicycle for so long. Ah! A child that small . . .

When I caught up to Lintang inside the classroom, he greeted me with a strong handshake. He talked without stopping, full of interest, in an amusing Belitong dialect, typical of those from remote areas. His eyes lit up as he glanced animatedly around the room. He was like an artillery plant. When drops of water fall on its petals, it shoots out pollen—glittering, blossoming, and full of life.

Bu Mus then gave out forms for all of the parents to write their names, occupations, and addresses. Each parent was busy filling out the form except for Lintang's father. The form was like an alien object in his hands. He stood up with a puzzled expression.

"Ibu Guru," he said slowly, "forgive me, I cannot read or write."

Lintang's father then added plaintively that he did not even know the year of his own birth. Suddenly Lintang got up from his seat and went over to his father, took the form from his hands, and exclaimed, "I will be the one to fill out this form later, Ibunda Guru, after I have learned how to read and write!"

Everyone was startled to see Lintang, such a small child, defending his father. His head was spinning around like an owl's. For him, the miscellany of our classroom—a wooden ruler, a sixth-grade student's clay vase art project sitting on Bu Mus's desk, the old-fashioned chalkboard, and the chalk scattered about on the classroom floor, some of which had already been ground back into dust—was absolutely amazing.

The pine-tree man watched his son grow increasingly excited with a bittersweet smile. I understood. This was a man who didn't even know his own birthday, imagining his son's broken heart if he had to drop out in the first or second year of junior high for the classic reasons of money or the unfair demands of life. For him, education was an enigma.

That morning would stay with me for dozens of years. That morning I saw Lintang clumsily grasping a large unsharpened pencil as if holding a large knife. His father had bought him the wrong kind of pencil. It was two different colors, one end red and the other blue. Wasn't that the kind of pencil tailors used to make marks on clothing? Or shoemakers to mark the leather? Whatever kind of pencil it was, it definitely was not for writing.

The book he'd bought was also the wrong kind of book. It had a dark blue cover and was three-lined. Wasn't that the kind of book we would use in second grade, when we learned how to write in cursive? But the thing I will never forget is that, on that morning, I witnessed a boy from the coast, my deskmate, hold a book and pencil for the very first time. And in the years to come, everything he would write would be the fruit of a bright mind, and every sentence he spoke would act as a radiant light. And as time went on, that impoverished coastal boy would outshine the dark nimbus cloud that had for so long overshadowed this school as he evolved into the most brilliant person I've ever met in all the years of my life.

3 ❁ GLASS DISPLAY CASE

It isn't very hard to describe our school. It was one among hundreds—maybe even thousands—of poor schools in Indonesia that, if bumped by a frenzied goat preparing to mate, would collapse and fall to pieces.

We had only two teachers for all subjects and grades. We didn't have uniforms. We didn't even have a toilet. Our school was built on the edge of a forest, so when nature called, all we had to do was slip off into the bushes. There was also an outhouse, but our teacher would have to accompany us there because snakes lurked inside.

We didn't have a first-aid kit, either. When we were sick, whatever it was—diarrhea, swelling, cough, flu, itching—the teacher gave us a large round pill that resembled a raincoat button. It was white and tasted bitter, and after taking it, you felt full. There were three large letters on the pill: APC—aspirin, phenacetin, and caffeine. The APC pill was legendary throughout the outskirts of Belitong as a magic medicine that could cure any illness. This generic cure-all was the government's solution to make up for the underallocation of health-care funds for the poor.

Our school was rarely visited by officials, school administrators, or members of the legislative assembly. The only routine visitor was a man dressed like a ninja. He wore a large aluminum tube on his back, and a hose trailed behind him. He looked like he was going to the moon. This man was sent by the Department of Health to spray for mosquitoes with chemical gas. Whenever the thick white puffs arose like smoke signals, we cheered and shouted with joy.

Our school wasn't guarded because there wasn't anything worth stealing. A yellow bamboo flagpole was the only thing that indicated this was a school building. A green chalkboard displaying a sun with white rays hung crookedly from the flagpole. Written in the middle was:

SD MD
Sekolah Dasar Muhammadiyah

There was a sentence written in Arabic directly under the sun. After I mastered Arabic in the second grade, I knew the sentence read, *Amar makruf nahi mungkar,* meaning, "Do what is good and prevent what is evil"—the primary principle of Muhammadiyah, the second largest Islamic organization in Indonesia, with more than thirty million members. Those words were ingrained in our souls and remained there throughout the journey to adulthood; we knew them like the back of our own hands.

When seen from afar, our school looked like it was about to tumble over. The old wooden beams were slanted, unable to endure the weight of the heavy roof. It resembled a copra shed. The construction of the building hadn't followed proper architectural principles. The windows and door couldn't be locked because they were not symmetrical with their frames, but they never needed to be locked anyway.

The atmosphere inside the classroom could be described with words like these: *underutilized*, *astonishing*, and *bitterly touching*. Underutilized, among other things, was a decrepit glass display case with a door that wouldn't stay closed. A wedge of paper was the only thing that could keep it shut. Inside a proper classroom, such a display case usually held photos of successful alumni or of the principal with ministers of education, or vice principals with vice ministers of education; or it would be used to display plaques, medals, certificates, and trophies of the school's prestigious achievements. But in our classroom, the big glass display case stood untouched in the corner. It was a pathetic fixture completely void of content because no government officials wanted to visit our teachers, there were no graduates to be proud of, and we certainly hadn't achieved anything prestigious yet.

Unlike other elementary school classrooms, there were no multiplication tables inside our classroom. We also had no calendar. There wasn't even a picture of the president and vice president of Indonesia or our state symbol—the strange bird with an eight-feathered tail always looking to the right. The one thing we had hanging up in our class was a poster. It was directly behind Bu Mus's desk, and it was there to cover up a big hole in one of the wall planks. The poster showed a man with a dense beard. He wore a long, flowing robe and had a guitar stylishly slung over his shoulder. His melancholic eyes were aflame, as if he had already experienced life's tremendous trials, and he appeared truly determined to oppose all wickedness on the face of this earth. He was sneaking a peek at the sky, and a lot of money was falling down toward his face. He was Rhoma Irama, the dangdut singer, a Malay backcountry idol—our Elvis Presley. On the bottom of the poster were two statements that, when I first started school, I could not comprehend. But in second grade, when I could read, I learned that it shouted: RHOMA IRAMA, HUJAN DUIT! Rhoma Irama, rain of money!

Imagine the worst possible problems for an elementary school classroom: a roof with leaks so large that students see planes flying in the sky and have to hold umbrellas while studying on rainy days; a cement floor continually decomposing into sand; strong winds that shake the students' souls with the fear of their school collapsing; and students who want to enter the class but first have to usher goats out of the room. We experienced all of these things.

4 ⚙ GRIZZLY BEAR

Like our school, Pak Harfan is easy to describe. His thick mustache was connected to a dense brown beard, dull and sprinkled with gray. His face, in short, was a bit scary.

If anyone asked Pak Harfan about his tangled beard, he wouldn't bother giving an explanation but instead would hand them a copy of a book titled *Keutamaan Memelihara Jenggot*, or *The Excellence of Caring for a Beard*. Reading the introduction alone was enough to make anyone ashamed of having asked the question to begin with.

On this first day, Pak Harfan wore a simple shirt that at some point must have been green but was now white. The shirt was still shadowed by faint traces of color. His undershirt was full of holes, and his pants were faded from being washed one too many times. The cheap braided plastic belt hugging his body had many notches—he probably had worn it since he was a teenager. For the sake of Islamic education, Pak Harfan had been serving the Muhammadiyah School for dozens of years without payment. He supported his family from a crop garden in the yard of their home.

Because Pak Harfan looked quite like a grizzly bear, small

children would throw fits at the sight of him. But almost immediately he won our hearts. We were spellbound by his every word and gesture. There was a gentle influence and goodness about him. His demeanor was that of a wise, brave man who had been through life's bitter difficulties, had knowledge as vast as the ocean, was willing to take risks, and was genuinely interested in explaining things in ways that others could understand.

Even that first day, we could tell Pak Harfan was in his element in front of the students. He was a guru in the true sense of the word, its Hindi meaning: a person who not only transfers knowledge but who also is a friend and spiritual guide for his students. He often raised and lowered his intonation, holding the edges of his desk while emphasizing certain words and then throwing up both hands like someone performing a rain dance.

When we asked questions in class, he would run toward us with small steps, staring at us meaningfully with his calm eyes as if we were the most precious of Malay children. He whispered into our ears, fluently recited poetry and Koranic verses, and then fell silent, like one daydreaming about a long-lost love.

Our first lesson from Pak Harfan was about standing firmly with conviction and a strong desire to reach our dreams. He convinced us that life could be happy even in poverty, so long as, with spirit, one gave rather than took as much as one could.

When he spoke, we listened, fixed in enchantment and observing intently, impatiently waiting for his next string of words. I felt unbelievably lucky to be there, amid these amazing people. There was a beauty in this poor school, a beauty that I wouldn't trade for a thousand luxurious schools.

Bu Mus then took over the class. Introductions. One by one, each student came forward and introduced him- or herself. Finally it was A Kiong's turn. He was asked to come up to the front of the room, and he was delighted. In between sobs, he smiled.

"Please say your name and address," Bu Mus tenderly told the Hokkien child.

A Kiong stared hesitantly at Bu Mus and then went back to smiling. His father made his way up through the crowd of parents, wanting to see his child in action. However, even though he had been asked repeatedly, A Kiong did not say one word. He just continued smiling.

"Go ahead," Bu Mus nudged once more.

A Kiong answered only with his smile. He kept glancing at his father, who appeared to be growing more impatient by the second. I could read his father's mind: *Come on, son, strengthen your heart and say your name! At least say your father's name, just once! Don't shame the Hokkiens!* The Chinese father had a friendly face. He was a farmer, the lowest status in the social ranks of Chinese in Belitong.

Bu Mus coaxed him one last time. "Okay, this is your last chance to introduce yourself. If you aren't ready yet, then you need to return to your seat."

But instead of showing dejection at his failure to answer, A Kiong became even happier. He didn't say anything at all. His smile was wide and his chipmunk cheeks flushed with color. Lesson number two: Don't ask the name and address of someone who lives on a farm.

And so ended the introductions in that memorable month of February.

5 ⚙ FLO

Belitong Island

The small island of Belitong is the richest island in Indonesia. It is part of Sumatra, but because of its wealth it has alienated itself. There, on that remote island, ancient Malay culture crept in from Malacca, and a secret was hidden in its land, until it eventually was discovered by the Dutch. Deep under the swampy land, a treasure flowed: tin. Blessed tin. A handful was worth more than dozens of buckets of rice.

If one plunged his arm down into the shallow alluvial surface, or pretty much anywhere at all, it would reemerge shimmering, smeared with tin. Seen from off the coast, Belitong beamed of shiny tin, like a lighthouse guiding ship captains.

The tin shone late into the night. Large-scale tin exploitation constantly took place under thousands of lights using millions of kilowatts of energy.

And blessed is the land where tin flows, because tin is always accompanied by other materials: clay, xenotime, zirconium, gold, silver, topaz, galena, copper, quartz, silica, granite, monazite, ilmenite, siderite, and hematite. We even had uranium. Layers of riches sat below the stilted houses where we lived our deprived lives. We, the natives of Belitong, were like a pack of starving rats in a barn full of rice.

The Estate

That great natural resource was exploited by a company called PN Timah. *PN* stands for Perusahaan Negeri, or "state-owned company"; *Timah* means "tin."

PN operated sixteen dredges. The enterprise absorbed almost the entire island's workforce.

The dredges' steel bowls were as long as football fields, and nothing could stand in their way. They smashed coral reefs, took down trees with trunks the size of small houses, demolished brick buildings with one blow, and completely pulverized an entire village. They roamed over mountain slopes, fields, valleys, seas, lakes, rivers, and swamps. Their dredging sounded like roaring dinosaurs.

We often made foolish bets, like how many minutes it would take a dredge to turn a hill into a field. The loser would have to walk home from school backward. We would follow along, beating on tambourines while he waddled backward like a penguin.

The Indonesian government took over PN from the colonial Dutch. And not only the assets were seized but also the feudalistic mentality. Even after Indonesia gained its freedom, PN's treatment of its native employees remained very discriminatory. The treatment differed based on castelike groups.

The highest caste was occupied by PN executives. They usually were referred to as *Staff*. The lowest caste was made up of none other than our parents, who worked for PN as pipe carriers, hard laborers sifting tin, or daily paid laborers. Because Belitong had already become a corporate village, PN slowly assumed the form of a hegemony. It was like feudalism: the caste of a PN worker followed him into nonworking hours.

The Staff—almost none of whom were Belitong-Malays—lived in an elite area called the Estate. This area was tightly guarded by security, fences, high walls, and harsh warnings posted everywhere in three languages: formal colonial-style Indonesian, Chinese, and Dutch. The warnings read NO ENTRY FOR THOSE WITHOUT THE RIGHT.

In our eyes—the eyes of poor village children—the Estate looked like it said: *Keep your distance.* That impression was reinforced by a row of tall pinnate trees dropping blood-red pellets on the roofs of the expensive cars piled up at the garage exit.

The luxurious houses of the Estate were built in the Victorian style. Their curtains were layered and resembled movie theater screens. Inside, small families lived peacefully, with two, maybe three children at the most. The houses were always peaceful, dark, and hushed.

The Estate was located on a high curve of land, giving the Victorian houses the appearance of nobles' castles. Each house consisted of four separate structures: the main chambers, the servants' quarters, the garage, and the storage unit. All of them were connected by long, open terraces encircling a small pond. Blue water lilies floated around the edge of the pond. In the center stood a statue of a potbellied child, the legendary Belgian peeing mannequin that always sprayed water out of its embarrassingly funny little piece.

The living rooms were filled with antique furniture, such as Victorian rosewood sofas. Sitting on these things, one felt like an exalted king. Expensive, abstruse paintings hung on the walls. My friend, if you were trying to get from the living room to the dining room and you weren't paying attention, you would get lost because of the abundance of doors in these houses.

The occupants of the houses ate dinner wearing their best clothes—they even put on their shoes for the meal. After placing their napkins on their laps, they ate without making a peep while listening to classical music, maybe Mozart's Haffner No. 35 in D Major. And no one put their elbows on the table.

On this serene night, the atmosphere of the Estate was very still. There was almost utter silence. The sound of a piano escaped from one of the tall-pillared Victorian homes. A small tomboy, Floriana, or Flo for short, was having a piano lesson. Unfortunately, she was a bit drowsy. Her chin rested on both of her hands, and she yawned over and over again. She was like a cat that had had too much sleep.

Her father, a Mollen Bas, head of all the dredges, sat beside her. He was infuriated by her behavior and embarrassed in front of the private piano teacher, a middle-aged, well-mannered Javanese woman.

Flo's father was capable of managing the shifts of thousands of workers, competent in solving the most difficult of technical problems, successful in overseeing million-dollar assets, but when faced with this small girl, his youngest, he just about gave up. The louder Flo's father scolded her, the wider her yawns became.

The private teacher started with the notations do, mi, so, ti, moving across four octaves, showing the finger position for each notation. Flo yawned again.

The PN School

The PN School was in the Estate compound, and it was a *center of excellence*, a place for the best. Hundreds of qualified students competed at the highest standard at this school, and one of them was Flo.

The difference between this school and ours was like the difference between land and sky. The PN School classrooms were adorned with educational cartoons, basic math tables, the periodic table, world maps, thermometers, photos of the president and vice president, and the heroic national symbol—which included that strange bird with the eight-feathered tail. There also were anatomy sculptures, big globes, and models of the solar system. They didn't use chalk but smelly markers, because their chalkboard was white.

"They have a lot of teachers," Bang Amran Isnaini, who once attended school there, informed me the night before my first day at Muhammadiyah Elementary. "Each subject has its own separate teacher, even when you are in first grade."

I couldn't sleep that night, I was so dizzy trying to count how many teachers the PN School had—and also, of course, because I was so excited about starting school the next day.

The PN School was Belitong's most discriminating club. On the first day of school, dozens of cars lined up out front. Hundreds of students were measured for not just one but three different uniforms. On Mondays they wore blue shirts with a beautiful floral print. And they were picked up by a blue school bus. Seeing the PN School students get off of the bus reminded me of a picture of a group of small, cute, white, and winged children floating off clouds in the Christian calendars.

The school accepted only children of the Staff who lived in the Estate. There was an official rule that regulated which rank of employees could enroll their children at the PN School. And, of course, on the gate hung that warning not to enter unless you had the right.

This meant that the children of fishermen, pipe carriers, hard laborers sifting tin, or daily paid laborers—like our parents—and especially native children of Belitong didn't have the least opportunity to receive a good education. If they wanted to go to school, they were forced to join the Muhammadiyah village school, which, if caressed by just a little bit of strong wind, could fall apart.

This was the most ironic thing in our lives: the glory of the Estate and the glamour of the PN School were funded cent by cent from the tin that was scraped out of our homeland. The Estate was a Belitong landmark built to continue the dark dream of spreading colonization. Its goal was to give power to a few people to oppress many, to educate a few people in order to make the others docile.

6 ❂ THOSE WITHOUT THE RIGHT

Without a doubt, if one were to zoom out, our village would appear to be the richest village in the world. The number of mines sprawled across the land was unimaginable, and trillions of rupiah were invested here. Yet, zooming back in, the wealth of the island was visibly trapped in one place, piled up inside the fortress walls of the Estate.

Just an arm's length outside of those fortress walls spanned a strikingly contradictory sight, like a chicken sitting next to a peacock. There lived the native Belitong-Malays, and if they didn't have eight children, they weren't done trying. They blamed the government for not providing them with enough entertainment, so at night they had nothing to do besides make children.

It would be an exaggeration to call our village a slum, but it would not be wrong to say it was a laborers' village, shadowed by an endless eclipse since the dawn of the industrial revolution. Belitong Island, one of the first places in Indonesia occupied by the Dutch, had been oppressed for seven generations when suddenly, in the blink of an eye, hundreds of years of misery were drenched in one night by a rain of torment: the arrival of the Japanese.

After three hundred fifty years, the Dutch said "good day" and the Japanese yelled "sayonara." Unfortunately, that wasn't the happy ending for us, the natives of Belitong. Our land was seized once again, but in a more *civilized* manner. We were freed, but not yet free.

From our yard, we could see the Estate's walls.

Our yard, overgrown with shrubs, velvetleaf, and shoe flowers, was boring. Our crisscrossed fence, which leaned over the edge of ditches filled with still, brown water and mosquito nests, was also boring.

Our stilted, worn-out house was crammed into the same area as the police station, the PN logistics building, Chinese temples, the village office, the religious affairs office, dorms for dock coolies, sailors' barracks, the water tower, Chinese-Malay stores, dozens of coffee *warung*—traditional roadside stalls—and pawnshops always full of visitors. At the edge of the village, tucked away in a corner, was the longhouse of the Sawang Tribe. Their house was long, and so is their story—which I promise to tell you later.

The Chinese-Malays, as they sometimes are called, have lived on the island for a long time. They were first brought to Belitong by the Dutch to be tin laborers. Most of them were Khek from Hakka, Hokkien from Fukien, Thongsans, Ho Phos, Shan Tungs, and Thio Cius. That tough ethnic community developed their own techniques for manually mining tin. Their terms for these techniques, *aichang*, *phok*, *kiaw*, and *khaknai*, are still spoken by Malay tin prospectors to this day.

As for the Malays, they lived like puppets—controlled by a small and comical but very powerful puppet master called a siren.

At seven o'clock every morning, the stillness shattered. The siren roared from the PN central office. Immediately PN coolies bustled about, emerging from every corner of the village to line up along the side of the road, jumping and jamming themselves into the backs of trucks which would bring them to the dredges.

The village fell quiet again. But moments later, an orchestra emerged as the women began crushing their spices. The sounds of pestles pounding against wooden mortars echoed from one stilted house to another, but when the clock struck five, the siren shrieked again. The coolies dispersed to go home. And that's how it went on, for hundreds of years.

My father said our family was still fortunate.

One of the extraordinary qualities of Malays is that no matter how bad their circumstances, they always consider themselves fortunate. That is the use of religion.

I remember something my father told me a few days before my first day of school. "My son, Muhammadiyah teachers like Pak Harfan and Bu Mus, fishermen, oil workers, coconut workers, and dam keepers live in such poor conditions. You must be grateful to Allah for what we have."

That was the first time I had heard Bu Mus's name.

Then my father said that he heard that she, the new young Muhammadiyah teacher, wanted to teach so village children could get an education.

That was the first time I accepted Bu Mus into my heart as a heroine.

Sahara, me, Kucai, Trapani, Harun, and Mahar were the children of PN coolies. Lintang was the son of a fisherman, Borek was the son of a dam keeper, Syahdan was the son of a boat caulker, and A Kiong was the son of a Chinese farmer.

If we say the families of Sahara, me, Kucai, Trapani, Harun, and Mahar were the jump rope of poverty, then the families of Lintang, Borek, Syahdan, and A Kiong played jump rope. When the winds were calm, they reaped a nice profit from shellfish and tapped rubber trees and were above the rope, having a little more money than we did. But during the prolonged rainy season, they were below the jump rope of poverty and barely scraped by as the poorest of the poor on the island.

And despite our varying degrees of poverty, there was someone even poorer than all of us, and she wanted to be our teacher. I couldn't wait to meet the young girl my father had mentioned.

"Call me Bu Mus," she said proudly, as if she had waited her whole life to utter those words. It was her first day teaching.

Bu Mus had just graduated from SKP (Vocational Girls' School), which was equivalent only to junior high school. It wasn't a teaching school but more of a school to prepare young women to be good wives. There, they learned how to cook, embroider, and sew. Bu Mus had been determined to go to the regency capital, Tanjong Pandan, to go to school at SKP so she could get a higher-level diploma than that offered by the elementary school where she would teach.

Upon graduating from SKP, she was offered a job with PN as the rice warehouse head secretary—a very promising position. She had even been proposed to by the son of a business owner. Her classmates could not for the life of them understand why Bu Mus had turned down those two attractive offers.

"I want to be a teacher," said the fifteen-year-old girl.

She didn't say the sentence defiantly or with gusto. But whoever was there when she spoke that sentence would know that

Bu Mus dug every letter of each word from deep in her heart, and that the word *teacher* bubbled in her mind because she admired the noble profession of teaching. There was a giant sleeping inside of her, a giant that would wake up when she met her students.

Her choice would later bring Bu Mus unimaginable hardships—no one else wanted to teach at our school because there was no payment. Being a teacher at a poor private school, especially in our village, was a profession—according to a village joke— embarked on only by those who weren't quite right in the head.

Yet Bu Mus and Pak Harfan filled their roles wholeheartedly. And after a day of teaching every subject, Bu Mus sewed lace food covers. She sewed late into the night; that was her livelihood.

Our never-ending problem was money. It was so bad that we often couldn't buy chalk. Whenever this happened, Bu Mus would bring us outside and use the ground as her "chalkboard." But all these trials gradually and unexpectedly made Bu Mus a strong young teacher—charismatic, in fact.

"Say your prayers on time, and your reward will be greater," she would advise.

Wasn't this the testimony inspired by Surah an-Nisa in the holy Qur'an, spoken hundreds of times by hundreds of preachers at the mosque and often echoed by members of the religious community? Somehow, when spoken by Bu Mus, those words were different and more powerful, resounding in our hearts. We would feel remorse when we were late for prayer.

On one occasion, we were whining about the leaky school roof. Bu Mus wouldn't hear of our complaints but instead took out a book written in Dutch and showed us a picture from one of its pages. The picture was of a narrow room surrounded by thick, gloomy walls that were tall, dark, and covered with iron bars. It looked stuffy and full of violence.

"This was Sukarno's cell in a Bandung prison. Here he served his sentence. But he studied every day and read all the time. He was our first president and one of the brightest people our nation has ever produced."

We were astounded. Our complaints fell silent. From that moment on, we never again complained about the condition of our school. One time, it was raining very hard, and thundering ominously. Rain spilled from the sky into our classroom. We didn't move an inch. We didn't want Bu Mus to stop the lesson, and Bu Mus didn't want to stop teaching, so we studied holding umbrellas. Bu Mus covered her head with a banana leaf. It rained nonstop for the next four months, but we never missed school, never, and we never complained, not even a little.

Bu Mus and Pak Harfan were our teachers, friends; our spiritual guides. They taught us to make toy houses from bamboo, showed us the way to cleanse before prayer, pumped air back into our flattened bicycle tires, taught us to pray before bed, sucked poison from our legs when we were bitten by a snake, and from time to time made us orange juice with their bare hands. They were our unsung heroes, a prince and princess of kindness, and wells of knowledge in a forsaken dry field.

7 ❀ HIS FIRST PROMISE

Filicium decipiens trees are usually planted by botanists to attract birds. Their bountiful leaves know no season. Gorgeous parakeets often visit them, and before attacking our filicium, those lovely green birds would first survey the area from the branches of a tall *ganitri* tree behind our school, scouting out the possibility of competitors or enemies. Then, with lightning speed, those voracious birds would dive down and plunder the small fruits of the filicium with their razor-sharp beaks. While eating, they constantly would turn their heads to the left and right, paranoid. Lesson number three: If you are gorgeous, you will not lead a peaceful life.

After the parakeets came a flock of *jalak kerbau* birds, relaxed as could be. They had no predators, not even humans. They enjoyed the fruit left behind by the parakeets, then defecated as they pleased—even when their mouths were full. As afternoon approached, a few ashy tailorbirds landed in silence on the branches of the filicium. Calm and beautiful, they pecked at caterpillars crawling on the tree, eating less greedily than the parakeets, and then flew off again, as noiselessly as they had arrived.

Like the birds, we oriented our days around the filicium.

That tree was a witness to the dramas of our childhood. In its branches we constructed tree houses. Behind its leaves we played hide-and-seek. On its trunk we carved our promise to be forever friends. On its protruding roots we sat around listening to Bu Mus tell the story of Robin Hood. And under the shade of its leaves we played leapfrog, rehearsed plays, laughed, cried, sang, studied, and quarreled.

When the school day was over, we complained about going home. When it came close to Sunday, our day off, we couldn't wait for Monday.

The whole first week, we didn't touch a book.

Bu Mus and Pak Harfan told stories all day long. We were intoxicated by magical stories from faraway lands that taught about life struggles and wisdom, like the moral stories from *The Arabian Nights*.

Then, the first day of our second week.

I came really early. I couldn't wait to see Bu Mus and Pak Harfan. I was surprised when I opened the door to the class. Off in the corner was a drowsy cow, and in the opposite corner, sitting just as calmly, was Lintang. Even though his house was the farthest, he always came earliest.

On that happy day, after practicing singing "Rukun Iman," "The Six Pillars of Faith," Bu Mus began to teach us the alphabet.

"Seven letters per week," she said. "Within a month, you will know all the letters, and after that, we will learn to write them!"

After three weeks, I was incredibly delighted, because I had discovered new, strange letters, like O, Q, and V. I saw these new letters in Indonesian words only every so often. Why did they make something that was rarely used? As I was sighing about that, my deskmate raised his hand.

"Ibunda Guru," he shouted excitedly.

Bu Mus looked over. "Yes, Lintang?"

"Can I have the enrollment form from the first day of school? I want to fill it out."

Bu Mus smiled. "Patience, Lintang. We've just learned the alphabet. Later, in second grade, when you learn how to write sentences, you can fill it out."

"I would like to fill it out now, Ibunda. I promised my father."

Bu Mus hesitated. "You can fill it out?"

"I can, Ibunda," Lintang answered with certainty.

Clearly doubtful, Bu Mus opened her desk drawer and pulled out the form. We all got up at once and crowded around Lintang.

He took a pencil from behind his ear, bit the end, and reached for the paper. As Bu Mus watched Lintang's thin and dirty fingers carve each letter of the words, I saw her get goose bumps.

Name of Student: *Lintang Samudera Basara*
Name of Parent: *Syahbani Maulana Basara*

We could only gawk. Lintang could write, and he could write *well*! Bu Mus just stared at the boy as if he were a pearl in a clam. A moment later, she said softly, "*Subhanallah*, my goodness, Lintang, praise Allah's holiness, praise Allah's holiness . . ."

Lintang filled in every last part of that form and, with a relieved smile, returned it to Bu Mus. We hadn't been in school for a month, and Lintang had fulfilled his first promise—to defend his father's dignity.

8 ☼ MENTAL ILLNESS NUMBER FIVE

Months became years, and before we knew it, we were approaching our teenage years. Our poor school was still poor, but it was increasingly fascinating.

Through our shared trials and tribulations, we gradually grew to be siblings and knew one another's quirks inside and out.

Syahdan. His body was the smallest, but he ate the most. He never turned down food. It was as if his mouth weren't able to differentiate between delicious and disgusting food; he inhaled it all. It was baffling, he was so small—where did it all go?

Syahdan's deskmate, the honorable A Kiong, was somewhat of an anomaly. God only knows what possessed his father, a devout Confucian, to enroll his only son at this Islamic school. It must have been because of the impoverished condition of his Hokkien family.

Nevertheless, when seeing A Kiong, anyone would understand why he was destined to end up at this poor school. He had the appearance of a true reject. He looked like Frankenstein, with a head shaped like a tin can and hair like porcupine quills. His eyes tilted upward like sword blades; his eyebrows were virtually nonexistent. And he was bucktoothed. One look at his face and any teacher would feel depressed imagining the difficulty of cramming knowledge into this head.

Surprisingly, A Kiong's tin-can head quickly absorbed knowledge, but it turned out that the friendly, sweet-faced, and intelligent-looking boy sitting in front of him nodding knowingly during lessons was not very bright. His name was Kucai.

Kucai was rather unfortunate: He suffered from serious malnutrition as a small child—a condition that had a big effect on his eyesight. His eyes couldn't focus correctly, so when he spoke, he thought he was looking at the person he was talking to, but his eyes were really gazing about twenty degrees to the left.

With all of Kucai's other characteristics combined— opportunistic, self-centered, a little deceitful—plus his know-it-all attitude, shamelessness, and populist tendencies, he met all of the requirements to be a politician. For that reason, we unanimously appointed him class president.

Being class president was not a pleasant position. He was supposed to keep us quiet, but he himself could not shut up.

One day, in our Muhammadiyah ethics class, Bu Mus quoted the words of Khalifah Umar bin Khattab, one of the apostles of the Prophet Muhammad: "Anyone appointed as a leader and who accepts anything beyond his determined wage is committing fraud."

Bu Mus was definitely furious about the spreading corruption in Indonesia.

"And remember, leadership will be justly rewarded or punished in the afterlife."

The entire class was stunned, but Kucai was visibly shaken. As class president he was worried about being held accountable for his actions after death, not to mention the fact that he already loathed looking after us. He couldn't take it anymore. He stood up and said very pointedly, "Ibunda Guru, you must know that these coolie children cannot be kept under control! Borek acts like a mental patient. Sahara and A Kiong fight nonstop. It gives me a headache. Harun does nothing but sleep. And Ikal, *masya Allah*—my God, Ibunda, that boy was sent by Satan!"

Kucai was much better than other politicians. While they smeared others' names behind their backs, Kucai just came right out and said it to our faces.

"I can't take it anymore. I demand a vote for a new class president!" he said emotionally. Years of built-up frustration exploded from his body. He stared at Bu Mus, but his gaze fell on the Rhoma Irama *Rain of Money* poster.

Bu Mus was shocked. Never before had one of her students protested so directly. She thought for a moment and forced her face to reflect neutrality. She instructed us to write the name of a new class president on a piece of paper and to fold it in half. "In accordance with the principles of democracy, it is your right to vote, and your choice must be kept confidential."

We folded up our pieces of paper and gave them to Bu Mus. The room was tense. Bu Mus opened the first piece of paper and read the name inside. "Borek!" she shouted.

The color drained from Borek's face and Kucai joyously jumped up and down—it couldn't have been any more obvious that he himself had voted for Borek.

"Paper number two," said Bu Mus. "Kucai!"

This time Borek jumped up and down.

"Paper number three . . . Kucai!"

Kucai smiled bitterly.

"Paper number four . . . Kucai!"

"Paper number five . . . Kucai!"

And so it continued until the ninth paper.

There were only nine papers because Harun couldn't write. But Bu Mus still respected his political rights. She shifted her gaze to Harun. Harun let out his signature smile, exhibiting his long yellow teeth, and shouted sharply, "Kucai!"

Kucai drooped as he admitted defeat.

Sitting off in the corner was our prince, Trapani. He was as fascinating as the *cinenen kelabu* bird, and he was our class mascot. He was a perfectionist with a most handsome face, the type of boy girls fell in love with at first sight. His hair, pants, belt, socks, and clean shoes were always spotless and impeccable. He smelled good, too. His shirt even had all its buttons.

Trapani didn't speak if it wasn't necessary, and when he did, his words were impeccably chosen. He was a well-mannered, promising young citizen who was a model of Dasa Dharma Pramuka—the Boy Scout promise. He wanted to become a teacher and teach in isolated areas when he grew up, to help improve education and the condition of life for backcountry Malays. Everything in Trapani's life seemed to be inspired by the song "Wajib Belajar," about battling illiteracy.

Trapani was very close to his mother. No discussion was interesting to him other than those related to his mother, perhaps because among six children he was the only boy.

Sahara, the sole female in our class, was like the parakeets— firm and direct. She was hard to convince and not easy to impress. Another one of her prominent characteristics was her honesty— she never lied. Even if she were about to walk the plank over a flaming sea and a lie could save her life, not one would escape her mouth.

Sahara and A Kiong were enemies. They would have huge fights, make up, and then fight again. It was as if they were destined to always be at odds. One time, Trapani was talking about a great book, *Tenggelamnya Kapal Van Der Wijk—The Sinking of the Van Der Wijk*—Buya Hamka's legendary literary novel.

"I've read that book, too," A Kiong commented arrogantly. "I'm sorry, but I didn't care for it. There are too many names and places, difficult for me to remember them."

Sahara, who really appreciated good literature, was offended. She barked, "*Masya Allah!* My God! Where do you get off criticizing excellent literature, A Kiong? Maybe if Buya writes a book called *The Bad Little Boy Who Steals Cucumbers*, it would be more suitable for your literary tastes!"

On the other hand, Sahara had a soft spot for Harun.

Harun, who was well behaved, quiet, and had an easy smile, was completely unable to comprehend the lessons. Nowadays people call it Down syndrome. When Bu Mus taught, Harun sat calmly with a constant smile on his face.

During afternoon recess, Sahara and Harun always sat together under the filicium. The two of them shared a unique emotional connection like the quirky friendship of the Mouse and the Elephant. Harun enthusiastically told a story about his three-striped cat giving birth to three kittens, which also had three stripes, on the third day of the month. Sahara patiently listened, even though Harun told this story every day, over and over again, thousands of times, all year around, year after year.

The number three was indeed a sacred number for Harun. He related everything to the number three. He begged Bu Mus to teach him how to write that number, and after several years of hard work, he could finally do it. The covers of all his schoolbooks soon had a big, beautiful, and colorful number three written on them. He was obsessed with the number three. He often ripped off the buttons on his shirt so there were only three left.

He wore three layers of socks. He had three kinds of bags, and in each bag he always carried three bottles of soy sauce. He even had three hair combs. When we asked him why he was so fond of the number three, he pondered for a while and then answered very wisely, like a village head giving religious advice. "My friends," he said knowingly, "God likes odd numbers."

I often searched Harun's face to try to figure out what was going on in his head. He smiled whenever he saw me doing this. He was aware that he was the oldest among us, and he treated us with care, as if we were his own little brothers and sister. There were times when his behavior was very touching. One time, unexpectedly, he brought a large package to school and gave each of us a boiled caladium tuber. Everyone got one. He himself took three. His demeanor was very adultlike, but he truly was a child trapped in an adult's body.

The seventh student, our honorable knight in shining armor, was Borek.

In the beginning, he was just an ordinary student. His behavior wasn't peculiar. But a chance meeting with an old hair-growth-product bottle from somewhere on the Arabian Peninsula forever changed the course of his life.

On that bottle was a picture of a man; he was wearing red underwear, had a tall, strong body, and was as hairy as a gorilla.

From then on, Borek was no longer interested in anything other than making his muscles bigger. Because of hard work and exercise, he was successful and earned himself the nickname Samson—a noble title that he bore proudly.

It was definitely strange, but at least Samson had found himself at a young age and knew exactly what he wanted to be later; he strove continuously to reach his goal. He somehow skipped the identity-searching phase that usually leaves people doubting themselves until they are older. There are those who never find their own identity and go through life as someone else. Samson was better off than they were.

He was completely obsessed with bodybuilding and crazy about the macho-man image. One day he lured me in, and curiosity got the best of me. I didn't understand how he knew the secret to building chest muscles.

"Don't tell anyone!" he whispered while glancing around. He jerked my hand, and we ran to the abandoned electric shed behind the school. He reached into his bag and pulled out a tennis ball that had been split in half.

"If you want to have a bulging chest like mine, this is the secret!" He was whispering again, even though absolutely no one else was around. I looked at the two halves with surprise and thought: *Apparently the secret to an amazing body is in this tennis ball! It must be a great discovery.*

"Take off your shirt!" demanded Samson.

What is he going to do to me?

"Let me make you a real man!"

The expression on his face indicated that he couldn't figure out why every man didn't use this method—a shortcut to the perfect appearance.

I was hesitant, but I had no other choice. I unbuttoned my shirt.

"Hurry up!"

Suddenly Samson forcefully shoved the tennis ball halves against my chest. I stumbled back and almost fell. He had caught me by surprise and I was powerless, my back against some planks of wood. To make matters worse, Samson was much bigger than I was and as strong as a coolie. I wriggled around trying to break free.

And then I understood. The tennis ball halves were supposed

to work like that strange thing with a wooden handle and a rubber cup that people use to unclog toilets. In Samson's crazy head, those tennis ball halves functioned as a tool to pump up chest muscles. Before I knew it, I was being tortured in Samson's strong grip by the powerful suctioning of the tennis ball halves.

I felt the life being sucked out of my insides by the cursed tennis ball halves. My eyes felt like they were going to pop out of my head. I choked, unable to speak. I signaled to Samson to stop.

"It's not time yet—you have to finish counting names and parents first, and then the results will show!"

Counting names and parents was our own foolish creation—doing something within the amount of time it took to say the full names of everyone in our class and their parents. For example: Trapani Ihsan Jamari Nursidik, son of Zainuddin Ilham Jamari Nursidik. Or Harun Ardhli Ramadhan Hasani Burhan, son of Syamsul Hazana Ramadhan Hasani Burhan. Malay names were never short. No way could I endure these things sucking the life out of me for the entire amount of time it would take me to count names and parents.

Then, all of a sudden, one of the wooden planks behind me fell and gave me room to gather my strength. Without stopping to think twice, I mustered the last ounce of strength left in my body, and with one roundhouse-style move I kicked Samson as hard as I could right between his legs.

Samson howled and groaned. I broke free from his grasp, jumped away, and bolted off. I stole a peek back and saw the boy-Hercules hurl over and clutch his legs before falling down with a thud.

For days my chest was encircled by two dark red circular marks, traces of unbelievable idiocy.

My mother asked me about the marks. I wanted to lie, but I couldn't. Muhammadiyah ethics class taught us every Friday morning that we were not allowed to lie to our parents, especially not to our mothers.

I was forced to expose my own stupidity. My older brothers and my father laughed so hard they were shaking. And then, for the very first time, I heard my mother's sophisticated theory on mental illness.

"There are forty-four types of craziness," she said with the authority of a psychiatric expert as she gathered tobacco, betel leaves, and other ingredients from her pillbox containers for making tobacco chew, squashed them into a small ball, and chewed the concoction. "The smaller the number, the more critical the illness," she said, shaking her head back and forth while staring at me as if I were a patient in a mental hospital. "When people lose their minds and wander the streets nude, that is mental illness number one. I think what you did with that tennis ball falls into the category of mental illness number five. Pretty serious, Ikal! You'd better be careful—if you don't use common sense, that number will soon get even smaller!"

Malay people believe that destiny is a creature, and we were ten baits for destiny. We were like small mollusks clinging together to defend ourselves from the pounding waves in the ocean of knowledge. Bu Mus was our mother hen. I looked at my friends' faces one by one: Harun with his easy smile, the handsome Trapani, little Syahdan, the pompous Kucai, feisty Sahara, the gullible A Kiong, and the seventh, Samson, sitting like a Ganesha statue. And who were the ninth and tenth of us? Lintang and Mahar. What were their stories? They were two young, truly special boys. It takes a special chapter to tell their tales.

9 ❀ CROCODILE SHAMAN

Lintang was uncharacteristically late one morning. We were astonished when we heard his reason.

"I couldn't pass. In the middle of the road, blocking my way, lay a crocodile as big as a coconut tree."

"Crocodile?" echoed Kucai.

"I rang the bell on my bike, clapped my hands, and coughed loudly so he'd leave. He didn't budge. All I could do was stand there like a statue and talk to myself. His size and the barnacles growing on his back were clear signs that he was the ruler of this swamp."

"Why didn't you simply go home?" I asked.

"I was already more than halfway here. I wasn't about to turn around just because of that stupid crocodile."

I could only imagine what Lintang was thinking at that moment: *The word* absent *isn't in my vocabulary, and today we study the history of Islam—one of the most interesting classes. I want to debate the holy verses that foretold Byzantium's victory seven years before it happened.*

"You didn't ask anybody for help?" asked Sahara apprehensively.

"There wasn't anyone else around—just me, the giant crocodile, and certain death," Lintang said dramatically. "I was almost hopeless. Then suddenly, from the currents of the river beside me, I heard the water rippling. I was surprised. I was frightened!"

"What was it, Lintang?" asked a wide-eyed Trapani.

"The shape of a man emerged from the swamp. He walked toward me in bowlegged steps."

"Who was he?" Mahar choked out.

"Bodenga."

We all gasped and clasped our hands over our mouths.

"I was more scared of him than of any crocodile!"

We knew. The man who had emerged from the moss was a man who didn't want to know anyone—but who in coastal Belitong didn't know him?

"Then what?" Borek asked nervously.

"He passed by me as if I weren't there. Then he approached the ruthless animal blocking the road. He touched it! He petted it gently and whispered something to it—it was so bizarre! The crocodile submitted to him. Seconds later," Lintang continued in a low voice, "it dove into the swamp. It was as loud as seven coconut trees crashing down!"

We were astounded, thinking about Lintang's struggle to get to school. "And what about Bodenga?" we asked in harmony.

"Bodenga turned back and headed my way. It was clear that he didn't expect any gratitude. I didn't have the guts to look at him. But he just passed by."

"Passed by? Just like that?" I asked.

"Yeah, just like that. But I feel lucky. Not many people have ever witnessed Bodenga's supernatural powers."

It was true that I had never witnessed Bodenga in action. Bodenga *had* provided me with my first life lesson on premonitions. For me, Bodenga symbolized all things related to the feeling of sadness.

No one wanted to be Bodenga's friend. His face was scarred, cratered. A man in his forties, he covered himself with coconut leaves and slept under a palm tree, curled up like a squirrel, sometimes for two days and nights at a time. When he was hungry, he dove down into the abandoned well at the old police station, all the way to the bottom, caught some eels, and ate them while he was still in the water.

Bodenga was a free creature. He wasn't Malay, not Chinese, not even Sawang—he wasn't anybody. No one knew where he came from. He wasn't religious and he couldn't speak. He wasn't a beggar or a criminal. His name wasn't anywhere in the village records. He was deaf because one day he dove into the Linggang River to fetch some tin and dove so deep that his ears bled.

Nowadays Bodenga was like a lone piece of driftwood. The only family that villagers ever knew was his one-legged father. People say he sacrificed his leg in order to acquire more crocodile magic. His father was a famous crocodile shaman. As Islam flowed into the villages, people began to shun Bodenga and his father because they refused to stop worshipping crocodiles as gods.

His father died by wrapping himself from head to toe in *jawi* roots and throwing himself into the Marang River. He deliberately fed his body to the ferocious crocodiles of the river. The only remain was the stump he had used as a second leg. Now Bodenga spends most of his time staring into the currents of the Marang River, all alone and far into the night.

One evening villagers came flocking to the National School's basketball court. They had caught a crocodile that had attacked a woman washing clothes in the Manggar River. Because I was still small, I couldn't push my way through the people surrounding the crocodile. I could see it only from between people's legs. Its big mouth was propped open with a piece of firewood. It was missing a leg.

When they split its stomach in half, they found hair, clothes, and a necklace. That was when I saw Bodenga surge forward among the visitors. He sat down cross-legged beside the crocodile. His face was deathly pale. He pitifully pleaded for the people to stop butchering the animal. They took the firewood out of its mouth and backed off. Crocodile worshippers believed that when they died they became crocodiles. Bodenga must have thought that this was the crocodile his father had become.

Bodenga cried. It was an agonizing, mournful sound. I saw his tears streaming down his pockmarked cheeks. I felt my own tears stream down my face, and I couldn't hold them back.

He tied up the crocodile and carried his father's carcass to the Linggang River, dragging it along the riverbank toward the delta. Bodenga hasn't returned since.

That incident created a blueprint of compassion and sadness in my subconscious. In the years to come, whenever I was faced with heart-wrenching situations, Bodenga came into my senses.

That evening Bodenga truly taught me about premonitions. And for the first time, I learned that fate could treat humankind very terribly, and that love could be so blind.

While Lintang didn't have an emotional experience with Bodenga like I did, that hadn't been the first time he was faced with a crocodile on his way to school. It's not an exaggeration to say that Lintang often risked his life for the sake of his education. Nevertheless, he never missed a day of school. He pedaled eighty kilometers round-trip every day. If school activities went until late in the afternoon, he didn't arrive home until after dark. Thinking about his daily journey made me cringe.

During the rainy season, chest-deep waters flooded the roads. When faced with a road that had turned into a river, Lintang left his bicycle under a tree on higher ground, wrapped his shirt, pants, and books in a plastic bag, bit the bag, plunged into the water, and swam toward the school as fast as he could to avoid being attacked by a crocodile.

Because there was no clock at his house, Lintang relied on a natural clock. One time he rushed through his morning prayer because the cock had already crowed. He finished his prayer and immediately pedaled off to school. Halfway through his journey, in the middle of the forest, he became suspicious because the air was still very cold, it was still pitch-black, and the forest was strangely quiet. There were no birdsongs calling out to the dawn. Lintang realized that the cock had crowed early, and it was actually still midnight. He sat himself down beneath a tree in the middle of the dark forest, embraced his two legs, shivered in the cold, and waited patiently for morning to come.

Another time, his bicycle chain broke, so he pushed the bike about a dozen kilometers. By the time he got to the school, we were getting ready to head home. The last lesson that day was music class. Lintang was happy because he got to sing the song "Padamu Negeri" ("For You Our Country") in front of the class. It was a slow and somber song:

> *For you, our country, we promise*
> *For you, our country, we serve*
> *For you, our country, we are devoted*
> *You, country, are our body and soul*

We were stunned to hear him sing so soulfully. His exhaustion didn't show in his humorous eyes. After he sang the song, he pushed his bike back home, all forty kilometers.

Lintang's father had thought his son would give up within the first few weeks, but he was proved wrong. Day by day, Lintang's enthusiasm didn't fade—he became addicted to unlocking the secrets of knowledge. When he arrived home, he didn't rest; he joined the other village children his age to work as a copra coolie. That was the price he paid for the "privilege" of schooling.

When Lintang was in first grade, he once asked his father for help with a homework question about simple multiplication. "Come here, Father. How much is four times four?"

His father paced back and forth. He gazed wistfully through the window at the wide South China Sea, thinking very hard. When Lintang wasn't looking, he quietly sneaked out the back door and ran like the wind, cutting through the tall grass. The pine-tree man ran at top speed as swift as a deer to ask for help from people at the village office. Not much later, like a flash of lightning, he slipped back into the house and was suddenly standing attentively before his son.

"Fffooh . . . fffooh . . . fourteen, son, no doubt about it, no more, no less," he answered while panting to catch his breath, but wearing a wide smile full of pride.

Lintang stared deep into his father's eyes, and he felt a pang in his heart. From that day on, his enthusiasm for school burned even more intensely. Because his body was too small for his big bicycle, he couldn't sit on the saddle. Instead, he sat on the bar that connects the saddle to the handlebars. The tips of his toes barely reached the pedals. Every day he moved slowly and bounced up and down greatly over the steel bar as he bit his lip to gather his strength to fight the wind.

Lintang's house was on the edge of the sea. The house was a shack on stilts, in case the sea rose too high. The roof was made of sago palm leaves, and the walls were *meranti* tree bark. Anything happening in the shack could be seen from outside because the bark walls were dozens of years old and cracked and broken like mud in the dry season. Inside, it was a long and narrow space with two doors, one in the front and one in the back. None of the windows or doors locked. They tied the frames shut at night with cheap twine.

Both Lintang's maternal and paternal grandparents lived with them. Their skin was so wrinkly you could grab it in handfuls. Each day the four grandparents bent over a winnowing tray to pick maggots out of their third-class rice, the only kind they could afford. They spent hours on that arduous task—the rice was that putrid.

There were also Lintang's father's two younger brothers: a young man who wandered around all day because he was mentally ill and a disabled laborer unable to work because he suffered from inflamed testicles—the result of a nutrition deficiency. With these people, plus Lintang, Lintang's five little sisters, and his mother, the long, narrow house was very crowded. There were fourteen people total, and all of them relied on Lintang's father.

Each day Lintang's father waited for skippers or neighbors with boats to give him work. He didn't get a percentage of the catch but was paid based on his physical strength. He was a man making a living by selling his bodily power.

Lintang could study only late at night. Because the house was so crowded, it was difficult to find an empty space, and they had to share the oil lantern. However, once he grasped a book, his mind escaped the cracks of the leaning bark walls. Studying was entertainment that made him forget life's hardships. For him, books were like water from a sacred well in Mecca's mosque, renewing his strength to pedal against the wind day after day.

Then, one magical night, under the twilight of the oil lamp and accompanied by the waves of the tide, Lintang's thin fingers paged through a photocopied version of an archaic book titled *Astronomy and Geometry*. All at once he was immersed in the defiant words of Galileo against Aristotle's cosmology. He was entranced by the crazy ideas of the ancient astronomers who wanted to measure the distance from the earth to Andromeda and the Triangulum's nebulas. He gasped when he found out that gravity can bend light. He was amazed by the roving objects of the skies in the dark corners of the universe that may have been visited only by the thoughts of Nicolaus Copernicus.

When he reached the chapters on geometry, Lintang quickly mastered the extraordinarily complicated tetrahedral decomposition, the direction axioms, and the Pythagorean theorem. This material was way beyond his age and education, but he contemplated the information in the dim circle of light provided by the oil lamp, and right at that moment, in the dead of the night, his contemplation exploded and he observed something magical. On the old pages in front of his face, each letter and number lit up as it entered his mind. It was as if he were sitting at the same table as the pioneers of geometry.

The next day at school, Lintang was puzzled to see us confused about a three-digit coordinate exercise.

What are these village kids so confused about? asked the voice in his heart.

Just as stupidity often goes unrealized, some people are often unaware that they have been chosen, destined by God, to be betrothed to knowledge.

Now, this happened during the month of August—always a bad-news month.

One problem after another struck our school. For years, financial difficulty was our constant companion, day in and day out. People always assumed our school would collapse within a matter of weeks. Still, thanks to Bu Mus and Pak Harfan, we came to see school as the best thing that could have happened to us—it was much better than becoming coolies, coconut graters, shepherds, pepper pickers, or shop guards. We were living proof of the proverb "What doesn't kill you will make you stronger." And while our class still had only ten students, after a few years of no new enrollees we finally had some underclassmen—not as many as we may have hoped, but there they were.

Yet there was no ordeal as difficult as this one. An old DKW motorbike with a sputtering exhaust pipe slid toward our school. Uh-oh. He was here again.

The driver of the DKW was an older man with thick glasses and a tiny body, his forehead broad and shiny. The pulsing veins on his brow gave the impression that he often forced his agenda upon others. The fact is, people who are used to reproaching others usually lose their grasp on good manners. This man was famous for his inability to compromise. One word from his mouth and an entire school could be shut down. Principals could be fired. Teachers could be barred from promotion until the day they retired, or exiled to an isolated island—one that didn't even appear on maps—to teach primitive children and short-tailed macaques. The sight of this man's glasses made all the teachers in Belitong tremble. This was Mister Samadikun—the school superintendent.

Years earlier, on that first day of school, we'd managed to slip through Mister Samadikun's fingers when Harun saved us by becoming our tenth student. Mister Samadikun was not happy when that happened. He'd wanted to shut down our school for quite some time—we made troublesome extra work for the officials in the Department of Education and Culture. They repeatedly pushed for our school to be banished from the face of this earth. Mister Samadikun himself once bragged to a superior, "Ah, let me take care of the Muhammadiyah School problem. With one kick I could bring them down."

In my fantasy, after those arrogant statements, Mister Samadikun and the officials made a toast, clinking glasses filled with sugar-palm milk, which was the favorite bribe of teachers who wanted to be promoted or transferred out of isolated areas.

So Mister Samadikun created an elegant and diplomatic condition to shut down our school. The condition was ten students, a condition dramatically fulfilled by Harun at the last minute. Mister Samadikun was extremely irked by our school, and especially by Harun.

He was personally responsible for making sure we took our exams at another school because they considered our school incapable of administering its own tests. He also was unhappy with us because we didn't have any awards. In today's competitive education system, schools like ours could render the entire system inefficient. In that case, Mister Samadikun was right. But doesn't the future belong to God?

Bu Mus was as white as a ghost when Mister Samadikun arrived for a surprise inspection. To make matters worse, she was by herself. Pak Harfan had been out sick for the past month. The traditional healer said he was sick because he had inhaled low-quality chalk dust for dozens of years.

Mister Samadikun peeked into the classroom. As soon as he saw the completely empty glass display case, a belittling expression came across his face. He was used to seeing trophies in display cases.

Because she was so nervous, Bu Mus made a fatal mistake before anything else even happened. "Please come in, Pak," she said politely.

Mister Samadikun glared at her and snapped, "Call me Mister!"

It was common knowledge: he didn't want to be called Pak Samadikun. Maybe it was an influence from his Dutch teachers, or perhaps it was to maintain his authority.

Whatever the reason, he would be called "Mister."

Mister Samadikun took out the facility inspection form. He sneered and shook his head repeatedly to make his disappointment known. In the column for chalkboard and furniture he was forced to add a new choice: below *(E) Bad*, he added *(F) Extremely Bad*. In the column for national symbols—photos of the president and vice president and the Garuda Pancasila state symbol—and the columns for first-aid kit and visual aids, he was forced to create an additional choice once again: *(F) Nonexistent*. In the toilet and lighting facilities column, he added *(F) Natural*.

And then came the column for student conditions. He drew a long, deep breath and looked at us. Most of us were not wearing shoes, and our grubby clothes were missing buttons. Mahar's shirt was completely buttonless. Mister Samadikun stopped dead in his tracks when he saw Lintang and me wearing slingshots around our necks. He *tsk-tsk*ed at the sight of the guava fruit stains covering Kucai's shirt. In the columns for condition and completeness of students, the choice *(F) Extremely Bad* wasn't sufficient enough to describe us. He added yet another choice of his own: *(G) Pathetic*.

Mister Samadikun asked, "Who has a calculator, compass, and crayons?"

Not one of us answered. Mahar raised his eyebrows. We were already in fifth grade and we had no idea what those things were.

Mister Samadikun turned to Bu Mus. "Bu Mus! I have never seen a classroom as appalling as this. You call this a school? This place is no different than a livestock pen!"

Backed into a corner, Bu Mus became even paler.

"Your children look like mouse-deer hunters, not students!"

Bu Mus took the insult, but it was clear that it did nothing to diminish her pride in us.

"There's no other choice. This school must be closed!"

Bu Mus was shocked. She could sit back and take the insults, but there was no way she would let her school be shut down.

"Impossible, Mister. We've been studying here for five years."

Bu Mus was truly courageous. Never before had a teacher been brave enough to challenge Mister Samadikun.

"What about these village children?" Bu Mus continued.

Mister Samadikun was furious. "That's your problem, not mine! Move them to other schools."

"Other schools? The closest public school is all the way in Tanjong Pandan. It's impossible to separate these small children from their parents. They can't afford to go to school there. The PN School is nearby, but they are not willing to accept children this poor."

Mister Samadikun got all worked up, huffing and puffing. We wanted to take Bu Mus's side, but we were frightened—except for Harun. He smiled the whole time; he had no idea what was going on.

"We have already met the ten-student requirement. If it's only a matter of the first-aid kit, we can—"

"It's not just that!" Mister Samadikun cut her off. "It's also Harun!"

Bu Mus froze; he had touched a sore spot. The subject of Harun had always been sensitive for her. She never hesitated to put herself on the line for him.

Unlike Bu Mus, Harun was very pleased that his name had been mentioned.

"What about Harun?" Bu Mus asked defensively.

"He can't go to school here. It's not the appropriate place for him. He has to go to a special school! On Bangka Island!"

Bu Mus tried to keep her cool. We knew how much she loved Harun. We also understood that Mister Samadikun had made up his mind, and that Bu Mus was just a village schoolteacher. Bu Mus's face got puffy. "Mister," she said weakly, "this school is the best place for Harun. He is very diligent and very happy to study with his friends. Please, don't send him away."

Mister Samadikun was unmoved. "Study? What could he possibly study?"

Harun did indeed receive special treatment. When we moved

up a class, so did he, even though he didn't have an official report card.

Bu Mus wanted to explain that Harun had developed very well at the school, that he had found happiness with us. She didn't understand psychology, but she did believe that being in a normal environment was what special children like Harun needed. But her mouth was locked.

Mister Samadikun called Harun forward. Prejudice was something unknown to Harun; the boy tried to greet Mister Samadikun in a friendly manner. He didn't know that the fate of our school lay in his hands. Without being asked, and while trying to lean on Mister Samadikun's shoulder, Harun told his timeless tale about his three-striped cat giving birth to three kittens on the third of the month, even as Bu Mus tried hard to stop him.

"All right, let's test what Harun has learned *over these past five years*." Mister Samadikun noticeably stressed *over these past five years* because he wanted to deny Bu Mus's hard work with Harun and he wanted to undermine her by demonstrating that the school wasn't suitable for Harun. Harun, with his pure heart, remained blissfully unaware of the struggle. His face sparkled with pride because he was going to be questioned—he felt important. "What are your aspirations, Harun?"

Harun looked at Mister Samadikun with great seriousness. He smiled secretively. For him, the question was like an amusing game. *Aspirations?*

"What he means is, later, when you grow up, what do you want to be, Harun? Do you want to be a doctor, an engineer, maybe a pilot?" Bu Mus gently asked.

"Ooohh," Harun said, sounding like someone snapping back into consciousness after a week-long coma.

"Thank you, Ibunda Guru," Harun said as he raised his head to look at Mister Samadikun. His eyes shone brightly, but then he lowered his head again. It was as if he knew his answer but was ashamed to say it.

"What do you want to be, Harun?" Mister Samadikun asked again.

He bashfully pointed at Trapani. Mister Samadikun and Bu Mus looked at Trapani. Trapani was puzzled.

"Don't be shy," coaxed Mister Samadikun.

Harun pointed at Trapani again. No one understood Harun's peculiar behavior, but I knew what was going on. One day, back when we were in first grade, Harun invited me to climb up to the top of the highest minaret of al-Hikmah Mosque. He wanted someplace quiet with no one around so he could tell me what he wanted to be when he grew up. Only I was entrusted with this information. So I wouldn't spill the beans, he bribed me with three boiled caladium tubers. I placed one hand on the three snacks and raised the other high in the air to swear that I would keep his secret.

To my mind, because Harun pointed to Trapani, he had spilled the beans himself and revealed his secret aspiration. I considered myself free of my caladium-tuber oath. So when Mister Samadikun kept pushing Harun to answer, I couldn't help it and I spoke up.

"When he grows up, Harun wants to be Trapani," I said. Everyone was taken aback. Harun smiled widely, lowered his head, and his body shook as he tried to hold back his laughter.

We all admired Trapani; he was the most polished and handsome of our group. So Harun quietly aspired to be Trapani when he grew up. The problem, of course, was that this aspiration was rather difficult to achieve, considering the fact that Harun was much older than Trapani.

Mister Samadikun shot Bu Mus a taunting glare. And still he wanted more.

"Okay, Harun, final test. What is two plus two?"

This time he had gone too far. Mister Samadikun had intentionally chosen a ridiculously simple question that even children not yet in school could answer, all for the sake of insulting Bu Mus.

Harun approached Mister Samadikun. He walked with authority. "Mister," he said calmly, "you are kidding, right?"

"No, Harun, this is serious. I want to know what you have been learning all this time."

"Ah, Mister, you've got to be kidding me! That is a simple counting question. I have already studied addition. I can do it up into the hundreds, no problem!"

"That's great, Harun."

Upon seeing Harun's confidence, Mister Samadikun's face went stiff. He was aware that he had made a fatal error. The question was too easy! He regretted asking such an easy question. At least he could have made it two *times* two.

Bu Mus hugged her chest. She was tense, but she believed Harun could answer. She had been intensively working with him on the subject of addition. We prayed to God almighty, hoping she was right. Sahara's and Mahar's eyes were glassy. We were hopelessly in love with our poor school; we didn't want to lose it. But we believed that for the second time, Harun would save us. He would be our unlikely hero.

"Of course I know." He folded his arms across his chest. "Piece of cake."

"How much, Harun?"

Harun's hand shot up as he confidently yelled, "Three!"

11 ☼ FULL MOON

"You have only one more chance, and if there's no improvement, you're finished!" Mister Samadikun threatened.

The unexpected and embarrassing inspection was over, and Mister Samadikun began going through the motions required to complete his report. He summoned a photographer to take pictures of our school from various angles. Each time the photographer took a shot, Harun tried to jump in the photo. When the photographer was snapping a shot of the backside of the school, Harun's head suddenly popped up above the windowsill, wearing a wide smile and displaying his long yellow chompers. He didn't have a clue that these photos were being taken to drag him down and close our school; he was focused on his poses in the pictures.

After the photos were printed and exhibited by Mister Samadikun, it was clear that the degree to which our school building leaned to one side had reached a disturbing level. It was more or less like the Leaning Tower of Pisa. We knew the report and the photos would be distributed as widely as Mister Samadikun could manage.

But Bu Mus didn't waver. She inspired us, as usual, by quoting a holy verse.

"Just be patient," she coaxed. "After hardships, easier times will surely come."

In just a few powerful words, without a long-winded speech, Bu Mus had inspired us with the determination to fight for our school, no matter what. That, my friend, is what they call charisma.

Even though she was worried, Bu Mus didn't let the Mister Samadikun problem get her down. Her attention had been stolen by Lintang.

Ever since Lintang filled out that form back in the first grade, Bu Mus had had a sneaking suspicion he was gifted. Later, like a blacksmith filing the blade of a knife, Bu Mus meticulously sharpened Lintang's mind. Gradually, in Bu Mus's steady hands, his intelligence began to shine.

Our entire class was enchanted with Lintang. My God, that seashell-collecting boy was sharp. His bright eyes radiated intelligence, and his forehead lit up like a lightbulb. Bu Mus and Pak Harfan didn't even know what to do with him.

He was the fastest at folding paper into geometric shapes; he was the best at reading. But his most obvious talent was math. While we still stammered through even-number addition, he already was skilled with odd-number multiplication.

The rest of us were barely able to dictate mathematical problems and he already was astute in dividing decimals, calculating roots, and finding exponents—he could even fully explain their operational relationships in logarithmic tables. His only weakness, if it could even be called a weakness, was his chaotic chicken-scratch handwriting. Maybe it was so bad because the motor skills of his fingers couldn't keep up with his racing logic.

"Thirteen times six, times seven, plus eighty-three, minus

thirty-nine!" Bu Mus challenged from the front of the classroom.

We took the rubber bands off our handful of twigs, took out thirteen of them—six times—and painstakingly added each set. We arranged six more piles of twigs numbering the same as the first. Each pile was counted one by one as a result of two phases of multiplication. Then eighty-three twigs were added and thirty-nine were taken away. It took us an average of seven minutes to solve a problem. It was definitely an effective method, but not efficient.

In the meantime, Lintang, who wasn't even touching a twig, closed his eyes for a moment. Not more than five seconds later, he yelled out, "Five hundred ninety!"

He wasn't even off by a digit. That was on the first day of second grade.

"Great, coastal boy, excellent!" praised Bu Mus. She was tempted to test the extent of Lintang's intellectual power. "Eighteen times fourteen times twenty-three plus eleven plus fourteen times sixteen times seven!"

We gripped our twigs. In less than seven seconds, without even writing down one digit, without hesitation or haste, without blinking, Lintang bellowed, "Six hundred fifty-one thousand nine hundred fifty-two!"

"Full moon, Lintang! Your answer is as beautiful as a full moon! Where have you been hiding all this time?"

Bu Mus made every effort to stifle her giddy laughter. It was out of the question for Bu Mus to laugh boisterously—her religious beliefs forbade it. Instead, she shook her head with approval as a sign of her salute and looked at Lintang as if she had been searching her whole life for a student like him.

We, on the other hand, were bursting with questions about how Lintang was able to do all that. This was his recipe: "First learn the odd number multiplication tables by heart—those are tricky. Leave the last digits out of two-digit multiplication problems; it's easier to multiply numbers that end in zero. Do the rest later, and don't eat so much that you are too full; it clogs your ears and slows down your brain."

His answer was innocent enough, but if you listened to it, even though he had just entered the second grade, by developing his own techniques for localizing the difficulty, analyzing it, and solving it, Lintang already showed signs of *high cognitive complexity.*

As time went by, Lintang soon found that the main feature of his intellect was his spatial intelligence—he was very advanced in multidimensional geometry. He could quickly imagine the surfaces of an object from different angles. He could solve complicated modern decomposition cases and taught us the technique of calculating the area of a polygon by breaking down its sides using the Euclidian theorem. I would have to say that these are not easy matters.

Lintang was not only bright, he was also intellectually creative. He was experimenting in formulating his own donkeybridge method for memorizing things. For instance, he designed his own configuration of the body: respiratory system, digestive system, motions, and senses for humans, vertebrates, and invertebrates.

So if we asked him how worms pee, we had to be ready to receive a precise, chronological, detailed, and very clever explanation about how the microvilli work. Then, as relaxed as a monkey picking out lice, he analogized the worm's urinary system to the excretion system of protozoa through the highly complicated anatomy of contractile vacuole. If no one stopped him, he would gladly carry on and explain the functions of the cortex, Bowman's capsule, medulla, and the Malpighian corpuscle in the human excretion system. Because of his own donkey-bridge design, Lintang would master the whole excretion system as easily as squashing a bloated mosquito.

Lintang was very excited whenever it was his turn to sweep Pak Harfan's office. When he was in there, he read about geometry, biology, geography, civics, history, algebra, and various other subjects in books from Pak Harfan's collection. Some of the books were in Dutch and English. Pak Harfan patiently guided Lintang and often let him borrow the books.

Lintang was obsessed with learning new things. Every piece of information was a fuse of knowledge that could blow him up at any moment.

The following incident occurred on the same day he was saved by Bodenga, the crocodile shaman.

"Al-Qur'an sometimes mentions names of places that must be interpreted carefully," Bu Mus explained during our history of Islam lesson, an obligatory subject in Muhammadiyah schools. Don't even dream of moving up to the next grade with a failing score in that class.

"For instance, *the nearest land* conquered by the Persian army in the year—"

"A.D. 620! Persia conquered Heraclitus's empire, which was also threatened by Mesopotamian, Sicilian, and Palestinian rebellions. It was also attacked by the Avars, Slavs, and Armenians," Lintang interrupted. We were stunned; Bu Mus smiled.

"That *nearest land* is—"

"Byzantium! The former name of Constantinople, the proud city of the great Constantine. Seven years later, Byzantium took back its independence, the independence that had been written in the holy book but denied by the non-Muslim Arabs. Why is it called *the nearest land*, Ibunda Guru? Why was the holy book defied?"

"Patience, my child. The answer to your question involves interpretations of Ar-Ruum—which embraces at least fourteen hundred years of knowledge. We will study interpretations later, when you are in junior high school."

"No way, Ibunda Guru. This morning I was almost swallowed by a crocodile. I don't have time to wait. Explain it all, and explain it now."

We cheered, and for the first time we understood the meaning of *adnal ardli*, literally "the nearest land," and interpretively the lowest land on the earth. That place was none other than Byzantium in the eastern part of the Roman Empire. We were amazed by Lintang's drive to challenge himself. If the heart is not envious of one with knowledge, then it can be illuminated by the rays of enlightenment. Like stupidity, intelligence is contagious.

"Come on, guys, don't let this curly-haired coastal boy be the only one to answer," urged Bu Mus.

That was about the time when I was tempted to answer, feeling hesitant, awkward, and unsure—which usually resulted in my being wrong. Lintang would correct my answers in the spirit of friendship.

I studied hard every night, but never was I close, not even a little, to surpassing Lintang. My grades were a tad better than the class average but way below his. I always was in Lintang's shadow. Since the first quarter of the first grade, I perpetually received the second rank—it would never change, just as the surface of the moon will always look to me like a mother holding her baby. My archrival, my number one enemy, was my friend and deskmate, whom I loved like a brother.

God didn't just bless Lintang with brains. He also blessed him with a beautiful personality. When we had trouble with subjects, he helped us patiently and always encouraged us. His superiority didn't threaten those around him, his brilliance didn't cause jealousy, and his greatness didn't give off the slightest hint of arrogance. He was a breath of fresh air for our school, which had been ignored for so long. Lintang and the magnetism of his mind slowly became our new life force. He marched to the beat of his own drum. He was the mantra in our *gurindam* rhymes— two-lined aphorisms.

Then came news that made our hearts race. Our school was invited to participate in an Academic Challenge in the regional capital, Tanjong Pandan. The challenge was held every year. It was truly prestigious.

It had been a very long time since we'd last participated. We always lost by a landslide. So to avoid being shamed, we had just decided not to compete at all.

Now Lintang could probably change that. Our competitors from the PN and state schools were awfully intelligent and had won at the national level, but Lintang gave us a sense of confidence. Would he be able to defeat them? Would his scrawny body be able to prop up our collapsing school—the school that was unlikely to even receive any new students the following year?

Lintang had no choice but to study diligently. Consequently, his first-quarter report card in the fifth grade was truly fantastic. The number nine filled the slots from faith studies, al-Qur'an, Fiqh, Islamic history, geography, all the way to English. For mathematics and other such subjects—geometry and natural sciences—Bu Mus dared to give him a perfect score: ten. His lowest grade was six—for art class. He couldn't compete with the eccentric young man with a skinny body and a handsome face sitting off in the corner. This enchanting boy was Trapani's deskmate. Mahar was his name. He always wore a mischievous smile.

12 ☼ HE BETRAYED HARMONY

Papilio blumei, the captivating tropical black butterflies with blue-green stripes, visited the tips of the filicium leaves. Moments later, they were followed by other species: the pure clouded yellow butterfly and the Danube clouded yellow butterfly.

Only experts can tell the difference between the two similarly named species. Their Latin names, respectively, are *Colias crocea* and *Colias myrmidone*. To the untrained eye, they are equally flawless in their beauty.

Unlike small birds with aggressive and exhibitionist dispositions, these mute creatures have a short life span and are completely unaware of their beauty. And even though there were hundreds of them, they were silent, fluttering as they wandered about. If one carefully observed them, one realized that their every movement, no matter how slight, was moved by harmony's heartbeat. They were an orchestra of color with instinct as their conductor, creating a vision even more stunning than the Garden of Eden. Seeing them made me feel like writing poems.

This afternoon, however, the heavenly butterflies weren't the only ones harmonizing. Listen.

". . . may my fwag fwutter . . ."

". . . the howy, stuwdy, symbol . . ."

". . . waving! Mawching! Mawching!"

A Kiong was "singing" Ibu Sud's "Berkibarlah Benderaku"— "May My Flag Flutter"—as if he were a drill sergeant. It was painful to hear.

While singing, he stared out the window and focused on the gourd vine on the low branches of the filicium. He didn't even glance at us. His ears seemed disconnected from his voice; their attention had been captured by the boisterous chatter of the stripe-winged, tiny prinia birds shouting over the buzz of female yellow-back beetles. A Kiong didn't care about the range of his voice and didn't bother trying to sing on pitch.

To be fair, we weren't paying attention to him, either. Lintang was engrossed in the Pythagorean theorem. Harun had fallen asleep and was snoring. Samson was drawing a picture of a man lifting a house. Sahara was absorbed in embroidering calligraphic Arabic symbols on her cross-stitch, which read KULIL HAQQU WALAU KANA MURRON, meaning, "Tell the truth, even when it's bitter." Trapani was folding, unfolding, and refolding his mother's handkerchief. Syahdan, Kucai, and I were busy talking about the PN School kids' uniforms and our plan to hang the Koranic studies teacher's bike in the branches of the *bantan* tree. Only Mahar listened attentively to A Kiong's singing.

Bu Mus covered her face with her hands. She was trying very hard to hold back laughter as she listened to the howling.

A Kiong finished. Bu Mus looked at me: my turn. After having been scolded by Bu Mus for always singing the song "Potong Bebek Angsa"—"Chop the Goose's Neck"—this time I decided to progress a little with a new song: "Indonesia Tetap Merdeka," or "Indonesia Forever Free," by C. Simanjuntak. When I began to sing, Sahara looked up from her cross-stitch and glared at me with disgust. I ignored her insult and continued spiritedly.

". . . Joyous cheers . . . joy for all . . .

". . . our country's been liberated . . . Indonesia is free . . ."

As I sang, I jumped from octave to octave. I had no control and even less harmony.

Tears ran down Bu Mus's face as she shook in silent laughter. I tried hard to improve the sound, but the harder I tried, the stranger the noise. This is what they mean by untalented. I struggled to finish. My classmates had no sympathy for me. They were suffering, too—from sleepiness, hunger, and thirst in the midday heat. My singing made it that much worse.

Bu Mus saved me by hastily asking me to stop before the great song was over. She looked to Samson.

Samson chose the song "Teguh Kukuh Berlapis Baja"— "Strong, Firm, and Coated with Steel"—also by C. Simanjuntak. The song fit with Samson's gigantic body, and he sang it in an earsplitting voice as he bowed deeply and stomped his feet.

". . . Strong, firm, and coated with steel!

". . . chain of spirit tightly bound!

". . . upright fortress of Indonesia!"

But he, too, knew nothing about the concept of harmony, and he turned the beloved song into one we did not recognize. He betrayed C. Simanjuntak.

Before he could get through the first verse, Bu Mus asked him to return to his seat. Samson froze; he couldn't believe his ears.

"Why am I being asked to stop, Ibunda Guru?"

This is what they mean by untalented and oblivious.

To make a long story short, singing was the least promising subject for our class. Not one of us was able to sing, and for that reason, Bu Mus put singing class at the end of the day. Its purpose was to pass the minutes while we waited for Zuhr—midday prayer—which marked the closing of the school day.

"We still have five minutes until the call to prayer. Hmm. We have time for one more," said Bu Mus. We were indifferent to this news. It was a languid afternoon. Now and again the stripe-winged prinias perched on the windowsill of our classroom, warbling emphatically.

"Let's see . . . who's next?"

It was Mahar.

"Please come up to the front, my child. Sing a song while we wait for the Zuhr call to prayer." Bu Mus returned to smiling in anticipation of yet another ridiculous performance by one of her students.

Up until this point, we had never heard Mahar sing. Whenever his turn came up, the call to prayer invariably sounded and he was spared the chance to perform. So we paid no attention when he got up and made his way to the front of the class. Once in front of the class, he did not sing his song right away. Already prepared to go home, he had slung his rattan bag over his shoulder. After a while he drew his arms together over his chest like someone in prayer. The backs of his hands were oily, like wax. He had scars all over his fingers, and his nails were mangled. Since the second grade, Mahar had worked after school as a coolie, grating coconuts at a Chinese produce stall. Hour after hour, until nightfall, he kneaded coconut leftovers, which caused his hands to develop a waxen appearance that never went away. The sharp blade of the grater, its engine cranked by an adult, sliced the tips of Mahar's fingers, deforming his fingernails in the process. The grater puffed out black smoke. The sound of it was harrowing, a sound of deprivation, hard work, a poor life without a choice. Mahar had to work to help his family survive. His father had already died, and his mother was very ill.

"I shall sing a song about love, Ibunda Guru, an agonizing love, to be exact . . ."

My God! We never gave prologues like that, and we never sang songs of that theme. We usually sang nationalistic songs, religious songs in Arabic, or children's songs.

"This song tells the story of someone with a broken heart. His beloved sweetheart was stolen by his good friend."

He fell silent and stared out through the window, past the drifting clouds. We were blown away when he opened his rattan sack and pulled out an instrument: a ukulele!

Mahar began gingerly strumming an introduction that broke the silence like the rumbling of distant thunder. His eyes were shut. Then, after a smooth prelude, he glided into the first verse of the song.

> *I was dancing with my darling to the Tennessee Waltz*
> *When an old friend I happened to see,*
> *Introduced her to my loved one, and while they were dancing,*
> *My friend stole my sweetheart from me.*

We gasped in awe. The song was none other than the famous "Tennessee Waltz," sung by Anne Murray! The vibration of Mahar's voice was flawless; his comprehension of the song was incredible. He actually looked as though he were suffering terribly from the loss of his beloved sweetheart. We were mesmerized, enchanted by Mahar's pained voice. When he finished, we gave him a standing ovation. Bu Mus tried hard to hide the tears in her eyes. That July midday, in the peak of the dry season, while we waited for the Zuhr call to prayer, a great artist was born in the poor Muhammadiyah School.

13 ✵ THE DAYDREAMER

Only after witnessing his performance did we know who Mahar really was. All this time he had been acting awkward, dressing eccentrically, talking nonsense, and we—unaware that all those quirks were reflections of his artistic talent—had deemed him a weird bohemian boy. We now discovered that Mahar balanced out the ship of our school, which had teetered to the left because of the pull of Lintang's brain. Lintang and Mahar created an intellectual and artistic set of goalposts in our classroom. With those goalposts in place, it became impossible for us to be bored.

Because Lintang and Mahar sat across from each other, the rest of us often ended up looking left and right, back and forth, as if watching a Ping-Pong match. Sandwiched between them, we were like the dimwits challenged by Columbus to make an egg stand up straight.

Once, during free time between classes, Lintang got up in front of everybody and drew a blueprint for how to make a boat from a sago tree leaf. The boat moved by a propeller connected to a motor, which had been taken from a tape recorder. It was powered by two batteries. He made mathematical calculations in order to manipulate the tape recorder motor to push the boat and explained to us the fundamental laws of hydraulics. His calculation could estimate the speed of the boat based on its mass. I was spellbound by the little sago-leaf boat spinning around in the bucket.

On another occasion he showed us a kite design and a glass-coated thread that would render us unbeatable in kite battles. The amazing thing was, he had many technical sketches and plans that remained raw. These seeds included his idea to lift heavy items from the bottom of the river; a plan for a strange building that defied the laws of architecture and civil engineering; and, last but not least, a plan to make humans able to fly.

As for Mahar, time after time he stole the stage. He had artistic insight—plus he knew about music because he hung out with the local radio broadcasters from Suara Pengejawantahan (The Voice of Manifestation) AM. He read some verses of poems about white birds on Tanjong Kelayang Beach, as well as parodies about Malays who suddenly became rich. He also played that remarkable ukulele. It could rock us to sleep.

Because he was so imaginative, Mahar became an even bigger fan of unreasonable legends and all things smelling of the paranormal. One could ask him about ancient stories and Belitong's mythology, and he knew everything from the fairy tale of the South China Sea dragon to the story of the monkey-tailed king believed to have once ruled our island.

Mahar also was crazy about Bruce Lee. The walls of his house were covered with pictures of the kung fu master in various poses. He begged Bu Mus over and over again for permission to hang up a poster of Bruce Lee posed in a raging dragon move, eyes glaring, with a double stick as his weapon and three parallel scratches on his cheek because he had been clawed by his enemy.

Mahar firmly believed that aliens not only existed, but that they would one day come down to Belitong Island disguised as male hospital orderlies in charge of giving vaccinations at the PN clinic, school guards, muezzins at the al-Hikmah Mosque, or football referees. Sometimes Mahar was positively ridiculous. For instance, he assumed himself to be the chairman of the international paranormal association that would lead the fight of human beings against aliens, using velvetleaves as weapons.

One evening, after a full day of heavy rains, a perfect rainbow stretched across the sky to the west, a half circle shining brilliantly with seven rows of color. It rose out of the Genting Delta like a sparkling carpet and planted itself deep in the pine forest on the Selumar Mountain. It curved and danced, looking like a million maidens floating down into a remote lake.

We invaded the filicium tree, claiming our own separate branches. The old tree became engulfed in boisterous debate as we offered our personal theories on the magical panorama sweeping across East Belitong. We so loved the stories we had to tell, it became a habit for us to climb the tree after every rainstorm in search of rainbows. And because of this, Bu Mus nicknamed us Laskar Pelangi. *Laskar* means "warriors"; *pelangi* means "rainbow": we were the Rainbow Troops.

The most entertaining stories came, of course, from Mahar. We pressed him to tell a story. He acted shy and hesitant at first. The look in his eyes implied, *This is a dangerous story! You all won't be able to guard this highly sensitive information!*

But after serious consideration, he would give in—not because of our begging, but because of his own irresistible desire to show off. "You know what, you guys?" he asked, gazing into the distance. "Rainbows are actually time tunnels! If we were to succeed in crossing the rainbow, we would meet our ancient Belitong ancestors and the Sawangs' predecessors."

Mahar looked regretful, as if he had just revealed a deep, dark family secret that had been kept for seven generations. He continued in a strained tone. "But you don't want to meet the primitive Belitong people or the Sawangs' forefathers," he commanded in all seriousness.

"Why not, Mahar?" A Kiong asked fearfully.

"Because they were cannibals!"

A Kiong covered his mouth with his hands and, having let go, almost plummeted from his branch. Ever since the first grade, he had been Mahar's faithful follower. He believed, with all of his soul, whatever Mahar said. He regarded Mahar as a master and spiritual advisor. The two of them had inducted themselves into the sect of collective foolishness.

Lintang patted Mahar on the back, appreciating his amazing tale, but smirking and faking a cough to disguise his laughter. We continued admiring the magnificence of the rainbow until the sun set.

The call for Maghrib prayer echoed among the high posts of stilted Malay homes, crying out from mosque to mosque. The time tunnel was swallowed by the night. We had been taught not to speak while the call to prayer sounded.

"Be quiet and listen attentively to the call to glory," our parents instructed.

I mused over Mahar's tale. More than being drawn in by the time tunnel, I was captivated by the part about the ancient peoples of Belitong.

We Malays are generally simple individuals who acquire life's wisdom from Koranic studies teachers and elders at the mosque after Maghrib prayer. That wisdom is taken from accounts from the prophets, the tale of Hang Tuah, and *gurindam* rhymes. Ours is an old race. There are some experts who say that Belitong-Malays are not Malay.

We don't put much stock in that opinion for two reasons: Belitong people themselves don't understand such matters; and because we aren't eager to be primordial. To us, people all along the coast—from Belitong up to Malaysia—are Malays, based on a mutual obsession with peninsular rhythms, the beating of tambourines, and rhyming. Our identity is not based on language, skin color, belief systems, or skeletal structure. We are an egalitarian race.

Last week, when the mosque's sound system was being fixed, we went to see the mess of cables, which had been called "magic new-age objects." While we were there, our seventy-year-old muezzin told us a story that stunned me.

The story was about his great-grandfather, who lived in a nomadic group, wandering the coasts of Belitong. They wore clothes made of bark and ate by spearing animals or trapping them in tree roots. They slept on the branches of *santigi* trees to avoid being attacked by predatory creatures. During the full moon, they lit fires and worshipped the moon and the stars above. I got goose bumps thinking about how close our community was to primitive culture.

"We've been allied with the Sawangs for a long time. They were skilled sailors living in boats, sailing from island to island. In Balok Bay our ancestors traded mouse deer, rattan fruit, areca nuts, and resin with salt made by Sawang women," the muezzin informed us.

Like fish living in an aquarium, we forgot about the water.

After all these years living side by side with the Sawangs, we had no idea they were actually an anthropological phenomenon. Like the Chinese, Sawangs made up an important element of our heritage.

Next to the Malays—and even more so next to Chinese—the Sawangs have a very different appearance. They are like the native Australian inhabitants, the Aborigines: they have dark skin, strong jaws, deep eyes, thin foreheads, Teutonic-like cranial structures, and broomlike hair.

PN employed the males of this tribe as coolies to haul sacks of tin from washing stations to ferries in ports. The ferries would then bring the tin to melting factories on Bangka Island. The women were employed as tin-sack weavers. The men and women occupied the lowest stratum among laborers in Belitong, but they were happy because they got paid every Monday. It was hard to say if the money would last until Wednesday—not a drop of stinginess ran in Sawang blood. They spent like there was no tomorrow and borrowed like they'd live forever.

Because of their money management problems, the Sawangs often became the victims of negative stereotypes in the circles of the Malay majority and the Chinese. All bad things were, without a doubt, associated with them. These attempts at discrediting the Sawangs reflected the character of a minority of Malays and Chinese afraid to lose jobs because of their own reluctance to perform hard labor. History has shown the Sawangs are a people of integrity, living exclusively within their own community, not sticking their noses in others' business, and employing a strong work ethic. They never got into trouble with the law. More than that, they never ran from their debts.

The Sawangs were quite happy to marginalize themselves. For them, life consisted of a foreman willing to pay them once a week and hard jobs that no other race was willing to do. They didn't recognize the concept of *power distance* because there was no hierarchy in their culture. People who didn't understand their culture would consider them impolite. The one and only exalted one among them was the head of the tribe, usually a shaman, and the position wasn't hereditary.

PN placed them in a longhouse with partitions. Thirty families lived there. There's no accurate record of their origins. It's quite possible that they are unmapped by anthropologists. Do policy makers know their birthrate is so low and their mortality rate so high that there are only a few families of pure-blooded Sawangs left? Will their beautiful language be swept away by the waves of time?

A thick black rope hung over the surface of the rolling waters, arcing toward the river's surface. One end was tied to a branch of an old, brittle rubber tree that reached up like an arm in the middle of the river's flow. It was Samson who had hurled it out there.

It was about seventeen meters from the edge of the river to the rubber tree branch in the middle. That meant the river was roughly thirty meters wide, and God only knows how deep. The current ran swiftly and briskly. The surface of the water glittered under the blaze of the sun.

A Kiong, positioned on the edge of the river, held the other end of the rope. He climbed up a *kepang* tree across from the rubber tree and then tied his end to one of its branches.

My body shook as I made my way along the rope, hand over hand, toward the rubber tree. The rope slid inch by inch through my choking grip. I hung like a soldier in a drill; my legs fell down from the rope every once in a while and skimmed the swift surface of the water, making my blood curdle. I could vaguely see my shadow on the opaque water. If I fell, I would be found stuck among mangrove roots near Linggang Bridge, about fifty kilometers from here.

All this effort—which, by the way, went against our parents' wishes—was for the sake of obtaining rubber fruit and increasing the worth of our bets in the *tarak* arena. The fruit was something of a mystery. Certainly the strength of its skin could not be deduced from its shape and color. Herein lay the appeal of the ancient and legendary game of *tarak*, a game in which two rubber fruits were stacked and then hit with the palm of the hand. Whichever fruit didn't break was the winner. *Tarak* was a game that opened the rainy season in our village, a warm-up for the far more exciting games to come when the rain flooded down from the sky. There was one fundamental key to *tarak*, which was that the rubber trees with the hardest fruits were always deep in the forest, and it took either an extraordinary amount of effort or intrepid yet foolish determination to obtain them.

As rain beat down more violently on the village, the aura of *tarak* slowly faded away. When *tarak* was no longer being played, it meant it was already the end of September. The entire world becomes depressed during the months that end in -*ber*—that is, the entire world excluding us. The sadness of the final months of the year was for adults to worry about. For us, the end of the year brought many fun things, and each had its own story. My friend, I will share them with you, one by one.

Up first was Lintang. He informed us that he had just bought a new, stronger tire for his bike. He had also repaired the bike's chain. His goal was to be able to carry his mother on the back of the bike. And for the first time, his mother would come to the school to receive his report card. Lintang's eyes lit up when he spoke of his mother. He usually got his report card with his father. It was clear as day that Lintang was extremely proud to be able to present his mother with his top-of-the-class report card.

Lintang and his parents were the first to arrive and take their seats on the long bench. Because they owned only one bicycle, Lintang's father departed from their home in the middle of the night to make the journey by foot. Once morning came, Lintang followed with his mother on the bicycle.

After all the parents and students had gathered, Pak Harfan delivered a short speech. He told all present that Lintang was the pride of the Muhammadiyah School. To pay his respects to Lintang's mother for making the long journey to school, Pak Harfan invited her to say a few words.

She was shy and hesitant at first. She had met with misfortune, suffering from polio as a child. She now walked with a cane. Lintang got up to hold his mother's arm.

Lintang's mother received his report card from Pak Harfan. Her hands quivered, holding on to it. She opened the first page, unaware that she was holding it upside down. Like Lintang's father, my father, and most of our parents, Lintang's mother could not read or write.

She thanked Bu Mus and Pak Harfan. Her dialect was hard to follow—it was very backcountry Malay. She said, more or less, that this was the first time she had left her village, and everyone smiled bitterly when she said it was so hard to believe that these days, reading and writing could change one's future.

She knew our school had been threatened with closure. She said that in her nightly prayers she always prayed Lintang would win the Academic Challenge so our school wouldn't be closed—a truly sincere hope.

It appeared that the coastal family had high hopes for Lintang's education. They believed their future could be better if

Lintang got his diploma. Lintang's mother finished by saying how proud she was of her oldest son. I looked over at Lintang. His eyes were glassy, and he lowered his head as his tears fell to the floor.

After Lintang's mother spoke, Pak Harfan invited Lintang to come up. With wet eyes, Lintang dedicated all of his grades on his report card to his mother.

Usually after Lintang's report card came mine. As I've said, I always got second place. However, this time it was different. Harun snatched second place.

As part of our struggle to save our school from Mister Samadikun's efforts to close it, as well as for the sake of appreciating Harun and making him happy, Bu Mus had made him a special report card. Even the numbers inside were special. Bu Mus spoke with Harun in a truly democratic manner. First of all, Harun asked, "Ibunda Guru, of all the subjects on this report card, which one is the most important?"

"Muhammadiyah ethics," Bu Mus answered convincingly, pointing at it on the lowest line of the report card.

Harun nodded and, even more convincingly, asked to be provided with the same grades as Lintang and Trapani. That action certainly made him the runner-up, defeating me. For that class, Harun demanded the grade of three.

"Three is a low mark, my child. You are very well mannered. I dare say you deserve an eight."

Harun froze. Bu Mus had said it was lamentable to get a three on your report card.

"The score of eight is rightfully yours. It is the highest grade I have ever given to any of my students for that class. Isn't that great? You got the highest score in the most valuable subject of study in the world."

Bu Mus was right, and we all agreed. Harun's exemplary behavior deserved to be rewarded with an eight. The ironic thing was that on the contrary, we, who had a *more normal* way of thinking, never received eights in ethics class.

Despite numerous attempts at persuasion, Harun didn't budge. Bu Mus stopped trying to convince him after he peacefully said, "God likes odd numbers, Ibunda Guru."

So the low number three was carved onto Harun's report card. His grade average would certainly drop. However, because he had taken all the tens from Lintang's card and other high scores from his idol Trapani's card, he remained runner-up.

Bu Mus had made a wise decision in making Harun's report card. His mother was as happy as a parent at her child's graduation ceremony. Harun grinned and waved his report card high in the air.

As the afternoon grew older, the joyous report card festivities came to a close. I went home riding on the back of my father's bike, but I couldn't tear my eyes away from Lintang and his parents as they left the school.

Lintang pedaled the bike and tightly gripped the handlebars, with his mother's cane slung over his left shoulder. She sat on the back of the bike, and his father walked alongside, pushing it.

Lintang's family was like the epitome of poverty for Malay and Indonesian traditional fishermen. They carried that misery in their hearts from generation to generation. They swallowed the bitterness of empty expectations for the future and their doubts about their children's education. This misery, of the *have-nots*, couldn't be heard by anyone's ears, not the *haves'* nor the state's.

But today the misery briefly disappeared for one family, covered by the near-endless marks of ten in the report card of their extraordinary young son.

The sky darkened. Lintang and his parents ran to take shelter under the leaves of the *gayam* tree. Millions of honeybees attacked the village from the mountain. The first rain had come.

15 ❈ THE FIRST RAIN

Belitong Island lies at the point where the South China Sea and the Java Sea meet. The location, sheltered by Java and Kalimantan, protects its coasts from extreme waves, but the millions of gallons of water evaporating from the surrounding seas in the dry season spill down on it for days on end during the months of the rainy season.

The first rain was a blessing from the sky, and we greeted it with joy. The heavier it rained, the louder the thunder roared, the faster the winds stirred the villages, the greater the lightning flashed, the merrier our hearts. We let the torrential rains shower our bodies. We ignored the threats of rattan whippings from our parents; they were nothing compared to the allure of the rain. We went anyway, strange animals making our way up from bottoms of ditches, over fallen trees and PN project cars drowning in floods, with the refreshing smell of rainwater reviving our chests.

We didn't stop until we were blue in the lips and couldn't feel our numb fingers. We ran around, played football, made sand castles, pretended to be monitor lizards, swam in the mud, shouted to the planes flying above, and screamed loudly and incoherently to the rain and thunderbolts in the sky.

The most fun game didn't have a name, but it involved *pinang hantu* tree leaves. One or two people sat on a leaf as wide as a prayer mat, while two or three people pulled. The outcome resembled sledding.

The game's climax came at the moment when the leaf-pullers, strong as horses, made a quick turn and intentionally pulled harder. Those on the leaf would be thrust to the side, the slippery mud smoothing out an otherwise sharp, rapid, and exhilarating skid.

I felt my body thrash about beyond my control and saw a huge wave of mud splash up from the right and cover the spectators in wet dirt. Syahdan acted as my copilot, imitating a long-haired daredevil riding his motorcycle through a flaming tunnel at the circus.

The severe angle of the turn made it difficult to round successfully; the leaf-pullers crashed into each other and tumbled around and around. As for Syahdan and me, we were flung from the leaf and sent into a spin before finally spilling into a ditch.

My head felt heavy. I groped it and felt small bumps emerging. My voice sounded strange, even robotic. A throbbing pain on the right side of my head was spreading to my eyes, something I usually felt after getting water up my nose. I looked for Syahdan, who had slid a bit farther. I found him sprawled out, motionless and half-covered in the ditch's water.

He wasn't breathing. He had fallen hard, like a pipe from a truck. I saw thick blood dripping slowly from his nose. We gathered around. Sahara started crying, all the color drained from her face. I slapped Syahdan's cheeks.

"Syahdan! Syahdan!"

I touched the blood vessel on his neck, imitating what I'd

seen on the TV series *Little House on the Prairie* at the village hall. Since I didn't know what I was searching for, I didn't find it. Samson, Kucai, and Trapani shook Syahdan, trying to wake him up.

We panicked; we didn't know what to do. I kept calling his name, but he still didn't move. Samson suggested that we lift him up. His body was already rigid. I held on to his head as we carried his body, running together. Sahara was wailing at this point. We were truly in a state of panic, but amid the rising urgency, the black curly head in my hands showed rows of decayed teeth as pointy as ice picks and let out a high-pitched laugh.

My copilot had faked his death! That rascal had lain still and held his breath so we'd think he'd died. We returned the favor by throwing him back into the ditch. He was elated, doubling over with laughter at our bewilderment.

The strange thing was, while falling, crashing, and rolling around were painful, they were nonetheless followed by loud laughter and teasing—which were the most appealing parts of the no-name game. We would play it over and over again. The falling incident wasn't caused by the physics-defying angle of the turn, speed, and mass, but by the voluntary silliness triggered by the rainy-season euphoria. The world may have been depressed, but the *-ber* months were glorious for us. The rainy season was a festival held for Malay children, for us, by nature itself.

16 ❀ HEAVENLY POETRY AND A FLOCK OF *PELINTANG PULAU*

Before the rains came, when the dry season had not yet left our village, trees withered, and passing vehicles kicked up dust from the red-pebbled roads; it clung to windowsills. My village was dry and smelled like rust.

The Chinese community became more vigorous in their routine: they bathed in the middle of the day, combing back their wet hair and trimming their nails. They were the only ones who looked a bit cleaner during the dry season. The Sawangs, on the other hand, idly hugged the posts of their longhouse. It was too hot to sleep under the corrugated, ceilingless roof, but they were too exhausted to go back to work.

The Sarong people, as I refer to them, spent all day and night out at sea. Soon enough, the months ending in *-ber* would be here and the winds would be too powerful. The dry season was their opportunity to make money.

The Malays got disheveled and spent a lot of time at home. None of them owned a refrigerator. Once in a while their children could be seen passing along the main road carrying blocks of ice and flavored syrup to make cold drinks.

The humidity didn't lift until late at night. As dawn approached, the temperature fell drastically, testing the faith of the Prophet Muhammad's followers, challenging them to get out of their beds and head to the mosque for Subuh prayer.

For the past few days, Lintang had been cheerful, as usual, but exhausted on account of the condition of his bicycle. The chain, which often snapped, was getting shorter because a link had to be removed each time it broke. The tires kept going flat. Then he had to push his bicycle the entire way to school. Finally, it could no longer be used.

With no other choice, Lintang had to walk the dozens of kilometers to school. There was a shortcut, but it was very dangerous—you had to cut through a swamp, home to many crocodile jaws. The middle was chest-deep. But if he had to walk to school, that was the route Lintang had to take to arrive on time.

Lintang often told stories about how, when he went down into the swamp, dozens of sunbathing crocodiles would follow with their sights set on him. For that reason, before he left for school, he always bathed himself in betel water—a traditional antiseptic.

When he got to the swamp, he bundled his clothes and books in plastic and held them up high as he waded through the water, and when he had to swim, he clenched the plastic with his teeth. He was always glancing around for crocodiles.

Today Lintang arrived sopping wet from his head down to his toes. During his escape from the crocodiles, his bundle of plastic had spilled open. He stood dazed in front of the classroom door. Bu Mus invited him in. He was happy to study even though his clothes were wet.

After school, Lintang approached me. His forlorn expression was, like the elongated dry season, highly uncharacteristic. I was surprised; sullenness was not one of Lintang's traits.

"What's wrong, buddy?" I asked, trying my hardest to smile.

Lintang took a handkerchief out of the pocket of his shorts. I remembered seeing his mother hold it when we got our report cards. He unfolded the handkerchief, revealing a ring.

"This is the wedding ring my father gave my mother," he said shakily. "My mother doesn't want me to miss school because of the bicycle. She said I have to study hard so I can win the Academic Challenge. She asked that I sell this ring for money to buy a new bicycle chain."

Lintang's eyes were glassy. My chest tightened.

We left for the market. The eighteen-karat ring was weighed on a portable scale: three grams. The low quality of gold made it look like an imitation, but it was Lintang's family's most precious possession. The ring sold for just about 125,000 rupiah, at that time about 50 U.S. dollars—just enough to buy a bicycle chain and two tires.

Lintang wouldn't let go of the ring. The gold dealer had to pry his fingers open one by one to take it. When Lintang finally let go, he let his tears go as well.

"You repay your mother's sacrifice by winning that Academic Challenge, Boi!" I said, hoping he would forget his sadness. Boi is a nickname for close friends among Belitong-Malay boys. Lintang looked at me earnestly. "I promise, Boi."

But all life's sadness and weariness had to be left behind, or at least set aside, because our class had big plans: camping.

While the PN School kids rode their blue bus to Tanjong Pandan for recreation, or visited the zoo and the museum, or went on *verloop*—Dutch for vacation—with their parents to Jakarta, we went to Pangkalan Punai Beach. It was about sixty kilometers away, and we made our way there in a lively flock, riding bicycles.

Even though we visited Pangkalan Punai every year, I never

grew tired of the place. Where the dozens of hectares of sand met the forest, I found a different sense of beauty.

As evening approached, I lingered at the top of a hill, listening to the faint sounds of fishermen's children, boys and girls, kicking buoys and playing football without goalposts.

At my back was a savanna as wide as the sea itself. Thousands of pipits settled on the tall grass, shouting among themselves, fighting for a place to sleep. From gaps between rows of coconut trees, I saw the giant boulders that are Pangkalan Punai's trademark, fencing in the lustrous blue South China Sea. Brackish river streams wound and curved from afar until finally merging with the sea, like floes of melted silver.

As night drew near, the orange and red rays of the sun fell below the *nanga*-leaf roofs of the stilted homes sticking out among lush *santigi* leaves. Smoke billowed from hearths burning coconut fibers to chase away bugs that appeared around Maghrib. The smoke, accompanied by the call to prayer, drifted slowly over the village like a ghost, faintly crawled up the branches of the sweet-fruit *bintang* trees, was swept away by the wind, and then was engulfed by the vast sea. Small buds of fire in oil lamps danced silently behind the small windows of the stilted houses scattered about below.

The enchantment of Pangkalan Punai hung over me until it moved me to write a poem.

I Dreamt I Saw Heaven

Truly, the third night in Pangkalan Punai I dreamt I saw heaven
It turns out that heaven is not grandiose, but a small castle in the middle of the forest
There were no beautiful maidens as is said in the scriptures

I walked along a small, narrow bridge
A beautiful woman with a pure face greeted me
"This is heaven," she said
She invited me to walk through a field of flowers
Under the colorful low clouds
Toward the veranda of the castle

On the veranda, I saw small lights hidden behind the curtain
Each light cut through the thick grass in the garden
Beautiful, unspeakably beautiful

Heaven was so very quiet
But I wanted to stay here
Because I remembered your promise, God
If I came walking
YOU would meet me running

As part of our camping program, we had to turn in an assignment—a composition, painting, or handmade object composed of materials collected around the beach. With that poem I received an art score a little bit better than Mahar's.

Mahar hadn't received the highest score because of a flock of mysterious birds the people of Belitong call *pelintang pulau* birds—"island crossing" birds.

Pelintang pulau birds were attention-grabbers anywhere, but nowhere more so than on the coast. Some thought they were supernatural creatures. The name of those birds sent shivers through the hearts of coastal people because of the myths surrounding them and the messages they bore. If a flock appeared in a village, fishermen would promptly cancel plans to sail; to them, the arrival of these mysterious birds portended a storm at sea.

Whatever those birds actually were, Mahar claimed he saw them while doing research for his art assignment, which he had decided would be a painting. He scrambled back to the tent to tell us what he had just seen. We dashed into the forest to witness one of the rarest species in Belitong Island's rich fauna.

Unfortunately, all we saw were empty branches, several long-tailed monkey babies, and a vacant sky. Mahar had trapped himself. Mockery ensued.

"If someone eats too many *bintang* fruits, he can get drunk, Mahar—blurred vision, a rambling mouth," Samson said, pulling the trigger. The derision began.

"Seriously, Samson, I saw a flock of five *pelintang pulau* birds!"

"'The sea's depth is immeasurable, a lie's depth is unpredictable,'" Kucai jabbed with a simple verse.

Despair emerged on Mahar's face. His eyes searched the branches above. Without a witness to back him up, he was powerless. I looked deep into Mahar's eyes. I did believe he had just seen those sacred birds. How lucky! Too bad Mahar had a reputation as a liar.

"Don't get caught up in lies and imagination, friend. You know, lying is forbidden to us. The prohibition appears over and over again in our Muhammadiyah ethics book," Sahara lectured.

The situation grew chaotic as news that Mahar had seen *pelintang pulau* birds spread to the village, prompting fishermen to cancel their plans to go to sea. Bu Mus was incapable of pacifying the situation. Mahar was cornered.

But that night the winds blew furiously, turning our tent upside down. Lightning flashed violently over the sea. Black clouds swirled menacingly in the sky. We ran for our lives, finding shelter in one of the villagers' homes.

"Maybe you really saw *pelintang pulau* birds, Mahar," Syahdan said shakily.

Mahar didn't say anything. I knew that the word *maybe* was inappropriate. The storm backed his story up, and the fishermen thanked him. But his own friends? They still doubted him. They made him feel like a persona non grata, an outcast.

The next day Mahar made a painting he titled *Pelintang Pulau Flock*. It made for an interesting theme. Five birds were portrayed as obscure shapes darting through the gaps of *meranti* treetops. The background was a gloomy cluster of storm clouds. The sea was painted dark blue, with a glinting surface reflecting flashes of lightning. Rendered as amorphous streaks of yellowish green, Mahar's birds moved with great speed. If the painting was glanced at casually, it vaguely looked like the birds made up five flocks, but the impression was of colorful strokes of fire. A truly spine-tingling painting. It was riveting.

The idea behind Mahar's painting was to try to capture the essence of the mysterious *pelintang pulau* birds. The anatomy of the birds was irrelevant to him. But Samson, Kucai, and Sahara held the opinion that the birds' shapes were unclear because Mahar hadn't actually seen them. Mahar retreated into cynicism, and his mood soured.

Disappointed, Mahar turned in his assignment late. That was the reason his score was lowered—because he exceeded the deadline, not because of aesthetic considerations.

"This time I didn't give you the best score, in order to teach you a lesson," said Bu Mus to an apathetic Mahar. "It is not because your work lacked quality; no matter what kind of work we do, we must have discipline. Talented people with a bad attitude are useless."

I felt this was a fair enough opinion. Mahar lost no sleep over the score he received for his works of art. More so now than usual, he was very busy. He was in the middle of brainstorming for the carnival on August 17—Independence Day.

17 ❀ LOVE AT THE SHABBY SUNDRY SHOP

Ah, adolescence was great.

At school, lessons became more useful. We learned how to make salty eggs, embroidery, and *menata janur*, a Malay wedding decoration. Better yet, we started stumbling through the English language: *good* this, *good* that, *excuse me, I beg your pardon*, and *I am fine, thank you*. The most enjoyable task was learning how to translate songs. It turned out the old song "Have I Told You Lately That I Love You" had a beautiful meaning.

Its lyrics, more or less, tell a story about a young child who always hated being sent by his teacher to buy chalk, until one day he left in irritation to buy it, unaware that destiny was waiting to mercilessly ambush him at the fish market.

Buying chalk was without a doubt the least enjoyable class chore. Another chore we really hated was watering the flowers. The various ferns, from the *Platycerium coronarium* to the dozens of pots of Bu Mus's beloved adiantum, had to be treated delicately, as if they were expensive Chinese porcelain. Careless handling of the flowers was a serious violation.

"This is part of your education," Bu Mus insisted earnestly.

The problem was, getting water from the well behind the school was hard work, even for coolies. Aside from having to fill two big buckets and scramble back with them on your shoulders, you also had to face the creepy old well. The well was so deep its bottom couldn't be seen, like it was connected to another world, or perhaps was a pit filled with demons. Anyway, the burden of life felt much heavier on mornings when you had to lower your head into that well.

Only when I watered the Canna "Striped Beauties" did I feel a slight consolation. To think that such a beautiful flower originates from the damp wilderness of the Brazilian hills. It is still in the *Apocynaceae* family, which is why it slightly resembles the allamanda, but the white stripes on its yellow flowers are a distinctive feature that no other canna possesses. Its plump green creeping leaves bear a striking contrast to the color gradation in its blossoms year-round, emanating a primeval beauty. The Persians called them heaven's flowers. When they bloom, all the world smiles. They are emotional flowers, so one must water them carefully. Not everyone can grow them. It's been said that only one with a green thumb and a gentle and pure heart can cultivate them, and that was Bu Mus, our teacher.

We had a few pots of Canna "Striped Beauties," and we agreed to place them in the most distinguished position among the *daun picisan* and succulents, which paled in comparison. When the season arrived and they bloomed simultaneously, they looked like a layered cake placed on a serving tray.

I was always hasty in watering the flowers so I could just get it over with, but when I got to the cannas and their neighbors, I tried to take it slowly. I enjoyed daydreaming, guessing what people would imagine if they were in the middle of this mini-heaven. Would they feel like they were in a prehistoric paradise?

I looked around the little flower garden located right in front of our principal's office. There was a little path of square stones leading to the garden, its left side overflowing with monstera, nolina, violces, peas, *cemara udang*, caladium, and tall begonias that didn't need watering. The flowers, unarranged, were rich with nectar, crowded with brightly colored unknown plants and various wild grasses and bushes.

A gourd vine snaked up our bell's post. Like a giant arm touching the wooden-planked walls of our school, it was unrestrained by the roof shingles hanging loose from their nails and the pomegranate twigs shading the office roof. The young vines of the gourd dangled in front of the office window; you could reach out and touch them. Javanese finches frequently hung from them. All morning long the place was abuzz with the sounds of beetles and honeybees. Whenever I really listened, after a while my body felt weightless, floating in air.

Curiously, our garden somehow appeared both cared for and neglected. The background of the garden was our collapsing school, like an empty building forgotten by time, accentuating the impression of a wild paradise.

If it weren't for the horrifying well of evil spirits, watering the flowers could very well have been a fun job.

But the job of buying the chalk was even more horrifying.

Sinar Harapan Shop—Ray of Hope Shop, the one and only place that sold chalk in East Belitong—was very far away. It was located in a dirty fish market. If you didn't have a strong stomach, you'd vomit from the stinking smell of salted radishes, fermented bean paste, starch, shrimp paste, *jengkol* beans, and kidney beans deserted in rusty bins in front of the store. Once you were inside, that smell mixed with the odor of plastic toy packages, the eye-watering scent of mothballs, the stenches of oil paint and bike tires strewn about, and the stink of stale tobacco that had been left unsold for years.

The owner of the shop was a hoarder. He collected useless junk, never willing to throw any of it away. The store's stench was amplified by the odor of the Sawang coolies' sweat as they went in and out with pickaxes, speaking in their own tongue, sacks of wheat flour slung leisurely over their shoulders.

This morning it was Syahdan's and my turn to buy the chalk. We got on the bike and made a serious deal—Syahdan would start out pedaling with me on the back until we reached the half-way mark, a Chinese grave; we'd switch there, and I would pedal to the market, and we'd do the same thing on the way home. There was one more finicky condition: every time we came to an incline, we'd get off and take turns pushing the bicycle, switching only after meticulously counted steps.

"Off you go, Your Majesty," Syahdan teased me as we hit our first slope.

He panted, but with a wide smile, as he bowed down like a bootlicker. Syahdan happily accepted tasks, no matter what they were, even watering the flowers, as long as he got out of class. For him, the task of buying chalk was like a little vacation and a good opportunity for him to try to flirt with the young shop ladies he had crushes on. I wasn't interested in playing along with his game.

We arrived at a low moon-cake-shaped shrine with a black-and-white photo of a serious-faced lady covered with a sheet of glass at the center of it. Drops of red candle wax were scattered around it. This was the grave from our agreement. It was my turn to pedal the bicycle.

I halfheartedly mounted the bicycle, and with the first turn of the wheel I was already angry with myself, cursing this task, the stinking store, and our stupid agreement. I grumbled because the bicycle's chain was too tight and it was hard to pedal. Other things I complained about: the law never siding with the poor; the saddle being too high; corrupt officials wandering around as free as wild chickens; Syahdan's body being so heavy even though it was so small; the world not being fair. Syahdan sat tight, fully enjoying his backseat, whistling the song "Semalam di Malaysia"—"A Night in Malaysia." He paid no heed to my blubbering.

We arrived at the fish market, which was deliberately situated at the edge of the river so that the waste could easily be disposed of. But it was on low land, and during high tide the river would bring the waste back to the narrow alleys of the market. When the water receded, the trash got stuck in table legs, piles of cans, broken fences, *kersen* tree stumps, and crisscrossed wooden posts.

That market of ours was the result of sophisticated city planning, courtesy of the most hickish of Malay architects. It wasn't decadent, but it was an exploding mess.

Buying chalk was insignificant business, so we had to wait until the owner of the shop finished dealing with men and women with their heads covered in sarongs.

A Miauw, the owner of Sinar Harapan Shop, was a terrifying character. He was fat. He always wore a tank top, shorts, and slippers. A little batik-covered debt book invariably was in his hand. There was a pencil tucked behind his meatball-like ear. A *sempoa*—an old wooden abacus—sat on his table. Its sound was intimidating.

His shop was really more like a discount warehouse. Hundreds of kinds of merchandise were stacked up to the ceiling. Besides the various fruits, vegetables, and other foods in the rusty bins, the shop also sold prayer rugs, pickled *kedondong* fruit in old jars, typewriter ribbons, and paint that came with a bonus calendar of women in bikinis. The long glass shelves displayed cheap face-whitening creams, water-purifying tablets, firecrackers, fireworks, BB gun bullets, rat poison, and TV antennas. If you were in a rush to buy Butterfly-brand diarrhea medicine, you couldn't expect A Miauw to find it right away. He sometimes forgot where things were. He was drowning in a whirlpool of merchandise.

"Kiak-kiak!" A Miauw summoned his coolie, Bang Arsyad, telling him to come quickly.

"Magai di Manggara masempo linna?" a Sarong man complained when he saw the price of oil lamp wicks. He said it was cheaper in Manggar.

"Kito lui, Ba? Ngape de Manggar harge e lebe mura?" Bang Arsyad passed the complaint on to A Miauw, the first question in Khek language, the second in Malay.

I felt queasy in that smelly shop, but the conversations entertained me. Three men with completely different ethnic roots had communicated using each of their mother tongues, their words jumbled yet understood. A Miauw was indeed an arrogant snob with an unpleasant voice. His face gave the impression that he was always looking for someone to browbeat. He was condescending, and his body stank like he ate too much garlic or something. But he was a devout Confucian, and in doing business he was undeniably honest.

Amid the harmony of our community, the Chinese were the efficient traders. Those who actually produced the product hailed from places unknown to us—we knew them only through the *made in* tags on the back of pants. The Malays were the consumers, and the poorer they grew, the more consumptive they became. Meanwhile, the Sarong people provided seasonal jobs to the Sawang, who hauled their purchases to their boats.

The chalk transaction was routine and always the same. After

I waited and waited and almost passed out from the smell, A Miauw would yell loudly and order someone to fetch a box of chalk. Then, from the rear of the shop, someone would shriek back, just like the white-rumped shama bird. I always assumed the sound came from a little girl.

A box of chalk was slid through a small slot the size of a pigeon-cage door. Only a soft right hand could be seen passing the box through the slot. The face of the hand's owner was a mystery. She was hidden behind the wooden wall in the back that separated the stockroom from the rest of the shop. The mysterious hand's owner never spoke one word to me. She passed the box of chalk through and then pulled her hand back immediately, like one feeding meat to a leopard. It went on this way for years, the procedure always the same, unchanging.

There was never a ring on her tiny fingers, but she wore a bracelet made of jade stones, and embedded in the tips of those upwardly curved fingers were extraordinarily beautiful fingernails, well cared for and far more enchanting than her jade stone bracelet.

I had never seen such beautiful nails on a Malay girl, let alone on a Sawang. The nails were so smooth they appeared transparent. The tips were cut with breathtaking precision in the shape of a crescent moon, creating a sense of harmony throughout her fingers.

The surface of the skin around her nails was very neat, probably because she had soaked it in an antique ceramic bowl filled with warm water and young ylang-ylang leaves. As they grew, the nails bowed down over the tips of her fingers, making them even more beautiful, like the bluish water quartz hidden at the bottom of the Marang River. So different from the nails of Malay girls, which widened and jutted out ungracefully as they grew, like the prongs of a rake.

I had been assigned the irritating task of buying chalk frequently, and my only incentive to carry it out was the chance to glance at those nails. Having gone there so often, I knew the mysterious young girl's nail-cutting schedule: once every five weeks on Friday.

I had never seen her face. She was uninterested in seeing mine. Every time I said *kamsiah*—thank you—after receiving the box of chalk, she never responded. Quiet as stone. For me, this young girl full of secrets was a manifestation of an alien from an unknown land. She was extremely consistent in keeping her distance from me. No saying hello, no time wasted on trivial matters. To her, I was as insignificant as the chalk itself.

There were times when I felt curious to see what the owner of these heavenly nails looked like. Was she as lovely as her nails? Were the nails on her left hand as gorgeous as those on her right? Or did she have only one hand? Did she even have a face? But all of these thoughts were just in my heart. I had no intention of sneaking a peek at her face.

Usually, after taking the box, A Miauw wrote in his debt book, and Pak Harfan would pay the bill at the end of the month. We children didn't deal with financial matters. Every time we passed through, A Miauw didn't bother to look at us. He flicked at the *sempoa* loudly with his fingers, as if to remind us of our mounting debt.

For A Miauw, we were unprofitable customers—in other words, we were just trouble. If once in a while Syahdan approached him to borrow the bicycle pump, he'd lend it to us, even as he exploded with complaints. He didn't like lending his pump to anyone—especially to us. I really hated seeing his tank top.

———

The air grew hotter. I felt like a vegetable boiling in soup. A Miauw barked a command to the mysterious girl to pass the box of chalk through the pigeon-cage door. With a powerful glance, A Miauw signaled for me to take the box.

I moved quickly through the garlic sacks, plugging my nose. But just a few steps toward the pigeon-cage door, a cool breeze blew into my ear, lingering a brief moment. I didn't realize my destiny had crept up on me in the decrepit shop, circling, then mercilessly grabbing hold of me. Without my knowing it, the coming seconds would determine the man I would become in the years ahead; right at that moment, I heard the girl yell loudly, "Haiyaaaaa!" Then came the sound of dozens of pieces of chalk falling to the tile floor.

Apparently the girl with the gorgeous nails had been careless. She had dropped the box of chalk, scattering it all over the floor.

I had to get down and crawl to pick up the pieces, one by one, from the gaps between sacks of wet raw candlenuts that emitted a dizzying smell. I needed Syahdan's help, but he was talking animatedly to the daughter of the *hok lo pan* cake seller as if he had just sold fifteen cows. I didn't want to interrupt his phony moment.

So I had no choice. Some of the chalk had fallen under an open door with a curtain of small seashells neatly strung together hanging in front of it. I knew behind that curtain the young girl was also picking up pieces of chalk. I heard her grumbling, "Haiyaaa . . . haiyaaa . . ."

All of a sudden she drew back the curtain, leaving our startled faces less than an inch away from each other.

We stared into each other's eyes with a feeling I cannot describe in words. Her hands loosened around the pieces of chalk she had gathered, sending them back down to the floor. My own hands gripped the chalk even tighter, and it felt like I was holding tubes of Popsicles.

At that moment it seemed as if all the hands on all the clocks in the entire world stood still. All moving things froze as if God had captured their movement with a giant camera from the sky. The camera flash was blinding. I saw stars. I was stunned; I felt like flying, dying, fainting. I knew that A Miauw was yelling at me, but I didn't hear it, and I knew that the shop was becoming smellier in its stuffy air, but my senses had already died. I guess she felt the same way.

"*Siun! Siun! Segere . . . !*" shouted the Sawang coolie, telling me to get out of the way quickly, but it sounded far away, echoing as if it had been yelled in a deep cave. My tongue was immobilized. I couldn't utter a single word, couldn't move. That young girl absolutely paralyzed me. The look in her eyes squeezed my heart.

She had an exquisite oval-shaped face, like Michelle Yeoh, the Malaysian movie star. Her clothes were fitted and fancy, as if she were going to attend a wedding, with a motif of small *portlandica* flowers. It was the moment of truth: the owner of the heavenly nails was indeed a strinkingly beautiful girl with an indescribable charisma.

Her cheeks flushed. She clearly felt awfully embarrassed. She got up and slammed the pigeon-cage door, paying no heed to the chalk or to me.

The slam of the door woke me from an intoxicating spell. I was swaying, dizzy, my vision flashing. I couldn't get up from the floor. My blood was tingling; my body felt clammy. I had just been hit by my very first love at very first sight—a most incredible feeling that only some are fortunate enough to experience.

———

Not bothering with the half-empty chalk box, I turned to leave the shop. I felt weightless, as if I were a holy man who could walk on water. A strange feeling of happiness settled on me, like nothing I had known before. It far exceeded the happiness I'd felt when my mother gave me a two-band transistor radio for complying with my circumcision.

As I prepared to return home, I glanced back inside the shop and caught sight of the girl sneaking a peek at me from behind the curtain. She was hiding herself, but not her feelings. Right there, among the stinky candlenut sacks, cans of kerosene, and sacks of *jengkol* beans, I had found love.

I flashed Syahdan the best smile I had, receiving only a puzzled look in response. I then hoisted up his small body and set him on the bicycle. I had become a man with unlimited strength, and I was more than willing to cart Syahdan on the back of the bike to anywhere in the world. My friend, if you really want to know, that is what they call being madly in love.

After school, Syahdan and I were summoned by Bu Mus to be held accountable for the shortage of chalk. There I stood, still as a statue, not wanting to lie, to answer, or even to deny any accusations. I was prepared with a full heart to accept the punishment, no matter how severe, including retrieving the bucket that Trapani had dropped yesterday into the well of horror. The only things on my mind were the girl with heavenly nails and the magical moment when I was blitzed by love.

The punishment was as I anticipated. I entered the well to retrieve the bucket, but miraculously, the well of horror seemed charming now. Ah, love!

18 ✲ MASTERPIECE

The August 17 Independence Day Carnival had the potential to raise our school's dignity. Prizes were to be awarded for Best Costume, Most Creative Participant, Best-Decorated Vehicle, Best Parade, Most Harmonic Participant, and—most prestigious of all—Best Art Performance.

Bu Mus and Pak Harfan had been pessimistic about the carnival because of our age-old problem: funding. We could never afford a good performance. The state schools could afford to rent traditional costumes that made their performances charming. The PN School was even more impressive. Their parade was the longest, their position the most strategic, and their formation the biggest. Their front line consisted of brand-new, basketed, colorfully decorated bicycles. The riders also were adorned in cute outfits. The bikes' bells rang loudly and simultaneously. Their second line was made up of cars decorated as boats and airplanes. On them rode small girls in Cinderella gowns and crowns. It was truly festive.

The PN School's parade was topped off with a marching band, the part I loved the most. The bellowing of dozens of trombones sounded like the thunderous explosion of trumpets on Judgment Day. The pounding of drums shook my heart.

At the climax of the carnival, the marching band formed two circulating squares while saluting the VIP podium. The podium was the place for the most respectable attendees, including the head of PN operations. Also in attendance were his secretary, who was always carrying a walkie-talkie, along with a couple of PN managers, village heads, wealthy sundry shop owners, the postmaster, the BRI Bank supervisor, the Sawang tribe chief, the Sarong people's chief, the Chinese community leader, the shamans, and various other heads, all accompanied by their doting wives. The podium was positioned in the center of the market, and most of the crowd gathered around it. The audience was likely to watch the carnival close to the podium, because that was where the carnival participants gave their ultimate performances. An intimidating jury also sat on the podium, ready to judge the performances.

The PN School typically snatched first to third place in all categories. Occasionally, state schools from the regency's capital, Tanjong Pandan, took some third-place rankings. We were ashamed; year after year, we put on the same lowly spectacle. But this time we had a glimmer of hope: Mahar.

For most of us from Muhammadiyah, the carnival was an unpleasant, if not traumatic, experience. Our carnival performance comprised merely a bunch of children led by two village teachers holding a banner with the symbol of our school. The banner was made of cheap fabric and drooped sadly between two yellow bamboo sticks. Behind them lined up three rows of students wearing sarongs, traditional Muslim caps, and Islamic outfits. They represented the founders of Sarekat Islam—the first Indonesian intellectual Muslim organization—and the founding fathers of Muhammadiyah.

Every year for the carnival, Samson donned a dam gate-keeper's uniform. He certainly did not do so because that was what he aspired to be, a dam keeper like his father, but because it was the only carnival-ready costume he had. Syahdan wore a fisherman's outfit, also in accordance with his father's profession. A Kiong, every carnival, chose an outfit like the gong keeper of a Shaolin temple.

Trapani had put on high boots, overalls, and a helmet. The uniform belonged to his father. He had dressed up as a PN laborer. Kucai, who lacked both boots and a helmet, was determined to join the parade in overalls. When asked, he explained that he was a low-level PN laborer on leave.

To be more dramatic, Syahdan brought along a sack of dragnet. Lintang blew a whistle because he was a football referee, and I ran around, back and forth, as the assistant referee. One handsome student had dressed rather neatly, sporting black shoes and dark trousers, a long belt, a white long-sleeved shirt, and carrying a big briefcase. That remarkable student was in fact Harun. It was unclear what profession he represented. In my eyes, he looked like someone who'd been kicked out by his mother-in-law.

That's the way we appeared year after year. It didn't symbolize our aspirations, because we didn't dare have any. It was suggested to every student to use our father's work uniform because we didn't have the funds to rent carnival costumes. Accordingly, we represented the jobs of the marginalized community, and in this context, Mahar was dressed as neatly as Harun. Mahar waved to the spectators a retiree ID card, as his father was already retired, while Sahara reluctantly sat out because her father had been laid off.

Given the reality of our situation, we had to face the pros and cons of participation each time the carnival came around. Trapani, Sahara, and Kucai suggested we not participate instead of performing and embarrassing ourselves. Bu Mus and Pak Harfan had another idea.

"The carnival is the only way to show the world that our school still exists on the face of this earth. Our school is an Islamic school that promotes religious values! We must be proud of that!" Pak Harfan said. "If we pull off an impressive performance, who knows, Mister Samadikun might be pleased and reconsider trying to close down our school. This year, let's give Mahar a chance to show us what he's got. You know what? He is a very gifted artist!"

Pak Harfan was rightfully proud of Mahar. Recently, Mahar had given Pak Harfan a good name by solving the problem of an overcrowded audience trying to watch the black-and-white TV in the village hall. Mahar came up with a solution to reflect the TV screen off a couple of mirrors, thereby allowing the village hall to accommodate a bigger audience.

We applauded Pak Harfan's speech and sang Mahar's praises, but Mahar himself was nowhere to be seen. It turned out he was perched on one of the filicium's branches, a mischievous grin on his face.

Mahar immediately appointed A Kiong as his general affairs assistant—his servant, basically. A Kiong told me that he couldn't sleep for three nights because he was so proud of his promotion. Mahar stayed up for three nights as well, meditating for inspiration. He couldn't be disturbed. I had never seen him act so serious.

All evening, Mahar sat alone in the middle of the field behind our school. He beat a tabla—traditional drum—searching for music; he didn't allow anyone to come near him. He stared at the sky and suddenly got up, jumped around, ran in circles, yelled like a madman, threw his own body onto the ground, rolled around, sat down again, and, without warning, dropped his head down like a suffering animal.

Was he creating a masterpiece? Would he be successful in redeeming our school after it had been looked down on in the carnival for so many years? Was he truly a pioneer, a renegade capable of phenomenal achievements? Should he even be carrying the burden to impress Mister Samadikun so he wouldn't close down our school? That's a heavy burden, my friend. After all, Mahar was just a child.

I watched him from a distance. One week passed. He didn't reveal his concept.

Then, on one bright Saturday morning, Mahar came to school whistling. It was clear to us he had been enlightened. We gathered around him. He looked at each of us directly, one by one, as if he were about to show a magical lightbulb to a group of little kids.

"No farmers, no PN laborers, no Koranic teachers, and no dam keepers for this year's carnival!" he yelled. "All the power of Muhammadiyah School will be united for one thing!"

We were bewildered.

"We are going to perform a choreographed dance of the Masai tribe from Africa!"

We all looked at one another, not believing our own ears.

"Fifty dancers! Thirty tabla drummers! Spinning around like tops, we are going to blow up the VIP podium."

Oh God, I was going to faint. We jumped up and down, imagining the greatness of our coming performance.

"With tassels!" shouted Pak Harfan from the back.

"With manes!" Bu Mus added. We were ecstatic.

Mahar was so unpredictable. His imagination jumped all over the place. Performing as a faraway tribe from Africa was a brilliant idea. That tribe was known to be meagerly dressed. The fewer the clothes, the less funding required. Mahar's idea wasn't brilliant just from an artistic point of view—it also accommodated our school's cash condition.

After that, every evening after school, we worked very hard practicing a strange dance from a faraway land. According to Mahar, it had to be performed quickly and energetically. We stomped our feet on the ground, flung our arms up to the sky, and formed a circle as we spun. Then we bowed our heads, jumped, turned, and dispersed in all directions, assuming the original formation once again. There could be no gentle movements; everything was fast, fierce, passionate, and fractured. The whole scenario was accompanied by tablas, their rhythm ceaselessly piercing the sky, the drummers dancing dynamically. We had to yell words we didn't know the meanings of: *Habuna! Habuna! Habuna! Baraba, baraba, baraba, habba, habba, homm!*

When we asked Mahar what those words meant, he acted as if he possessed knowledge that spanned the continents and replied that it was a traditional African rhyme. I had just found out that African people shared a custom with Malays: an obsession with rhyming words. I tucked that knowledge away in my memory.

However, I was mistaken about the meaning of the dance. I had formerly been under the impression that the eight of us—Sahara had opted to sit out, and Mahar himself played the tabla—were to be a Masai tribe, happy that our cows were pregnant and giving birth. But to my surprise, Mahar said we were the cows themselves; following some enthusiastic dancing, we were going to be attacked by cheetahs. They circled us, disrupted the harmony of our dance formation, and then pounced on us. Chaos overcame the cows, but at that moment the Morans, or famous Masai soldiers, came to our rescue. The soldiers would battle the cheetahs to save us, the cows. Mahar adroitly orchestrated the cheetahs' movements. They looked exactly like animals that hadn't eaten in three days.

The choreography represented an exciting drama—the collective fight of man versus beast in the wilds of Africa, an exemplary work of art, Mahar's masterpiece.

Do you know, my friend, what happiness is? It's what I felt then. I was completely taken in by art. I would perform with my best friends. Maybe my first love would be watching.

19 ☼ A PERFECTLY PLANNED CRIME

And the day of the carnival arrived. It was a day that made our hearts race.

Mahar fashioned the cheetah costumes out of canvas painted yellow with black spots, transforming our underclassmen into convincing representations of the wild animals. Shocks of dyed yellow hair topped their painted faces.

Others performed as tabla drummers. Their bodies were painted shiny black, but their faces were painted snow white, and the result looked rather strange. The Morans—the famous Masai traditional soldiers—were smothered in red paint. Armed with spears and red whips, and wearing headdresses made of woven wild grass, they were very fierce indeed.

Mahar paid extra-special attention to us, the eight cows. Our costumes were the most artistic. We wore dark red shorts that went from our belly buttons down to our knees. Our entire bodies were painted light brown like African cows, save for our faces, which were painted with streaks. Anklets with bells and tassels were fastened around our ankles. They jingled with every step we took. Around our waists hung sashes made with chicken feathers. We also wore various exotic accessories, like big clip-on earrings and bracelets made from tree roots.

Then there were our crowns—huge, made from long, wound pieces of fabric. Sewn onto the fabric was a miscellany of goose feathers, bark, wildflowers, and miniature flags.

The most ordinary-looking of our accessories was a necklace made from *aren* (sugar palm) fruits strewn together like skewered meat on a rattan string. No one suspected that in these common-place necklaces lay Mahar's secret weapon. He'd stayed up for three nights making these; they were the peak of his creativity.

For the final touch, Mahar fastened a faux horse mane made of plastic twine to our backs. Before the parade began, we gath-ered around, held hands, and lowered our heads to say a prayer.

As we had predicted, the greeting from the spectators lining the street was outstanding. Nearing the VIP podium, we heard the thunderous sounds of drums, tubas, horns, trombones, clari-nets, trumpets, and saxophones. It was the PN marching band in action!

The pinnacle of their performance was when they halted be-fore the front of the VIP podium and played "Concerto for Trum-pet and Orchestra." The concerto's beautiful intro was unveiled by fifteen *blira* players dinging three different sounds on their in-struments. These were then joined by the beats of cymbals, until their tempo and tone were drowned out as dozens of snare drums took over. The audience was not yet finished swaying with the snare drums when the color guards flooded the street with an attractive contemporary dance.

Thousands of spectators applauded, their cheers growing even louder as three majorettes, the queens of charm, skillfully twirled and tossed their batons. The young ladies, straight off the pages of a girlie calendar, wore miniskirts, black stockings, and Cortez high-heeled boots that came up to their knees. Their white gloves extended to their elbows.

They were dazzling, but we weren't discouraged. We soon formed our lines, waiting impatiently for our turn.

As the marching band took its leave, basking in applause, Mahar and the tabla drummers attacked the VIP podium. They walloped the tablas with all their might, moving like hundreds of monkeys fighting over mangoes. Mahar led the audience's imagination into Africa. Without prompting, they cheered for the beating tablas.

In the course of the tense wait, my neck, chest, and ears began to feel hot, then itchy. And it seemed that my friends were all experiencing the same thing. Then it dawned on us: the itch was being caused by the sap from our *aren* fruit necklaces.

The intensity of the itch quickly escalated, but there was nothing we could do about it, because to take off the necklaces, we'd first have to remove our crowns, which weighed about two pounds and had been fastened to our heads by wrapping some of the fabric strips around our chins three times. Clearly, Mahar had intended the crowns' design not only to enhance the glory of our costumes but also to lock the necklaces onto our bodies. We were helpless, and Mahar signaled that it was our turn to take action.

I will never forget what happened next. We attacked the arena with Spartan-like spirit. The audience's applause erupted. At first we danced according to the choreography. Then we, the cows, began to move a bit peculiarly, diverging from the plan, for we were being attacked by an unbearable itch.

We tried not to scratch because it would ruin the choreography. We were highly determined to defeat the PN marching band. We endured the misery. The only way to divert the itch's torture was to jump around like crazy. We roared, butted heads, pounced on one another, crawled, rolled around on the ground, and squirmed. We were like a can of worms poured onto a sizzling asphalt road. Nothing we did was in the choreography.

The tabla drummers were burning with enthusiasm as they saw us ignite with their music. They accelerated their tempo to keep pace with us. The spectators assumed that the sound of the tablas wove some sort of magic that placed us, the eight cows, under a trance. Their amazement grew.

According to the choreography, the next part of our performance was an attack by cheetahs. We, possessed by the unbearable itch, fought back. Confused, the cheetahs ran for their lives. It was not supposed to go this way; according to the plan, we should have been frightened and fleeing until the brave Masai soldiers came to our rescue. But we couldn't just do nothing; if we stood still, the itch would make our veins explode.

The cheetahs rallied, and again we countered. The diversion from the choreography had unexpectedly brought out the true character of animals, which can be both vicious in some situations and fearful in others. I glanced at Mahar, who was delighted with our improvisations. He must have manipulated the situation, expecting this very outcome. The sound of his tabla became livelier. He smiled from ear to ear. I had never seen him so pleased.

The street grew hotter as the Masai soldiers burst onto the scene to save us. Then a real battle broke out. Dirt flew up from the street and swirled around us. Out of the chaos rose hysterical yells, animal roars, the thumping of tablas. Our choreography had the character of dance drumming from sub-Saharan tribes. This was *adzohu*, the manifestation of the struggle to survive represented through the metaphor of human movement. The vibrations of the dance shook one's very soul, as if they were drawn from the mystical rituals of the cycle of life. The spectators were stunned. The photographers ran out of film.

After the performance, we ran to find water. The closest source was a dirty watercress pond in the back of a sundry shop, teeming with spoiled fish that couldn't be sold. What could we do? We plunged in.

We didn't see the spectators give Mahar a standing ovation. We didn't see the tears of pride running down Bu Mus's and Pak Harfan's faces. We didn't even hear the praise from the head of the jury for our magnificent interpretation of the dance from a distant land. We also didn't know that, at that moment, Mahar was accepting the trophy for this year's Best Art Performance. It was the first time that trophy was taken home by a village school. It was the trophy that could prevent our school from ever being mocked again.

While the glorious ceremony was going on, we were soaking in the pond's muddy waters, scrubbing our necks with velvetleaf. We could imagine Mahar smiling as he was showered with praise. After years of our ridicule, he had gotten both his revenge and his most coveted award. He was a genius. It must have been a sweet revenge for him, very sweet—as sweet as *bintang* fruit.

20 ☼ LONGING

One special Monday morning, after years of misfortune, the Belitong Muhammadiyah School smiled for the first time.

We held a small ceremony in front of our glass display case, which seemed to join us in smiling. For the first time, it would hold something truly worthy of its shelves: a trophy.

The previous day, the chairman of the carnival judge panel had handed the trophy over to Mahar, ending its forty-year stay in the PN School's prestigious glass display case.

Conversely, a Muhammadiyah village school that had stood for almost one hundred years—the oldest school on Belitong Island, maybe even in all of Sumatra—for the very first time had received a trophy. So despite his outlandishness, despite his eccentric appearance, despite his chaotic vision and methods, Mahar was the first person to go down in history as achieving something phenomenal for our school.

Our celebratory ceremony closed with a photograph. Bu Mus had deliberately called a professional photographer to take our picture so we could show Mister Samadikun that we, too, could get a trophy.

Bu Mus had promised us, both personally and in the name of the school, that if we got a perfect test score or won a special award, she would give us a prize of our choosing—as long as it was something she was *capable of fulfilling*. The right to select a prize now lay in Mahar's hands.

"What is it that you want the most, child?"

Mahar couldn't have been happier. He opened his bag and took out a rolled-up piece of paper.

"And what might that be?" asked Bu Mus.

Mahar unrolled the paper, grinning as he revealed Bruce Lee in a mid–raging dragon move with three parallel scratches on his cheek and a double stick ready to strike his enemy on the head. We knew what Mahar meant. He had begged Bu Mus over and over again to hang the Bruce Lee poster in our classroom. Now he saw a golden opportunity.

Bu Mus was dismayed. "Wouldn't you like something else, Mahar?"

Mahar shook his head.

"You're sure? There's no other request?" Bu Mus said with a hint of frustration.

Mahar shook his head again. "Destiny is circular, Ibunda. You have to trust that one day this Bruce Lee poster will be useful." And that—calmly, philosophically, innocently was how Mahar convinced Bu Mus.

The next day, Bruce Lee's face was spread over the wall in front of our class, hanging directly above the chalkboard. But somehow he looked different. His smile seemed as serene as Rhoma Irama's on the *Rain of Money* poster hanging next to him.

It was truly extraordinary—the master of kung fu and the master of dangdut now presided over our classroom. After closer inspection, I found there was a similarity between them: both had melancholic eyes full of determination to oppose all wickedness on the face of this earth. Very impressive.

Good things tend to breed more good things, as the old Malay proverb goes. And it was true—the presence of that trophy lifted our spirits. We received a small sum of money with the carnival prize, money we could use to fulfill Mister Samadikun's requirements: a new chalkboard and a first-aid kit. Bu Mus filled the first-aid kit with APC pills and worm-extract medicine. The rest of the money was used to order a picture of the president, vice president, and Garuda Pancasila from Cahaya Abadi, literally "Eternal Light"—the store for model school materials in Tanjong Pandan.

After we got our trophy, how happy the days were. We often gazed at it for long periods of time, talking about it everywhere we went. But amid the euphoria, I was often struck by emptiness.

Those days, I felt lonely in the midst of festivity. I often drew away from my friends, sitting by myself under the filicium, not wanting to talk to anyone and not wanting any company. I didn't even understand myself, always daydreaming, unsatisfied by food, unable to sleep well. I was struck by an odd feeling that I had never known before. Everything I thought I knew was turned upside down by a new word that had taken over my life: longing.

Every day I was attacked by longing for that young girl with the beautiful fingernails. I felt breathless all the time. I longed for her face, her smooth nails, her smile when she looked at me. I even longed for her wooden sandals, the wild hairs over her forehead, the way she pronounced her r's, and the meticulous way she rolled her sleeves.

I soon understood that I wasn't the type of boy who could

stand longing. I thought very hard about how to lighten this burden. I finally arrived at the conclusion that my longing could be treated only by frequently buying chalk. And for that, Bu Mus was my sole hope.

I begged her to give me, and me alone, the task of buying chalk. I conferred with my classmates to take over their turns for buying chalk. I even approached the class president, Kucai, and addressed the Laskar Pelangi leader, Mahar, for support.

For a bribe of two packages of tamarind candy, Kucai was willing to change the chalk-buying schedule, which had already been made for a year's worth of turns. He, like most politicians in this country, was that easy to buy. The schedule now contained one name, and that was mine. Nary a word of protest came from my friends, who were perfectly happy to be freed from riding a bicycle to the rotten shop to buy chalk from obnoxious A Miauw. So what I had to do to change the schedule was not difficult at all. But, my friend, I saw it differently. In my eyes, my efforts to become the one and only chalk buyer were part of a blood-and-sweat struggle. I exaggerated to anyone who would listen that it took me three months and a sack of tamarind candy in order to bribe Kucai to select my bid for the task of buying chalk, when the reality was that I had no rival. Love made me a hopeless romantic. All of this additional drama made her even more beautiful to me. How lucky was I, this boy, to be in her proximity when buying chalk!

Bu Mus was baffled by my sudden enthusiasm for buying chalk. "Don't you hate buying chalk more than anyone, Ikal? For mercy's sake, isn't it you who always says that the chalk store is putrid?"

She wasn't interested in debating with me. Surely, the instincts she developed over years of teaching rang bells in her head, warning that my sudden change of heart had to do with *cinta monyet*—monkey love, or puppy love. But with full compassion and an irked smile, she consented while shaking her head back and forth.

"As long as you don't go losing any of the chalk again. You should know that chalk is bought with money from contributions of the religious community!"

Syahdan and I soon became a solid team for the task of procuring chalk. I was in charge of the purchasing. Syahdan didn't need to pedal at all; it was enough for him to sit on the back and hold on tight to the boxes of chalk and keep his lips sealed. We enjoyed the thrill of keeping the secret.

Of course, Syahdan, by my recommendation to Bu Mus, always accompanied me. He was happy to miss class and also to be free to try to flirt with the daughters of the *hok lo pan* shopkeepers.

Upon our arrival at Sinar Harapan, I entered the sundry shop and stood at attention in the dead center of the ocean of junk. I fanned eucalyptus oil under my nose to fight the rancid smell. I wiped sweat from my brow as I waited for the magical moment when A Miauw ordered the white-rumped shama behind the seashell curtain to get the chalk.

I approached the pigeon-cage door. She slid her hand out. My heart pounded every time it happened. She still didn't say a word, and neither did I. But she no longer pulled her hand back so hastily, as she had before. She gave me the chance to admire her nails. That was enough to keep me happy until the next week.

And so it went on for months and months. Every Monday morning I could meet the other half of my heart, even though it was only a set of nails. And that was as far as our relationship progressed. No greetings, no words, just hearts talking through beautiful nails. No introductions, no face-to-face interaction.

Our love was an unspoken love, a simple love, a shy love, but it was beautiful.

Sometimes she tapped her nails or teased me by not letting go of the chalk box when I grabbed it, leaving us to play tug-of-war. She often clenched her fist; maybe it was her way of asking, *Why were you late?*

I prepared myself time and time again to hold her hand, or to tell her how very much I missed her. But every time I saw her nails, my courage vanished under the pile of *jengkol* beans. After our meeting, I would suffer for a week, but it was suffering mixed with an inexplicably strange happiness, combined with a longing that began to choke me the moment she pulled her hand back into the slot.

If there's anything this world never has enough of, it's love. Time passed, and my heart felt more tumultuous. I couldn't bear not seeing her miraculous nails for a whole week. So, slyly and casually, I often took several pieces of usable chalk and either buried them under the filicium or gave them to Harun, who was ecstatic to have them. The chalk would be just about gone by Thursday, and I would be sent to the market on Friday morning. I was happy to cut back three days of longing.

I tried to compensate for my deviousness by sweeping the school, cutting the grass, watering the flowers without being asked, and washing Bu Mus's and my classmates' bicycles. They were perplexed by my behavior. *Cinta monyet* is truly confusing!

Two seasons had passed, the Sarong people had gotten off their boats twice, and I still didn't know the name of that young girl with the beautiful nails.

For days I tried to muster up the courage to just ask her. But since I lost my ability to speak when her hand came out, I assigned Syahdan to dig up some information. The assignment thrilled him—he was like a Malay secret agent, stealthily sneaking and tiptoeing around.

"Her name is A Ling!" he whispered one day while we were reading al-Qur'an in the al-Hikmah Mosque. "She's a student at the National School!"

Bam! Taikong Razak's *kopiah*—traditional hat—struck Syahdan's book stand.

"Watch your manners before the book of Allah, young man!"

Syahdan flinched and went back to reading al-Qur'an. The National School was a special school for Chinese kids. I stared at Syahdan seriously.

"A Ling is A Kiong's cousin!"

I felt like I had just swallowed a *rambutan* seed, big as a grape, and it was stuck in my throat. A Kiong, that tin-headed boy! How in the world did *he* have a cousin with heavenly nails? These past few days he had had to stand while studying at school because five boils had emerged on his bottom, rendering him unable to sit. But he had been insistent on attending school.

I couldn't describe how I felt about all these new revelations. The fact that A Ling was A Kiong's cousin made me both excited and anxious. Syahdan and I had some serious discussing to do about this new development.

In the end, we came to the conclusion that we must disclose the situation to A Kiong. He was our only shot at penetrating the seashell curtain in Sinar Harapan Shop.

We ushered A Kiong to the flower garden behind our school and sat on a small bench near a cluster of beloperone plants and blooming hibiscus, the perfect place for discussing love.

A Kiong listened intently to my story, but he showed no reaction. His face didn't change at all. The gist of our story completely escaped him. His stare was empty. I guess A Kiong didn't know the first thing about the concept of love.

"It's as simple as this, A Kiong," I said impatiently. "I will give you letters and poems for A Ling. Give them to her when you pray together at the temple, understand?"

He raised his eyebrows. His spiky hair stood on end and his round pudgy face looked even funnier than usual. When he relaxed his eyebrows, his chubby cheeks fell down as well. He was a boy with a peculiar but amusing face.

Why don't you just give them to her yourself when you see her every Monday morning? It doesn't make any sense!

A Kiong didn't actually say that, but that's what his furrowed brow meant. I answered him from my heart, telepathically. *Hey, Hokkien kid, since when has love ever made sense?*

Drawing a deep breath, I turned myself around and stared off into our school field. I acted as if I were in a soap opera. I picked dracaena leaves, crumpled them in my hands, and then tossed them up into the air.

"I'm shy, A Kiong. Near her, I am paralyzed. I'm a compulsive man. Compulsive men are always careless. If her father found out, I couldn't even begin to imagine the consequences!"

I got those breathtaking lines from *Aktuil*, a magazine my older brother subscribed to. I probably hadn't used them correctly, but I didn't care.

Upon hearing a dialogue that resembled the ones from radio dramas (very popular at the time), Syahdan hugged the *petai cina* tree beside him. I ran out of words trying to explain to A Kiong that, in the world of love, sending letters carried a higher romantic value because they carried an element of surprise.

I guess A Kiong picked up on the hopelessness in my voice.

He may not have been the smartest student, but he was a loyal friend. As long as he could help, he never turned down a friend in need. My theatrics melted his heart.

But because of his inherited sense of entrepreneurship, he demanded compensation. I didn't mind doing his math homework.

Through A Kiong, my love poems relentlessly flooded the fish market. It was an easy task for him, and he began to relish his rising math grade. He was completely unaware that his actions could potentially cause a terrible clash between him and his uncle A Miauw.

I always pushed A Kiong to tell me what A Ling looked like when she received my poems.

"Like a duck seeing a pond," he answered with a good-natured tease.

One beautiful evening, I sat on a round stone in our flower garden and composed a poem:

Chrysanthemum Flower

A Ling, look up
And see high in the sky
Those white clouds drifting your way
I sent chrysanthemum flowers to you

As I slid the poem into an envelope, I smiled. I couldn't believe I could write poetry like that. Perhaps love has the ability to bring things into the open, like hidden abilities or characteristics, things we don't know live inside us.

21 ❀ SNATCHING RITUAL

Mujis, the mosquito-spraying astronaut, told us that the other day he sprayed the PN survey office and saw the big map of tin exploitation.

"Three dredges are pointing toward this school!" he said sternly.

Mujis could even name the IBs.

"IB nine, IB five, and IB two."

"IB" is the local way of saying "EB," *emmer bager*, Dutch for "dredges."

Mujis's news was horrifying, since whatever stood in the way of the dredges would surely be destroyed. But as usual, Bu Mus lifted our spirits. She asked us to pray so that nothing bad would happen to us. We soon forgot the threat of the dredges. Especially me, because I was taken aback by even more surprising news.

Here's the story. On the way back to school after buying chalk, while I was pedaling, Syahdan read something off the bottom of the chalk box in his hands: *Meet me at Chiong Si Ku.*

What? A message from A Ling! It must have been A Ling's

writing! The hidden message made me lose control of the bicycle, which wobbled and plopped itself down into a ditch. I tried to save the chalk and the writing on its box. Syahdan and I dove into the dark mud. The chalk was saved, but we were not. We were soaked.

When we got to the school, I took the chalk out of the box and put it in another one so I could bring A Ling's message home with me.

At home, I read the message over and over. The message stayed the same any way it was read: she wanted to meet with me. Backward like in Arabic, from the front, from above, from far away, or from close up. Reflected in the mirror, rubbed with candle wax, read with a magnifying glass, read behind a fire, sprinkled with wheat flour, read while held behind my legs with my head between my knees, looked at for a long time like a 3-D picture. The message was always the same: *Meet me at Chiong Si Ku at the red temple veranda.* It was straightforward Indonesian, not idiomatic, not scientific, not metaphorical. I just couldn't believe it. But in the end I concluded that I, Ikal, would soon meet with my first love! It was indisputable. Let the world be jealous.

Chiong Si Ku, or "the Snatching Ritual," was held every year—in fact, it still is. It's a lively event where all the Belitong-Chinese gather. Each and every family member attends, and their relatives return to Belitong from all over Indonesia in hordes just to take part. There are many other entertaining activities tied in to the old religious ritual, like pole climbing, a Ferris wheel, and Malay music. Chiong Si Ku had developed into the most highly anticipated cultural event on the island. All the major elements of our community came together to celebrate: Chinese, Malays, Sarong people, and Sawangs.

The central focus of the Snatching Ritual is three large tables, each twelve meters long, two meters wide, and two meters high. Piled on top of the tables are all kinds of offerings—household items, toys, and various foods—provided by the Chinese community. At least 150 things, such as pans, transistor radios, black-and-white TVs, cakes, biscuits, sugar, coffee, rice, cigarettes, textiles, soy sauce, canned drinks, buckets, toothpaste, syrup, bike tires, mats, bags, soap, umbrellas, jackets, sweet potatoes, shirts, pails, pants, mangoes, plastic chairs, batteries, and assorted beauty products, are heaped together in big mountainous piles on the large tables. At midnight, everything goes up for grabs or, more precisely, can be snatched by anyone. That's why Chiong Si Ku is also called the Snatching Ritual.

The main draw is a small red pouch called *fung fu*, hidden in the mountains of other things. *Fung fu* is coveted by everyone because it is a symbol of luck. Whoever finds it can sell it back to the Chinese community for millions of rupiah.

The three tables are arranged in front of Thai Tse Ya, a shrine to the ghost king constructed from bamboo and colorful paper. It stands five meters tall with a stomach that's two meters wide. That paper ghost is terrifying. His eyes are as big as watermelons. His long tongue looks like it wants to lick the greasy pork meat roasting beneath him. Thai Tse Ya represents man's worst characteristics and bad luck. All evening and night, Confucians from all over Belitong Island flow in to pray in front of Thai Tse Ya.

Thai Tse Ya was across from the temple, and I was supposed to meet A Ling on the red temple veranda.

A Kiong and his family entered the temple yard for prayer. He smiled at me. I replied to his smile with a grimace because I was nervous. I was a wreck thinking about what a young Chinese woman would think of a Malay village boy like me. Being in the middle of their environment made me uneasy. Would it be best if I just went home? No, my longing was already like a bleeding wound.

I had been waiting for A Ling ever since I had finished doing the Isha prayer. Those wanting to witness the ritual and the accompanying entertainment began arriving in great numbers. There was no sign of her—maybe I had come too early. I should have come late or not at all.

The superstars of the Snatching Ritual were the Sawangs. They were successful every year because of their solid organization. They researched the position of valuable items from the start of the evening, the angles from which they should attack, and how many people were needed.

The larger Sawangs were assigned to intercepting other snatching groups to make way for the smaller-bodied Sawangs to jump on the tables. The rest of them lurked underneath, ready to seize whatever fell off the tables. The group consisted of about twenty people.

I had been waiting for two hours. A Ling still hadn't shown up. Thousands of spectators and hundreds of eager participants began to fill the temple yard. The dangdut bands boomed. The Ferris wheel spun happily up into the bright sky. Shouting traders peddled various things. It was all very lively. The balloon sellers rang high-pitched bells, making me even more restless.

A few snatchers from the Sarong people's community showed up. They covered their heads like ninjas; only their eyes were visible. Then, not much later, some Chinese snatchers got together. There were no fewer than six groups.

The snatchers were visibly desirous as they waited for the moment at midnight when a Confucian priest would strike a large water jar. When the jar broke, the snatching could begin.

I didn't care about any of that. My thoughts were focused on A Ling. Where could she be? Didn't she know my chest was pounding because I wanted so badly to meet her?

Then I saw the Malays who would participate in this year's Snatching Ritual. Instead of being in groups, they were scattered, and I already knew why. Rather than focusing on their course of action for the ritual and winning the competition, they occupied themselves with internecine political tussles. They bristled at criticism and very rarely were willing to engage in introspection. They always held different opinions and were more than happy to argue. It didn't matter if the overall goal was not reached, as long as they didn't lose face during the petty debates. And it can certainly be said that the tendency was for the thickest and the least educated among them to expound most loudly.

If the Malays succeeded in actually forming a team, every single one of them wanted to be the leader. So in the end, a solid team was never formed, and they ended up operating individually and fighting solitarily. Consequently, all they managed to bring home were sugarcane, a few packages of coconut cookies, half a pair of socks, a couple of doll heads, some coconut seeds that the Sawangs hadn't bothered with, a water pump—or just its plug, to be more exact—and bruised and battered bodies.

But once again, I didn't care about the Snatching Ritual or the customs of the snatchers. My focus remained on A Ling, even though by now another hour had crawled by in vain.

Suddenly all eyes turned to a tall, thin figure. He was a Sawang man and was highly respected in the Snatching Ritual. For years and years, his ethnic group assigned him to the special task of hunting down the *fung fu*: the extremely valuable red cloth. Bujang Ncas was his name.

He came wearing a black robe, like a boxer. A Sawang child

always trailed behind him and took his robe off for him when he joined up with the rest of the Sawang snatching team.

I had seen Bujang Ncas in action before. He leapt onto the table with the agility of a squirrel. He wore a level expression. He didn't tolerate the greed of the other snatchers. He paid no heed to the roars of the hundreds of rugged men engaged in a brutal struggle. He skillfully tiptoed over the sea of things. His sharp, lively eyes glanced to and fro. And within no time at all he pinpointed the *fung fu*. Somehow he always managed to find it, even though the priest hid that small red sacred cloth neatly within the folds of a woman's nightgown, or in one of the hundreds of cookie tins nearly impossible to open, or in a sack of candlenuts, or in the gaps of a sugarcane, or inside a pomelo.

Bujang Ncas tucked the *fung fu* into his waist. Then the living legend of the Snatching Ritual took a single jump and landed on the earth without uttering a noise, as if he had the power to make himself weightless. A moment later, he disappeared into the crowd. He ran off with the supreme symbol of the Snatching Ritual, swallowed by the dark, the smoke, and the aroma of incense.

Because I was tense from my prolonged wait for A Ling, my stomach rose and made my gut ache. My legs were exhausted, my head was dizzy. Nonsensical thoughts began to possess me. Was A Ling just as I had pictured her all this time? Was what I had imagined of her different than reality? Maybe she never really cared about me.

My thoughts were interrupted when I heard the glass jar break. The surprise snapped me out of it, and I ran like hell to safety as thousands of snatchers attacked the three tables.

And then I witnessed one of the most astounding human phenomena in existence. Even though I saw it every year, it never failed to take my breath away. Mountains of hundreds of things on top of three tables vanished in less than one minute—twenty-five seconds, to be more exact. Those who successfully climbed onto the tables systematically tossed things down to their colleagues waiting below. Those acting alone climbed atop the tables, swooped down and seized whatever they could, and proceeded to stuff it into their sacks; this, too, was done at lightning speed. Occasionally they couldn't get their bags off the table because the contents were beyond their strength limitations.

Dozens of snatchers were fighting over something, and a brawl broke out in the middle of the heap. They toppled back, collided, and then fell headfirst to the ground. The spectators didn't even have a chance to clap—they were too dumbfounded by the tremendous yet horrifying scene.

Those who didn't bring sacks put whatever they could into their pockets, and even into their clothes—they looked like clowns. In such a fast-paced situation, the brain no longer functions logically—even grains of rice and sugar were being shoved into pockets. If their pockets and pants were full, they put what they could into their mouths. They took as much as possible of whatever they could get their hands on, as long as it was still on the tables. If need be, they would even put things in their nostrils and ears.

If one was fortunate enough to snatch a transistor radio, it was a futile hope to expect to bring it home in one piece, because that very radio was being snatched by fifteen people at once, and all that was left in the end was the knob or the antenna. The principle wasn't to get the antenna—it was to make sure no one else got the fully intact radio. The case of the destroyed and unusable radio was a trivial matter. The Snatching Ritual is a manifestation of human greed. It is irrefutable proof of anthropological theories that egoism, greed, destruction, and aggression are all fundamental characteristics of *Homo sapiens*.

In less than thirty seconds, the Snatching Ritual—which people had been awaiting for a full year—was already over, leaving nothing but thick dust, heavily injured snatchers, and tables as broken as my heart in its wake.

I had now been waiting for almost five hours, from Isha prayer until midnight—A Ling had not shown up. She had broken her promise. Maybe she was picking bean sprouts and had forgotten her promise? Didn't she know how much the message on the chalk box meant to me? She wasn't even coming.

I was tired of listening to the Malay dangdut song "Gelang Sipatu Gelang," a song that asked those in attendance to go home because the show was over. I stared blankly at the traders tidying up. I was sad to see the masses leave. My hope was broken.

I wanted to pedal my bike away as fast as possible and then throw myself into the Linggang River. But just as I was about to ride off, I heard a voice directly behind me. It was as soft as tofu. It was the most beautiful voice I had ever heard in my life, like the tinkling of a harp from heaven.

"What's your name?"

I turned around fast and immediately felt as if my feet were no longer touching the earth.

I couldn't utter even a fragment of a word because right there, precisely three meters away, there she stood, the distinguished Miss A Ling herself!

She had come from a completely unexpected direction; all this time, she had actually been inside the temple watching me. At the last minute, when I was about to give in to despair, she came and turned my feelings of disappointment upside down.

After three years of knowing her, knowing her nails only, it was just seven months ago that I first saw her face. After writing her dozens of poems, and after immense longing, only after this night would she know my name.

I stuttered like a Malay learning al-Qur'an.

She only smiled; it was a very sweet smile. She wore a *chong kiun*, an enchanting dress for special occasions, and in this festive month of June, she came down to earth like a Venus of the South China Sea. The dress followed the curves of her body, from her ankles up to her neck, and it was fastened with a high button shaped like a nail. Her slender body rested on top of a pair of blue wooden sandals.

At that moment I felt inadequate. For me, A Ling was like a person who would always belong to someone else. I was no more than an entry in her address book that she'd forget a week after this meeting.

She read my mind. She grasped her *kiang lian*, her necklace. Its surface was a jade stone engraved in Chinese writing that I didn't understand.

"*Miang sui*," she said. "Destiny."

A Ling took me by the hand. We ran from the temple yard toward the Ferris wheel.

The Ferris wheel operator had already killed the lights. He was getting ready to go home. A Ling begged him to let it go around one more time. The operator apparently understood the plight of a couple drunk with love.

"I read your poem 'Chrysanthemum' in front of my class," said A Ling. "It was beautiful."

I was soaring.

And then we were silent, just silent, spinning around on the Ferris wheel, not wanting to get off. My heart swelled at the sight of the Ferris wheel's lights illuminating the sky. That was the most beautiful night of my life.

22 ❀ TUK BAYAN TULA

What Mujis, the mosquito sprayer, had said turned out to be true. One day, four men wearing construction hats and carrying drills came to our schoolyard. They were PN's *juru cam*—surveyors. Their job was to gather land samples to find out the level of tin. If the tin level was indeed high, they would steer the dredges our way to extract it.

We were already strangled by daily difficulties, and Mister Samadikun's threat to close our school had not yet vanished—would our troubles now be compounded as we faced the dredges?

But for the time being, we were temporarily distracted, as a dashing man showed up in a uniform. His pocket was emblazoned with an emblem that announced: PRAMUKA (Boy Scouts). He asked, "Are there any Pramuka here?"

Bu Mus shook her head no. Because we couldn't afford it, we had never formed a Boy Scout troop. Our daily clothes didn't even have all of their buttons—we couldn't afford Scout uniforms.

The man said he needed the help of Scouts from various schools to look for a young girl lost on Selumar Mountain.

"But we do have Laskar Pelangi," Mahar volunteered.

"What is Laskar Pelangi?"

Mahar solemnly went on to explain the connection between rainbows and the ancient cannibalistic people of Belitong. Bu Mus and the uniformed man were left scratching their heads, both at a loss for words.

"We are ready to help," Mahar said convincingly.

It was already late afternoon by the time we arrived at the slopes of Selumar Mountain. The police, the search-and-rescue team, different Scout troops, and members of the community at large wanting to help were all ready to climb the mountain to look for the lost little girl. Apparently the little girl was from the Estate, a student of the PN School who had wandered away from her large group of classmates while hiking. Her family and teachers were panicked and crying.

A chorus of dog barks, people calling her name, and megaphone clamor rang out. From the shrieks of the megaphone, we knew the lost little girl's name: Flo.

It was almost night. The expressions on everyone's faces grew even more concerned. Last year, two boys had gotten lost; three days later they were found huddled under a *medang* tree, dead from starvation and hypothermia.

The contours of Selumar Mountain are unique. From any angle, the forest looks the same. A person may feel like he knows his whereabouts and, without realizing it, lead himself farther and farther into the wilderness.

Maybe Flo was lost in the south, headed toward the currents

of the Linggang River's tributaries, full of rapids. There, on the evenly spread-out level land, lay death traps, *kiumi*—quicksand that looked solid, but which, once stepped upon, immediately swallowed the entire body whole.

But if Flo was unfortunate enough to be lost in the north, it could be said that she had walked through death's very gates. There was no return. That area was blocked off by a cruel river called the Buta River. The river culminated in a gorge. *Buta* means dark, blind, clueless, trapped with no way out—death.

The river's surface was placid like a lake, still like glass. But beneath the calm surface lay huge crocodiles and black bottom-dwelling snakes. The crocodiles of the Buta River had a strange disposition. They had their sights set on monkeys hanging on low branches, but they even snatched at people on boats. Old Australian pines grew down to the middle of the river. Some of them had died, their figures like giant ghosts hovering over the river's surface.

Night fell. Flo had been missing for ten hours. No ray of hope illuminated our search. That poor child, alone in the pitch-black forest. Maybe her leg was broken or she was unconscious. Maybe she was under a tree—sobbing, scared, and cold.

Amid all the panic, several people suggested we enlist the help of an old man named Tuk Bayan Tula.

Tuk Bayan Tula was an infamous shaman. They said he could fly like the fog and hide behind a skinny blade of grass. He could turn off a lamp with the blink of his eyes. He was more powerful than Bodenga, the crocodile shaman, more powerful, in fact, than any other shaman. He was the only shaman in this world capable of crossing the sea through sheer wizardry. With the simple utterance of a mantra, he could kill someone over on the island of Java. Malay villagers believed Tuk Bayan Tula was half human and half divine—half ghost, to be more exact.

Tuk Bayan Tula was, like Bruce Lee, Mahar's all-time idol. Just as A Kiong desired to be Mahar's spiritual student, Mahar longed to be the spiritual student of the shaman.

So a few people were dispatched to meet Tuk Bayan Tula on Lanun Island—Pirate Island—where he lived. They set out on a PN speedboat.

Morning approached and the delegation returned. They were greeted by all with the irrational hope for a miracle. We'd searched for Flo everywhere, and there was still no sign of her.

The delegation brought a piece of paper from Tuk Bayan Tula and told us a story that raised the hair on the backs of our necks.

"The shaman lives in a dark cave," they said. "His eyes flashed like a parrot's. He wore nothing more than a sheet of fabric wrapped around his body."

Mahar's mouth was agape.

"When he walked, his feet didn't even touch the ground!"

For years I had been taught at the Muhammadiyah School to believe in the righteousness of rational thinking and to avoid the polytheistic world of shamanism, so it was hard for me to believe any of this. But this information was accepted by the members of the delegation, and they were not just coffee-stall know-it-alls making things up to toot their own horns. Mahar now admired Tuk Bayan Tula even more.

The head of the delegation unrolled the paper from Tuk Bayan Tula and read it aloud: *If you want to find the girl, look for her near the abandoned shack in the field. Find her soon or she will drown under the mangrove roots.*

I was taken aback by the message. It was threatening, or, to be more precise, intimidating. But it was undeniable that this message held a certain power. If Tuk Bayan Tula was truly a shaman, that message held the fate of his reputation. There were no ambiguous or hidden words.

If we wanted to test his ability, we had to forsake logic and follow his instructions. And if Flo wasn't soon found near the abandoned shack in the field, or dead in the gaps of the mangrove roots, then the legendary Tuk Bayan Tula was nothing more than a roadside dice-roller.

Because the farmers practiced field rotation, it was hard to determine if a field had an abandoned shack or not. There were in fact many abandoned shacks on the slopes of the mountain, and they made great hideouts for tin thieves, who dug up tin from the mountain and sold it to smugglers disguised as fishermen at the mouth of the Linggang River. The tin was then sold in Singapore. The unauthorized prospectors built shacks and sometimes disguised their mining sites with agricultural fields.

PN treated unauthorized prospectors and smugglers very harshly, inhumanely. The prospectors' and smugglers' actions were regarded as subversive criminal acts. In the peaceful mountains where the prospectors were seen as thieves, and on the sea where the smugglers were seen as pirates, the law didn't apply: if they were caught, their heads were blown off on the spot with an AK-47 by the "tin special police."

Based on Mahar's directions, Team Laskar Pelangi moved to the north, to the deadly path of the Buta River.

We stopped in dozens of fields and shacks. We scoured the gaps of mangrove roots. We found nothing. Our voices were hoarse from shouting Flo's name.

For each shack we searched that did not contain Flo, Tuk Bayan Tula's reputation lost one credit. And as midday approached, Tuk Bayan Tula's reputation was just about depleted. Mahar looked offended each time we complained about finding an empty shack, and more so upon hearing Samson's insults. "If that shaman can turn himself into a parrot, then we shouldn't even have to search like this."

Finally we arrived at a big protruding boulder. We gathered there to rest and preserve what remained of our strength. This was the end of the northern slope, and after this, about a half kilometer down, lay the perils of the Buta River.

Still no Flo. As far as the northern slopes were concerned, Tuk Bayan Tula's message had proved false. With a walkie-talkie, we monitored the progress to the west, east, and south; Flo had not been found in those places, either. Tuk Bayan Tula was a liar from all four points on the compass.

Mahar's face swelled up. He looked like he had been betrayed by the love of his life. I was sad, too, thinking of the terrible fate that had befallen Flo. It was quite possible that she'd never be found. Or maybe she would be found, but only her crow-pecked skeleton. Most heartbreaking of all would be if she died just a few hours before help arrived. It's difficult to hold on to life in cold nighttime temperatures without a crumb of food.

Harun patted Mahar's shoulder. Mahar slumped down in silence. His eyes stared down to the Buta River and the swamp of lilies. We got up, packed our supplies, and got ready to head home. Before we left, Syahdan decided to give the plastic toy binoculars around his neck a try. He focused them on the periphery of the Buta River. We had already gotten off the boulder when Syahdan shouted. It was a shout of destiny.

"Look, there's a mango tree at the edge of the river!"

Mahar immediately seized Syahdan's binoculars. He ran to the edge of the boulder and looked down. "And there's a shack!" he said with renewed spirit. "We have to go down there!"

The rest of us were stunned by his crazy idea. Kucai, who had kept his mouth shut until now, thought Mahar's foolishness had exceeded limits. As class president, he felt responsible.

"What are you, crazy?" he barked. The look in his red eyes was sharp. "Let me explain something for your thick skull. There can't possibly be a field down there. No one in their right mind would have a field on the edge of the Buta River unless they wanted to die for nothing!"

Mahar stared coolly at Kucai.

"Use your brain! Come on, let's go home!" Kucai capped off his rant.

Mahar didn't budge. Harun, the eldest among us, gently advised Mahar, "Come on, let's go home . . . this mountain has already taken one child. Come on, Mahar, let's go home."

Mahar seemed indifferent. We began to leave, and, as we moved, Mahar said very calmly, "You can all go home. I'll go down alone."

So we all went down together, even though we knew we couldn't possibly find Flo down there. We cursed Syahdan for casually looking through the cheap child's toy. But it was too late for regrets.

So we headed toward the region of death—the floodplain of the Buta River—only to accompany Mahar. We accompanied him to satisfy his ego and protect him from his own stupidity. We hated his fanaticism for the shaman Tuk Bayan Tula, but he was still our friend, a member of Laskar Pelangi. If later Flo was not found, I knew in my heart that I would be the first one to give Mahar a noogie. Ah, friendship is sometimes demanding, and it sucks. Lesson number four: Don't ever be friends with someone who is obsessed with shamans.

The terrors of the Buta River were no exaggeration. Swampy water in the underbrush of the thatch palm trees looked like a kingdom of evil spirits and a breeding ground for all kinds of ghosts. Monitor lizards of all shapes and sizes slithered around, completely unaffected by our presence and not the least bit afraid—some of them even behaved as though they wanted to attack.

Few people had ever been here, and among those who had, the most foolish would have to be us. We took quiet, cautious steps. We all took machetes out of our sarongs and formed a straight line to watch the back of the one closest to us. We heard something snap shut along with a big splash of water. It was the shutting of an unfathomably large crocodile's mouth. Snakes were dangling from the branches of trees.

The shack was about one hundred meters ahead of us. The closer we got, the clearer and more mysterious it became—it was actually in an abandoned field. Who was the extraordinarily brave person who had had a field here?

The field was very close to the edge of the Buta River. Definitely dangerous. The owner surely wanted to be close to the water without regard for his own safety. A stupid move. Perhaps his stupidity had ended his life, and that was the reason this field was unattended. Only a troop of monkeys and a dray of squirrels controlled it now.

A branch from the rose-apple tree near the shack was shaking like it was about to crash down. This was clearly the doing of a greedy long-tailed monkey.

We approached the rose-apple tree with caution and devised a strategy of attack. Covered in the luxurious leaves, the monkey was having a big celebration in the branches and was unaware of our presence. We wanted to catch it red-handed and give it a fright: a small way to entertain ourselves during our frustrating search for Flo.

We jumped under the branches and yelled loudly to surprise the monkey. But as soon as we did, the situation reversed itself. We were beyond surprised to see a white, happy-looking monkey perched on a branch like some child play-riding a horse. It appeared to have just woken up and had not yet had a chance to wash its face. It roared with laughter at our pale and confused appearances. Flo, that rascal, had been found!

23 ✿ FROM MY ROOM, YOUR FACE WILL NOT TAKE FLIGHT

In a book, I saw him riding a horse, holding on to the animal's stomach like Kubla Khan. His eyes gleamed as if the god of spears had pierced his heart. My blood bubbled as he crept toward a male moose. I couldn't bear turning the final page when he said he would throw away the love of mixed Tutuni and Chimakuan women. All this was because he wanted to preserve the Pequot Native American blood flowing through his veins—and the most saddening part was that he was the last of his tribe.

It was a riveting story. I never grew tired of it, even after repeated readings. How was it written so I felt as though I were there, in the middle of the Yellowstone prairie, when I didn't even know where that was?

"It's the power of literature," said the postman.

Literature, asked my heart, *what's that?*

We often helped the postman during school holidays. Our poor village postman. He worked alone, starting after Subuh prayer at dawn, taking care of the post office and thousands of letters. In the afternoon he received letters, packages, and outgoing money orders. In the evening he opened the post office and sorted the letters; then he delivered them by bicycle throughout the village. Sometimes this task continued on into the night.

I carried the weight of the postman's struggle in my heart. I made an effort to wake up in the middle of the night to pray earnestly. I squeezed my eyes shut: *O God, I don't yet know my goals for the future. But when I do grow up, please, God, please make me anything besides a postal worker, and don't let it be a job that starts at Subuh. I promise You, I will never hang the Koranic studies teacher's bike in the bantan tree again.*

The postman gave us a little money for shouldering the postal sacks and let us read books with stories like the one about the Yellowstone Native Americans. The books actually belonged to PN School children who had already returned to Java or other areas. These undeliverable books were kept in the post office.

Working at the post office was our school holiday activity. At night we slept at the al-Hikmah Mosque. At the mosque, we told each other all kinds of stories. We never tired of telling the story of the day we searched for Flo at the mountain and of Tuk Bayan Tula's proven message. That had been the first time Mahar demonstrated what would become his signature gesture, the one he'd do whenever he felt he was in the right: he lifted his eyebrows and his shoulders in unison with a righteous, repeated nod, not unlike a penguin after mating. It was obnoxious.

One day, when I was helping the postman put outgoing letters in his bag, I was surprised to see a letter with my name on it: Ikal.

I secluded myself behind the post office. I opened the letter beneath a *rambutan* tree. My heart raced. The letter contained a poem:

Longing

Love has truly been troubling me
The moment you glanced my way
At the Snatching Ritual on that fateful day,
It caused me to have a sleepless night,
For from my room, your face would not take flight.

Who are you,
The one who has me constantly daydreaming?
You are nothing more than a bothersome boy
But, even so, it is for you
I long.

Njoo Xian Ling (A Ling)

My eyes were transfixed on the paper. My hands shook. I read it again, and a bitter hunch slipped into my heart. I was happy but also stricken with a dark feeling of sadness—as if something terrible would soon happen to me. I turned around. I saw the post office's fence slowly turn into tightly packed human legs. In the gaps between legs, there was a man squatting on his heels across from a tailless crocodile carcass. He looked at me. Tears flowed down his pockmarked cheeks.

At that moment, I knew the pain that had struck the crocodile shaman, Bodenga, when I had witnessed him on the National School's basketball court all those years ago: a traumatic event ingrained in my young mind. It is a trauma that comes back to me whenever I get a bad feeling. And that afternoon, after many years, for the first time, Bodenga visited me.

24 ❀ I WILL BRING YOU FLOWERS FROM A MOUNTAINTOP

Selumar Mountain isn't extremely tall, but its peak is the highest point in East Belitong. To enter our village from the north, one has to pass the left shoulder of the mountain. It resembles an upside-down boat: strong and vaguely blue. Along the ascent and descent, on the edge of the left shoulder, were the homes of the Selinsing and Selumar residents. The twin villages were separated by a deep valley, flooded by the peaceful Lake Merantik.

The ascent to Selingsing Village was short but steep; making the trip on a bicycle tested one's stamina. Young Malay men trying to impress their sweethearts wouldn't stoop to ask their girls to hop off the back of the bike on the way up, determined to pedal up to the peak using all of their power, teetering along the road.

After conquering the ascent, the bicycle would dive down into its descent. The young man would allow himself a satisfied smile and ask his sweetheart to hold his waist tightly, convincing her that if she chose him, he would later be a dependable husband.

Then the bike would go around two bends, following the course of Lake Merantik's valley. Next came the ascent to Selumar Village. And here any sweetheart would understand if she were asked to get down, because while the ascent to Selumar was not quite as steep as Selinsing's, its distance was much longer. It was this that made the ascent to Selumar less realistic for proving one's love.

Nevertheless, when the peak was reached—that is, the peak of Selumar Mountain's left shoulder that I mentioned earlier—all the exhaustion would pay off. Spread out wide in front of your eyes would be beautiful East Belitong, bordered by a long blue coast, sheltered by pure white and bright clouds, and neatly lined with pine trees.

From the peak of that shoulder, one would see houses scattered along the banks of the Langkang River's estuaries, winding like snakes. They were fenced not with bamboo but by fields of wild grass.

If you travel along this path, don't rush down from Selumar's peak toward the valley. Stop and take a rest. Lean for a while against an *angsana* tree, where baby yellow-tailed squirrels play. Listen to the orchestra of pine needles and the shrieks of small birds fighting with black bumblebees for rose-apple nectar under the sun. Enjoy the sweet composition of the landscape: the mountain, the valley, the river, and the sea. Loosen your shirt and breathe in the fresh southern winds carrying the aroma of *andraeanum* petals from the heart flower, which swells up with fertility as its descendants grow in high places. It's named the heart flower because of the shape of its petals. Many call it the love flower.

I'm not sure whether the aroma originated from the *andraeanum* or from its symbiotic partner, a kind of fungus called *Clitocybe gibba*—the stemless mushrooms working hard to cover the roots of the taro family. Those mushrooms sprout up in a more humid climate when the west winds blow in toward the very end of the year. They have a plump, low, and sturdy form.

Laskar Pelangi often picnicked on Selumar Mountain, and we'd already grown a little bored with its attractions. Usually we didn't trek all the way up to the top; we were satisfied going 75 percent of the way. Besides, the granite on the slope up there made the climb a slippery one. But this time I was enthusiastic and determined to push up to the peak. My friends welcomed my enthusiasm. Nothing extraordinary had happened yet and they were already talking about the breathtaking scenery that we would witness from the peak: the bridge over the Linggang River and the barges of glassy sand leaning up against the pier.

But I didn't care about any of that. I was on a secret mission. The secret had to do with the amazing scenery at the highest point of Selumar Mountain, but it was also about a pair of gorgeous flowers that grew only at the highest elevations: the red needle flower and, if I was lucky, the sweet *muralis* flower would still be in bloom this week.

I call the *muralis* the flower of mountain grass—my own term. Because this flower likes to scatter itself about, six or seven of its offspring had infiltrated the zebra grassland. Its calyx is as wide as the thumb, and it is a dull yellow propped up by a light green stem with no uniform size: spontaneous and cute. If you were to pick at least fifteen of them, taking off their leaves and throwing in a few of those red needle flowers to make a bouquet— the heart of any woman receiving it would melt.

After three hours of climbing, we arrived at the top. All of Laskar Pelangi was gushing about the view spread out below us.

"Look at our school," yelled Sahara. It was a pathetic-looking building, even from afar. No matter what distance or angle it was viewed from, our school still looked like a copra shed.

Mahar began telling fairy tales. According to him, Selumar Mountain was a dragon that had coiled itself up and had been sleeping for centuries.

"This dragon will wake up later on Judgment Day. This mountain peak is his head. That means his head is under our feet at this very moment! Its tail coils in the mouth of the Linggang River."

A Kiong was shocked.

"So don't be too noisy, or you'll be punished by the spirits," Mahar continued, not yet satisfied with making a fool of himself.

A Kiong ate up Mahar's tale. To show his admiration, he gave Mahar a boiled banana from his provisions. He was like a primitive man paying a tribute to a shaman for curing scabies. Mahar snatched his tribute and shoved it down his throat, completely unaware of the power he held over A Kiong. We all laughed, but A Kiong stayed serious—for him, this situation was no laughing matter.

I didn't laugh, either. I couldn't take my eyes off a four-sided red box down below.

I investigated the wild grass fields on the mountain's peak, picking the buds of the wild red needle and *muralis* flowers and tying them together with shrubs.

It was truly a beautiful view from the mountaintop, like a song. Its introduction was the gathering of white clouds hanging low as if I could reach them. The vocals, the long whistles of *prigantil* birds, sounded near and high-pitched. The refrain: thousands of doves invading the lilies spread out below like a giant carpet. And then the song faded out in the forest of mangroves.

It was not for this fantastic scenery and the flowers that I made every effort to climb Selumar Mountain. No matter how overcome I was by the beauty, the real reason I was at the highest point in East Belitong was that red box down below. That red box was the roof of A Ling's house.

25 ❁ BILLITONITE

A bright Monday morning. A poem wrapped in purple paper covered with fireworks. A bouquet of flowers from the peak of Selumar Mountain, tied with a light blue ribbon. I had kept them fresh in a ceramic vase overnight.

These were the props for my love saga, set to continue this morning. The scenario had existed in my head for weeks, and it went like this: When A Ling pushed the chalk box out, I would put the flowers and poem into her hand. No words necessary. Let her take in the beauty of the flowers from the mountaintop. Let her read my poem and get a taste of something more delicious than Chinese New Year's cake.

After A Miauw gave his order, I approached the chalk box opening. But when I was about two steps away, I stopped dead in my tracks, startled by the rough hand emerging—not A Ling's hand!

This hand was very peculiar, like an evil copper blade: muscular, dirty, black, and oily.

A black coral bracelet coiled three times around the arm. Heads of venomous *pinang barik* snakes ready to lunge were carved at each end of the bracelet. The area just below the elbow was encircled by a tight aluminum bracelet, like the one often worn by brutal giants in *wayang* stories. The heads of the coiled bracelet were in the shape of a jagged key, the kind usually used to break the law. There were no tattoos, taboo for religious Malays, but the fingers were choked by three threatening rings.

The ring on the index finger held the largest *satam* stone I had ever seen.

Satam is a unique meteoric material found in only one place on earth: Belitong. Its place of origin is out of this world. It is pitch black because of its composition—carbonic acid and magnesium. It is denser than steel and impossible to be shaped.

Satam is hidden in the holes of old tin mines and it can't be found when sought—only good luck can bring it out from the bowels of the earth. In 1922, the Dutch named *satam* "billitonite." That was how our island got its name: Belitong. (In the local dialect, it was a sacred name, *Kuake*.) Later—I don't know why, maybe because backcountry Malays rarely use the letter *u*—the vulgar minions of the New Order government changed that name to Belitung.

Without any aesthetic consideration whatsoever, the owner of that copper hand mounted the sacred object on plain cheap brass. But it was worn proudly, as if its wearer were the ruler of the world.

On the middle finger sat the leader of all the intimidating rings and the revealer of its owner's sneaky tendencies: a big human skull grinning eerily with hollow eyes. This ring was made of stainless steel nuts obtained by conspiring with PN machinery washers.

The process of changing the stainless steel nut into a ring would make anyone shudder. After roughly shaping it with a lathe, the unbreakable nut was manually filed for weeks. Coolie-level PN employees usually made the rings. It was a secret culture of resistance against PN: that ring was symbolic of the people's oppression. Weeks of secret hard work yielded nothing more than a hideous, shiny ring. To this very day, it's a practice that makes no sense to me.

And the fingernails, ugh! Good Lord, they were shaped as if they'd been cursed. The difference between A Ling's fingernails—with which I had been enchanted for years—and these was like the difference between heaven and earth. These nails were thick, dirty, long, and unkempt. They were cracked at the tips. Basically, they looked like crocodile scales.

I hadn't recovered from my shock when I heard a loud tapping. I was being urged to take the chalk that had been pushed forward. Then I heard an unfriendly grunt. But most disturbing of all was that I didn't meet A Ling. Where could she have gone?

"What's going on?" Syahdan asked when he came to see what was taking me so long. "Whose hand is that?"

I couldn't answer. My throat tightened up.

That hand was not foreign to me. It was none other than Bang Arsyad's, A Miauw's coolie's. I remember when he carved the *pinang barik* snake heads into the black coral given to him by a Sarong man some time ago. He told me it took three weeks for the coral from the ocean floor to be shaped into a three-coil bracelet. The coral, long and taut at first, was conquered by smothering it with brake oil and patiently smoking it over a hearth.

Syahdan took the chalk box. Bang Arsyad pulled his hand back. It disappeared like an animal slithering into its hole.

A Miauw, who had been watching me since the beginning, approached me. He stood beside me and drew a deep breath.

"A Ling is going to Jakarta," he said slowly. "She'll take the nine o'clock flight. She has to stay with her aunt, who lives alone. She can go to a good school there."

I was stupefied. I couldn't believe my ears. The feeling that something bad would soon happen, drawn from my recent Bodenga flashback, had come true. My spirit was crushed.

"If it is meant to be, you will meet again someday," A Miauw said, patting my shoulder.

I lowered my head like someone observing a moment of silence. I clutched the bouquet of flowers and my poem.

"She asked me to pass along her greetings and wanted me to give you this."

A Miauw gave me a necklace. It was the jade necklace I had seen A Ling wear for years. *Miang sui* was written on the jade: Destiny. Then he gave me a box wrapped in purple paper covered with fireworks, exactly the same as the paper concealing my poem. A nearly impossible coincidence. I knew it! From the beginning, God had watched over this extraordinarily beautiful love.

I took the box, and at that moment I felt all the merchandise in the store fall on me. I wanted to stay and ask A Miauw so many things, but I was tongue-tied.

My chest tightened. I looked around and a sudden thought crossed my mind. I grabbed Syahdan to go home.

I pedaled as fast as I could from Sinar Harapan toward the school. Dozens of kilometers, steep grade after steep grade, I never slowed down. Exhaustion wasn't an option; I had to get to the schoolyard.

At 8:50 a.m., we arrived at the school. Syahdan returned to class. I ran across the yard toward the filicium tree. I climbed into the tree and sat on my branch, my usual position for watching rainbows.

Gradually, a little after nine, a Fokker F28 emerged in the

offing, headed from Tanjong Pandan to Jakarta. A Ling was on that plane. The longer I watched, the blurrier the plane became, not because of the distance, but because of the tears welling up in the corners of my eyes. Then the plane was gone. My soul mate had been torn away from me; the sky was empty again. Goodbye, my first love.

26 ❄ FURIOUS GENIE CHILDREN

I dreamed that a mysterious atomic bomb exploded in Belitong. A giant mushroom cloud descended from the sky, carrying with it radioactivity, mercury, and ammonia. Everyone scattered in confusion, searching for cover, slipping into water channels or jumping into drains. Many perished on the spot, and those who survived became dwarfed, putrid-smelling creatures.

Seeing the dwarfed appearance of the people of Belitong, the central government in Jakarta felt shamed before the world and refused to admit that they were citizens of the republic. We had no choice but to hold a referendum.

While only a few Malays wanted to separate from the unitary state of the Republic of Indonesia, the government took the referendum as Belitong's declaration of its status as a free nation. Belitong could no longer support itself, because its natural resources had been sucked dry over hundreds of years. The island collapsed.

At that moment, Bodenga—the long-lost crocodile shaman—reemerged to take over the government. He oppressed those who had previously treated him and his father unjustly. They were herded into and flushed down the Marang River, left to the crocodiles. The dwarfed people held on for dear life, but to no avail. Within no time at all they perished, floating in the river like poisoned fish.

I couldn't think straight. I had nightmares and I was haunted by bizarre fantasies. If I heard birds chirping, it became the drone of a mystical bird carrying news of death. I thought everyone—shopkeepers, the postman, coconut graters, civil service police, and coolies—was conspiring against me.

A Ling's departure left pain and sorrow in my heart. I wanted to burst into Sinar Harapan Shop. But I knew that such dramatic action—the kind I had seen in Indian movies—would be greeted only by bottles of bean paste and heaps of rotten shrimp seasoning. I was miserable, just miserable.

And then, mirroring again the conventions of Indian films, the separation made me ill. Some time ago, I had laughed at my neighbor Bang Jumari, who suffered from severe diarrhea and shivers because my older cousin, Kak Shita, had broken up with him. I could not get over how such an absurd reaction was possible. But now the same fate had befallen me. I had been absent from school for two days with a high fever. All I wanted to do was sprawl out on my bed. My head was heavy, my breaths were short. My mother gave me *askomin* syrup, but I did not recover. It turns out lovesickness cannot be cured by worm-extract medicine.

And then Syahdan, Mahar, and his faithful follower A Kiong came to visit me.

Mahar wore a jacket that came down to his knees. A Kiong hurried behind him lugging a suitcase like a nursing student doing an internship. It was a very special suitcase because it was covered in *peneng sepeda*—the stickers used back in the day to show that the bicycle tax had been paid—and various government symbols, giving the impression that my two classmates were important regional government officials.

A Kiong and Mahar didn't say a word. With a snap of his fingers, A Kiong ordered Syahdan to step aside.

Mahar stood right next to me and looked me over from head to toe. His face was serious, like a doctor's, and in no time at all he had finished his diagnosis. He shook his head as a sign that the case before him was no laughing matter. He drew an apprehensive breath and looked to A Kiong.

"Knife!" he yelled suddenly.

A Kiong quickly spun the combination to the suitcase and took out a rusty kitchen knife. Syahdan and I looked on anxiously. The knife was handed over to Mahar, who received it like a surgical specialist.

"Turmeric!" Mahar ordered once again, loud and clear.

A Kiong hastily groped for something in the suitcase and then handed Mahar a piece of turmeric the size of a thumb. Without much fuss, Mahar cut the turmeric, ground it up, and painted a big X on my forehead with a move so fast that I didn't have a chance to avoid it. Then, as if they both knew the next step in the procedure without need of a command, A Kiong took gardenia leaves from the suitcase and tossed them to Mahar, who caught them nimbly and proceeded to mercilessly slap them all over my whole body while chanting.

Not only that, but while Mahar was slapping me with gardenia leaves, A Kiong was spraying me with water. I tried to evade and repel them, but I couldn't get away because Mahar and A Kiong were a unified, fast, and systematic team.

Not much later, they stopped. Mahar let out a sigh of relief. A Kiong's silly face echoed Mahar's sigh.

"Three genie children were furious because you peed on their kingdom near the school well," Mahar explained, as if my soul would have been beyond help had he not come when he did. There was no sign of guilt or mischief on his face.

"They gave you the fever," he continued, putting his doctor's equipment back in the suitcase and elegantly handing it to A Kiong.

"But never fear, my friend, I have banished them, and you can come back to school tomorrow!"

And then, without bidding farewell, the two of them went home. A Kiong hadn't uttered even a single word. And there I remained with Syahdan, like a mangy, wet cat caught in the rain.

27 ❀ EDENSOR

I returned to school, but my heart was not cured. I shut myself off for days, overcome with a feeling of emptiness. It wasn't easy to forget A Ling. A void filled my chest, and my longing made it hard to breathe. I went to our shaman, Mahar, for answers.

"Boi, what could this sickness be that has befallen me?"

It was a frustrating question. In all honesty, I knew what had befallen me—I was suffering from the loss of my love. But an eccentric like Mahar just might have a magical answer that could make me see my situation in a different light. Like most broken-hearted people, I was thinking irrationally.

Mahar stared at me, slightly irritated, and said, "What did I tell you? Watch where you pee!" He turned and left.

Two weeks after A Ling's departure, during a break period, I—crestfallen, of course—showed Lintang the box she had left for me with her father. There was a picture of a tower on the box.

"Lintang, what's this picture of?"

Lintang examined the box.

"That's a picture of the Eiffel Tower, Ikal. It's in Paris, the capital city of France," Lintang said, his tone a bit surprised. "Paris is a city of smart people; artists and scholars live there. They say it is a beautiful city. Many people dream of living there."

When I got home from school, I lay down listlessly on my bed and stared at the box. I opened it. Inside were a diary and a book with a blue cover.

I opened the diary and, to my surprise, the pages were filled with every poem I had ever sent A Ling. The poems had been copied, one by one, into the diary. This answered the mysterious question of why she always returned my poems.

I took out the blue book. It was called *If Only They Could Talk*, and it was by a writer I had never heard of: James Herriot. I didn't know why A Ling had given me this book. I told myself that if it was boring after the first page, I would cover my face with it, because I also wanted to sleep.

Herriot began unusually. First, he told the story of his work tending to a cow giving birth. He wore no shirt, and the barn had no door. The wind blew fiercely. Snow entered the barn and pelted his back. He said that such things had never been written in a book.

After those sentences, I continued on to the next one and the next one and the next one; soon I was reading paragraph after paragraph. I devoured it chapter by chapter without stopping. Sometimes I even read the same paragraph over and over. All of my hopelessness and tears of longing for A Ling were whisked away, page by page.

The book told of the struggles of a young veterinarian during the depths of the Depression of the 1930s. The young doctor, Herriot himself, worked in a remote village called Edensor somewhere far off in England.

I felt, with each one of Herriot's sentences, a new spirit being blown into the crown of my head. My mouth hung open and I held my breath when I read the description of the village of Edensor. The scattered slopes of hills looked like they were cascading. I imagined high mountaintops whose slopes plunged into green hills and vast valleys. In my head, I pictured rivers winding through the bottoms of the valleys among the willow trees and farmers' houses made of cobblestone.

I was mesmerized by the small village of Edensor. I soon realized that there were other beautiful things in this world besides love. Herriot's lovely description affected me so completely that when he told about the little round-pebbled lane outside the home where he practiced, I could smell the *astuarias* running along the livestock fences down the lane. When he described the meadows spread out over the hills of Derbyshire surrounding Edensor, I wanted nothing more than to stretch out over them and rest my tired heart, to let my face be kissed by the calm and cool village winds.

That evening I finished reading Herriot's tale and immediately adopted it as a representation of A Ling and the picture of my feelings for her. Now I understood why she had given me this book.

I was cured. I had a new love right inside my worn-out bag. That love was Edensor. After 480 hours, 37 minutes, and 12 seconds of mourning my loss of A Ling, I decided to stop feeling sorry for myself. Instead of reminiscing over the stinky Sinar Harapan Shop and the moment my heart was badly broken there, I was now diligent about visiting the municipal library in Tanjong Pandan. There, I loyally read books about the secret to success, how to socialize effectively, steps to becoming a magnetic individual, and a series of books about managing self-development.

I focused on studying and stopped making strange and unreasonable plans. I found my new life motto by a stroke of luck in an old newspaper clipping at the library. The clipping contained an interview with John Lennon, who said, *Life is what happens to you while you're busy making other plans!*

I scoured all the roadside stalls in Tanjong Pandan for a John Lennon poster until I found a big picture of his face. The next day, I went to Bu Mus to ask permission to hang it in our classroom.

"Young man," my teacher said, furrowing her brow, her forehead crinkled up, "can you tell me, honestly, what prestigious achievement you have accomplished to deserve the right to hang that poster here?"

Bu Mus glanced over at Bruce Lee. Bruce Lee glanced at Mahar, Mahar glared at me.

I explained to her about the prestige of years of unrewarded dedication to buying chalk. Her ears perked up.

"Uh-huh, unrewarded, you say? Do you suppose these ears of mine are deaf? That they haven't heard the talk in the fish market—that you played with fire every Monday visiting A Miauw's daughter?"

Ah! Caught red-handed!

"Do you think I didn't know that on Fridays you tampered with our chalk so you could meet the girl?"

I was caught by surprise; it turned out Bu Mus knew everything. She had been wise to my behavior all this time.

I froze. I asked Bu Mus's forgiveness. I kissed her hand while promising that after I returned the chalk I had buried near the filicium tree, I would return to class. Then I tried to change the subject.

"What we need most in our classroom, Ibunda Guru, is inspiration!"

I went on to relate the inspirational advice of John Lennon.

Bu Mus may have been a village teacher, but she had progressive views. Maybe she was also impressed with my sincere apology. After fulfilling the terms of my inspirational apology, I was allowed to hang the poster.

So, amazingly, three posters and one glorious symbol hung in our classroom. A motto was printed on each:

Rhoma Irama: *Hujan duit (Rain of Money)*.

John Lennon: *Life is what happens to you while you're busy making other plans!*

Bruce Lee: *The dragon kung fu—fight to the death.*

The Muhammadiyah symbol: *Do what is good and prevent what is evil.*

28 ☼ A HIDDEN TREASURE BENEATH OUR SCHOOL

A gloomy day.

Today we were the recipients of four kinds of bad news.

The first: Pak Harfan was seriously ill. He couldn't even get out of bed.

The second: Mister Samadikun was not the least bit impressed with the picture of our carnival trophy. He sent it back to us. The threat to close our school was still very much alive. Our final inspection could come today, tomorrow—in other words, our school could be shut down at a moment's notice.

The third: An increasing number of PN inspectors started coming. They even came into our classroom and drilled for samples of our floor. From the head of the team, we learned that the level of tin down there was twelve—meaning that by their estimate, there were about twelve hundred kilograms of tin per one thousand cubic meters of land.

"Very high—levels this high haven't been seen since the time of the Dutch."

Our spirits were sunk because all of this meant only one thing: the dredges would surely come to plow down our school.

Bu Mus's face crumpled up.

"Not only that," someone from the team whispered in a secretive manner, "we also found ilmenite with tantalum. There may even be some uranium."

Tantalum and ilmenite together form an expensive commodity—ten times more valuable than tin.

We felt the sting of irony. Underneath our decrepit and collapsing school—the school where we fought in poverty every day to continue our lives—lay a hidden treasure worth trillions of rupiah.

The fourth: Mahar.

"Did you do your homework?" Bu Mus asked Mahar as she launched into a long spiel scolding him about his over-the-top behavior. He had, she lamented, already turned down the path leading to the realm of the occult. One of our favorite classes, gym, was canceled for the day for the sake of an intervention. We all came into the classroom to help bring Mahar back to the right path.

Mahar lowered his head. He was a handsome, smart, and artistic young man, but he was very stubborn about his convictions.

"Ibunda, the future belongs to God."

I saw the trial facing the teacher. Her face was washed out. My mother once said that the teacher who first opens our eyes to letters and numbers so we can read and count will receive endless rewards until the day she dies. I agreed with her—but that is not the only thing a teacher does. She also opens hearts.

"You have no positive plan; you never read or do your homework anymore. The time for shamanism and turning your back on Allah's verses is up." Bu Mus was beginning to sound like the morning news anchor on Radio Republik Indonesia.

"Your test scores have taken a sharp dive. Your third-quarter exam is right around the corner. If the score is bad and can't bring your average up, I won't let you join us for the final-quarter test. That means you cannot take the national examination to move up in school."

This was getting serious. Mahar's head sank down even farther. The sermon continued.

"Live according to the teachings of al-Qur'an and the hadiths: that's the guiding principle of Muhammadiyah. *Inshallah*, God willing, later when you are older, you will be blessed with a halal livelihood and a devout spouse.

"Mysticism, paranormal science, superstition, they are all forms of idolatry. Polytheism is the most serious violation in Islam. What about the good deeds we learn in faith studies every Tuesday? What about all of the lessons? What have you learned of the godless peoples of the past? Where are your Muhammadiyah ethics?"

The room was tense. We hoped Mahar would ask forgiveness and say that he'd learned his lesson. Unfortunately, he replied with an objection.

"I look for wisdom in the dark world, Ibunda. I am embittered because I want to know. Later, in a mysterious way, God will give me a devout spouse."

How dare he! Bu Mus tried very hard to contain her emotions. I knew she wanted to lay in to Mahar. Her patient face grew red. She left the room to calm herself down.

We all stared at Mahar. Sahara's eyebrows came together, her stare brutal. "Go out there and apologize! You don't even know how lucky you are!" she snarled.

Kucai, as the head of the class, took his turn. He said, "Opposing a teacher is the same as opposing a parent: insubordination! Haven't you heard that the punishment for insubordination is a hernia? The base of your thigh will be as big as a pumpkin!"

Mahar's face bore a strange expression. He looked both remorseful and determined to stand his ground—to stick to his version of things, naturally. Just as we were about to protest against him, Bu Mus reentered the room with more breaking news.

"Listen carefully, young man. There isn't a drop of wisdom in polytheism! The only thing you'll get from practicing mysticism is lost, and the longer you stick with those beliefs, the more lost you'll become in the bottomless pit of polytheism. And the devil himself will help you fan each ember you toss into that fire!"

Mahar cowered, but it didn't stop there. Bu Mus continued, "Now you have to straighten up because—"

Before she could finish her ultimatum, Bu Mus was interrupted by a greeting: *"Assalamu'alaikum."*

She stopped midsentence and spun around to face the doorway, where two people stood: a man with an important-looking face and a boyish young girl. The girl was tall and thin. She had short hair, white skin, and a pretty face.

The important-faced man tried to give a friendly smile. "This is my daughter, Flo," he said slowly. "She no longer wishes to attend the PN School and has been absent for two weeks now. She insists on attending this school here."

The man scratched his head; he was at a complete loss. His speech indicated that he was through trying to reason with his child.

Bu Mus smiled bitterly. Trials came in endless succession.

She was dizzy with worry about the sick Pak Harfan; weary from fighting our battles alone. And adding to Mister Samadikun's threat were the inescapable dredges, the deviant Mahar, and now a girl who, with her tomboy mien, would surely prove unruly. Today was Bu Mus's unlucky day.

Flo herself was indifferent—she didn't even crack a smile. She just stared at her father. She looked like she had an assertive character and knew exactly what she wanted. Her father returned her stare in kind, his own full of defeat. He went around our class to inspect everything. Maybe it reminded him of a Japanese interrogation room. The look in his eyes was sad as he conceded, "So I turn my child over to you, Bu Mus. If she gives you trouble, you know where to find me. And I am sorry to have to say this, but she will surely give you trouble."

We laughed. Flo still seemed indifferent, as if her father's words held no meaning. Her father smiled resentfully and excused himself.

"All right, then, welcome to our class. Please take a seat next to Sahara," Bu Mus said to Flo.

Sahara was absolutely delighted. She wiped off the empty seat next to her. But Flo looked our way, pointed at Trapani, and declared, "I only want to sit next to Mahar."

Unbelievable! The first sentence from her rich little mouth, mere minutes after setting foot in the Muhammadiyah School, was defiant! Defiance was not an ordinary occurrence here. We addressed our teacher not just with the normal respectful term, Guru, but with an even higher term, Ibunda Guru.

Bu Mus's face grew cloudier. She had just been thinking about Mahar and this new tomboy student and how they would destroy the Muhammadiyah ethics of this school—and now they wanted to be united? Life was laden with trials.

Flo's face made it clear that she was unwilling to compromise. Bu Mus was forced to make a difficult decision. She signaled to Trapani to step aside. Flo rushed over to fill Trapani's old seat beside Mahar. Mahar immediately displayed his three annoying signature traits: raising his eyebrows, shrugging his shoulders, and nodding his head. It was a nauseating sight for us, but he was elated. Just as he had expected, God had mysteriously granted him a partner. A prayer had been answered on the spot. Consequently, Trapani lost his deskmate. Because we had no other desks, he had to sit next to the notoriously temperamental Sahara. Sahara herself was extremely displeased about this and did not want to accept Trapani as her deskmate. She roared, her brows furrowing.

On those first days, we were dazzled by Flo's array of school supplies, but to her they were unremarkable.

She had six different bags to match her daily outfits. Friday's bag was the most interesting because it had fringes like the bags we had seen in Indian films.

Flo looked out of place sitting in our classroom. All our furniture was unfit for her. She was like a swan lost in a pen of ducks. What was this rich girl looking for in this poor, possessionless school? Why did she want to trade the sparkling PN School for this copra shed? Whose yard did she steal an apple from, to deserve being tossed out of the Estate's Garden of Eden?

It turned out she wasn't expelled from the PN School or kicked out of the Estate. She wanted to switch to the Muhammadiyah School of her own free will, without pressure from any other parties, and she was sound of body and spirit—it was only her mind that wasn't quite right.

When we asked her why she switched, she answered in a high-fed, wealthy voice, with a lisp. Her answer made the hair on the back of our necks stand up: "Because I liked your dance at the carnival. It was magical."

That answer unlocked the mystery of why she wanted to sit next to Mahar. According to Mahar's own maxim, fate is circular, and in our classroom the circle of fate had united two ghost fanatics.

It was strange, but at the barren Muhammadiyah School, Flo was enthusiastic, as if something had moved her. She was never absent even one day and was very well mannered toward our teacher. She arrived earlier than anyone, even Lintang. She swept the school, drew buckets of water from the creepy well, and watered the flowers with diligence. The poor Muhammadiyah School was a bridge to her soul.

Flo was very close with Mahar. People seeing the two of them would assume they were a couple, a handsome young man and a pretty tomboyish girl always together, equally crazy. But they didn't have that kind of emotional connection. They were crazy together, but their true sweetheart was the dark world of shamanism.

Mahar made a lot of progress with Flo around. He was further drawn to mythology and the relationships between the supernatural and anthropology, folktales, archaeology, the strength of healing, ancient sciences, rituals, and guiding beliefs. He thought of himself more or less as a scholar of the paranormal. Flo was a true adventurer. She was less concerned with mystical happenings, or their scientific aspects, and more interested in experiencing as many hair-raising things as possible. Flo's only use for deep mystical experiences was to test herself, to see how much fear she could tolerate. She was addicted to trembling in the dangerous ghostly world. Even compared to Mahar, Flo was crazy.

One cool evening after a heavy rain, our Flo took an oath to be a member of Laskar Pelangi. A rainbow bowed across the sky and thunder reverberated throughout East Belitong. Flo pledged to be a friend.

29 ✺ PLAN B

Because of Edensor Village and the story in *If Only They Could Talk*, I was able to move beyond feeling sorry for myself. I left behind the blueprint of my beautiful first romance.

This is the amazing thing about being a child: the ability to quickly mend a broken heart after years of love—five years, to be exact! Ah, it turned out I had been in love with A Ling since the second grade, and even though we met only that one time, it was love. Yet I was able to recover swiftly, and with the help of a book. Magical. Sometimes adults need years to remedy a broken heart. What is it that makes us grow more negative with age?

I remembered A Ling as the most beautiful part of my life. And I still set off with Syahdan to buy chalk every Monday morning, even though I was now greeted by a bear claw with the nails of a carcass-eating vulture. I remained diligent and with the same instinct for love and the same enthusiasm.

When I wasn't buying chalk, I occupied myself by reading practical psychology books on self-development and becoming more fanatical about John Lennon's inspirational sentence.

The books suggested that I find my talents, and I had no doubt what those talents were: I had an affinity for writing, and I was a skilled badminton player.

I always won first place in our badminton district. I had the trophies lined up at home. There were so many trophies that my mother used some as weights to hold down wash piles, as door stops, or as supports for the chicken pen walls. She used one as a hammer to crack open candlenuts. There was even a trophy from my latest competition with a pointy top that my father used to scratch his back.

I always defeated my opponents. They practiced hard for months and months. They ate half-cooked eggs every morning with *jadam* and bitter honey for extra strength. But they were helpless before me.

Sometimes I took action with a drop shot and a double somersault, returned smashes while chatting with the spectators, and hit the shuttlecock while rolling on the floor. I often took straight shots from between my legs with my back to my opponent, and it wasn't a rarity for me to do so left-handed!

Seeing me play, weak-minded opponents would become distraught and, if they were lured into expressing their anger, would guarantee their own loss. When I was competing, the market was quiet, the coffee stalls were closed, kids were let out of school, PN coolies left work early, government employees left work for a while—that is, if they had gone to work in the first place—and community representatives with no work to do lined up alongside the court way before the match.

"The curly-haired mouse deer" was what they called me. The badminton court next to the village administration office thundered with excitement. Those who couldn't find a place to stand alongside the court climbed nearby coconut trees to see me in action.

I thought all of these facts were more than enough reason to call badminton, as they say in the self-development books, my *main ability*.

My other great interest was writing. There was not much proof to confirm my ability, or lack thereof, in this field other than A Kiong's comment that my letters and poems to A Ling often tickled him with laughter. I wasn't sure what that meant—it could have been because they were either really good or really bad.

So I began to home in on those two fields. I practiced badminton every day. If I was exhausted, I looked at John Lennon's picture for a while, with his thin smile and round glasses, and my enthusiasm was reignited.

As the self-development scholars explained, a constructive individual has to make a plan A and a plan B.

Plan A meant mobilizing all of your resources to develop your main abilities—in my case, these were definitely badminton and writing. This plan covered every detail, from step one all the way up to the peak of glory. Every time I read this plan, I had trouble sleeping.

I was extremely happy to have a clear formula figured out for my plan A: to become a famous badminton player or writer. If possible, maybe both. If not, one would do. And if I couldn't become either of them, anything would do, really, as long as I didn't become a postal worker.

When I looked at the other Laskar Pelangi members, I knew they all had their special plan A's, too.

Sahara, for example, wanted to be a women's rights activist. The inspiration for this aspiration came from the tremendous oppression of women she saw in Indian films.

A Kiong wanted to be the captain of a ship. He said it was because he liked to travel. I was doubtful. This must have been his aspiration because of the big shape of the captain's hat. I suspected he wanted to cover part of his tin-can head with the big hat.

Kucai, from the moment he became aware that he had the qualities of a politician—sly, populist, and shameless, with a big mouth and an irresistible desire to debate—had a clear aspiration: to be a member of the Indonesian legislative assembly.

Out of the blue and without hesitation or timidity, Syahdan announced that he wanted to become an actor. He didn't seem to have the slightest capacity for acting. In our class performances, he couldn't even play a role with lines because he always made mistakes. So Mahar always gave him the simple role of fanning the princess. He was often incapable of doing even that.

"Aspirations are prayers, Syahdan," Sahara advised him. "If God granted your prayer, can you imagine what would become of the Indonesian film industry?"

As for Mahar, he wanted to be a renowned psychic, respected even by those who opposed him.

Samson's aspiration was the simplest. He was a pessimistic individual. He wanted only to be a ticket checker and security guard at the village movie theater. This was because his hobby was watching movies, and the security job carried a very macho image. In the meantime, the good and handsome Trapani wanted to be a teacher. And Harun, as always, wanted to be Trapani.

It was all because of Lintang. If there had been no Lintang, we wouldn't have dared to dream. The only thing in our heads—and the head of every other boy in Belitong—was that after elementary school, or maybe junior high, we would sign up to be PN *langkong*; in other words, we would be prospective employees, then work our whole lives as miners, and then finally retire as coolies. That was what we saw happen to our fathers and their fathers before them, generation after generation.

But Lintang and his extraordinary abilities gave us confidence. He opened our eyes to the possibility that we could become more than we had ever dreamed. He gave us encouragement, even though we were full of limitations.

Lintang himself aspired to be a mathematician. If he achieved it, he'd be the first Malay mathematician. Wonderful! I was moved whenever I thought of it; I had quietly fallen in love with Lintang's plan. So I prayed, frequently, that he'd achieve his dream. Suppose, just suppose, that God asked someone to sacrifice his or her dream so Lintang could achieve his. I would sacrifice mine for Lintang.

Lintang was in the midst of preparing for the Academic Challenge. He shone brighter every day. Would he be able to surpass the intelligence of the PN students with their national-level Academic Challenge prestige? Was Lintang really the genius we took him to be all this time? We were nervous that our admiration may have been a nearsighted distortion. We hoped he wasn't merely the champion of our little pen, a big fish in our little pond.

Now, according to my reading, a positive individual also needs an alternative backup plan with a proper name that is very hard to say: *contingency plan*.

This alternative plan is also called plan B.

Plan B is for when plan A fails. The procedure is simple: If you fail, throw plan A far away and look for a new talent. After you find it, follow the same procedure you did with plan A. It was a superb life recipe, no doubt the work of psychological experts conspiring with human resource professionals and book publishers, of course.

The problem was that, other than badminton, I had no other talent. Actually, I did have another talent, one I couldn't be held accountable for: the ability to fantasize. I was rather ashamed to admit it.

The beauty of my plan B was that it didn't require me to completely abandon plan A. The experts themselves probably hadn't yet thought this far. The gist of it was, if I failed in the field of badminton and wasn't successful as a writer—if the publishers would sell my writings only as scrap paper—then I would move on to plan B: to write a book about badminton!

Nothing had happened yet, but I was already fantasizing about my book's endorsements. The back cover would have praise from a former winner of the Thomas Cup: *"There's never been a sports book like this before. The writer truly understands the meaning of mens sana incorpore sano."*

A famous love specialist from Jakarta would write: *"This book is a must-read for the obese having trouble in the bedroom."*

The Indonesian minister of youth and exercise would give this comment: *"An exhilarating book!"*

The Indonesian minister of education would make a touching confession: *"I hadn't read in a very long time. Then this book came along, and finally I read again!"*

A beautiful former winner of the Uber Cup would admit, *"Reading this book made me want to hug the writer!"*

30 ☼ HIS SECOND PROMISE

There we were, in a rowdy oval room in an art deco–style building. We were backed into a corner: Sahara, Lintang, and I. Once again, our reputation was on the line.

This was the Academic Challenge. Our spirits were low after seeing the state school and PN kids carrying textbooks we'd never laid eyes on. Their covers were thick and shiny. They must've been expensive.

The risk here was higher than the one we faced in the carnival. The Academic Challenge was an open arena to demonstrate intelligence or, if you were unlucky, an unthinkable amount of stupidity. We had been through painstaking preparations with Bu Mus. She had high hopes for this competition, even higher than for the carnival. She collected example problems and worked hard training us from morning until evening. For her, succeeding here was the perfect way to convince Mister Samadikun not to condemn our school.

Unfortunately, no matter how hard Bu Mus tried to strengthen our minds, advise us, persuade us, and push us to stay strong, we were still terrified. The thick books with the shiny covers in the hands of the PN kids made all of our weeks of hard work and memorization vanish in an instant.

I tried to imagine myself meditating on a green meadow in the gentlest place in my imagination: Edensor. That usually calmed me down. This time, it failed.

We shrank behind a large, beautiful, cold mahogany table. The room teemed with supporters from all the schools.

The most dominant supporters, of course, were those rooting for the PN School. There were hundreds of them, and they wore special shirts with loud writing on the back: VENI, VIDI, VICI— I CAME, I SAW, I CONQUERED. It was enough to break their rivals' spirits.

The PN School's Academic Challenge team members were the best of the best. They were specially chosen according to very high standards. This year, they'd prepared even more thoroughly and scientifically than normal—a new young teacher, famous for his intelligence, had designed a simulation of the competition with bells, a jury, a stopwatch, and various potential questions. He taught physics. Drs. Zulfikar was his name. *Drs.* distinguished him as having earned a bachelor's degree.

Our supporters were led by Mahar and Flo. There weren't that many of them, but they had tremendous enthusiasm. They brought two Muhammadiyah flags and various other things usually carried by football fans. The PN students considered Flo a traitor and gave her brutal stares. However, just like Lintang, Flo didn't care. Even though it was almost certain that our team would be put to shame by PN's team, Flo didn't hesitate one bit to defend her school.

Among our supporters were Trapani and his mother. They were holding hands. I saw all the schoolgirls whispering, giggling, and constantly looking over at Trapani. The older he got, the more handsome he became. He was tall and slim, with clean white skin and thick black hair. His eyes were like unripened walnuts: calm, cool, and deep.

Trapani had been chosen for our team. His overall score was higher than Sahara's—but his geography score was lower. The structure of our team was as follows: math, natural sciences, and English were all in the hands of Lintang; I was pretty good in civics, history of Islam, Fiqh, and, to some extent, Indonesian. Our weakness was geography, and the expert in that was none other than Sahara. And so, for the sake of our team, Trapani, with an open heart, gave Sahara the chance to compete. He was a handsome young man with a big soul.

Bu Mus appreciated Trapani's sacrifice and gave him permission to hang any picture of his choosing in our classroom. Trapani took advantage of this sweet offer and hung up his parents' old-time wedding picture from the Seruni Salon in Manggar. It was an elegant black-and-white photograph.

Similarly, perhaps to help Trapani be strong, Lintang brought along a photograph of his mother and father as newlyweds. In it, the bride and groom were wedged between two big jugs overflowing with plastic flowers. And behind them was a paper backdrop featuring a sedan parked in an open meadow, surrounded by a happy-looking family. Maybe it was supposed to look like somewhere in Europe.

"Brace yourself, Ikal," Trapani said.

Lintang opened his rattan sack, studied his parents' newlywed photo, slipped it back into his bag, and returned to being still.

I couldn't stop fanning myself. Not because I was hot but because my heart was raging with fear. Never had even one village school won this competition; it was an honor just to be invited.

Since dawn, when we boarded an open-bed truck after Subuh prayer to bring us to the capital of our regency, Lintang had been mute. His mother, father, and little sisters came along. It was their first time to Tanjong Pandan, Lintang included.

Sahara sat in the middle. Lintang and I sat on either side of her. Lintang leaned forward listlessly. He felt inferior, discouraged, and shy in this completely foreign environment. He looked exhausted, like someone carrying the entire burden of defending our reputation. Occasionally he glanced over at his mother, father, and younger siblings in their poor clothing, sitting huddled together in the corner, looking confused in the boisterous atmosphere.

"To hell with self-confidence! The important thing is to listen carefully to the questions, hit the button quickly, and answer correctly!" I said to encourage Lintang and Sahara. They didn't seem to care.

Lintang and Sahara couldn't be counted on anymore. I saw the hands of other contestants start to test the buttons in front of them. Sahara, who had been assigned and specially trained to push the button for our team, wasn't even able to bring her finger close to the round device. A paralyzing stage fright gripped her. The noisy sounds of the buttons and microphones terrified us. We didn't test them out at all. We lost before the fight even began. The Muhammadiyah supporters read our fear. They were very uneasy.

The head of the jury rose from his seat, introduced himself, and announced the start of the competition. My heart raced, Sahara was deathly pale, and Lintang was silent.

I lacked the courage to face the audience. Bu Mus and Pak Harfan didn't even have enough courage to face us. Pak Harfan was hunched over. Maybe because expectations for our performance were so high, he was disappointed at our palpably broken spirits. Bu Mus turned toward the big lamp in the center of the room, which looked like an octopus king. This competition was the most important event in their teaching careers. A single event exemplifying all the things they had to prove to Mister Samadikun, it put their very reputations as teachers on the line.

Not much later, a woman asked the audience to calm down so she could begin the questioning. The moment of truth had arrived. The contestants were rapt, ready to listen to the barrage of questions and attack the buttons. It was nerve-racking.

The first question reverberated throughout the room.

"She's a Frenchwoman between myth and reality—"

Buzz! Buzz! Buzz!

The question was not yet finished. Someone had pushed the button prematurely. All in attendance were startled. A coarse arm had just attacked the button in front of us with lightning speed—it was Lintang's arm!

"Team F!" yelled the woman asking the questions.

"Jeanne d'Arc, Loire Valley, France!" Lintang said—without blinking, without any hesitation, with an incredibly nasal French accent.

"One hundred points!" yelled a man sitting at the jury table as he was greeted by a thunderous applause from the Muhammadiyah supporters. The woman continued.

"Question number two: Use an integral to calculate the area bounded by functions y and x, where y equals two-x and x equals five."

With no delay, Lintang attacked the button and shouted out, "The integral limits are five and zero, and two-x minus x times dx equals twelve-point-five!"

Incredible! Without any doubt, without writing any notes, without even blinking.

"One hundred!" the man yelled once again.

Our supporters clamored and clapped their hands.

"Question three: Calculate the area in the integration region of three and zero for a function of six plus x minus x to the second degree."

Lintang closed his eyes for a moment, as he often did when Bu Mus asked questions in class. Less than seven seconds later, he wailed, "Thirteen-point-five!"

"One hundred!"

Right on, no haste and no hesitation.

The attendees were astounded by Lintang. The other contestants were stupefied. Bu Mus moved forward. The worry on her face had disappeared. Her lips mumbled, "*Subhanallah, subhanallah*, Allah is most holy . . ."

Lintang's mother and father watched intently as Lintang swept through the math and natural science questions. Questions from other categories went to our competitors, especially PN's team. Still, when the first round was over, we had a definite lead.

In the second round, our competitors gradually began to gain ground. To make matters worse, Sahara and I had answered a few questions incorrectly, costing us points. In the third round, the PN contestants, intelligent like Lintang, had caught up to our score; they even surpassed it a few times.

Every time a PN team member answered correctly, hundreds of supporters cheered loudly. Ours did the same. The happiest of all was Harun. He truly enjoyed the festivity. I saw him clapping nonstop and shouting encouraging words, but he wasn't looking at us. He was looking out the window. It appeared he was encouraging a group of girls playing *kasti* out in the yard.

At last, the final round arrived. PN's team and ours kept

trading the lead. We were down, but the difference between us was only one hundred points. The competition had reached a critical point: a correct answer would determine the winner, an incorrect answer carried fatal consequences.

We had the chance to tie, but then the woman asked the question "'Pleng Chart Thai' is—"

With absolute certainty, I hit the button and shouted out, "The Chinese national anthem!"

And I was wrong.

"Minus one hundred!"

Everyone cursed me. How foolish. It was clear from the name itself the answer was Thailand. But because of A Ling, everything in three-word phrases, for example Njoo Xian Ling, made me think of China.

My stupidity landed us in a serious situation. We were down two hundred points. Defeat danced in front of our eyes. It was truly saddening. Lintang's greatness would be overshadowed by Sahara's and my incompetence—especially mine. Sahara and I hadn't been able to perform up to Bu Mus's expectations in our fields of expertise. I felt at fault. Sahara was very angry with me. She whispered heatedly into my ear, "Boi, listen up! If any of the questions are about geography, don't you dare interfere! Shut your mouth and watch yourself!"

Sahara was a straight shooter.

"This is what happens when a task is given to a nonexpert! Wait for the destruction!"

Amazing! Even in this critical situation where we were about to lose, Sahara could still quote hadiths, and she could still quarrel—it was truly her hobby. What she meant was that she was the geography expert, and any question having to do with any country's residents, agricultural produce, and national anthems should be answered only by her. Her griping wasn't for nothing; while elbowing me in the ribs, Sahara went straight for the next question.

"What is Brunei Darussalam's national anthem?"

Buzz!

"Team F!"

"Allah Peliharakan Sultan!"

"One hundred!"

But we were still on shaky ground, down by one hundred points.

The second-to-last question was about a man named Ernest Rutherford.

"What did this New Zealand–born man contribute to science?"

"He was a pioneer in separating nuclei into smaller particles," Lintang answered calmly.

"One hundred!"

Our supporters' enthusiasm erupted again because of the tied score: eighteen hundred to eighteen hundred. There was only one question left. Everyone left their seats to jostle their way up front. Bu Mus and Pak Harfan looked like they were praying. Even the questioner was tense. "Listen carefully. This is the last question," she said shakily. "A scientific breakthrough regarding color concepts in the early sixteenth century started intense research in the field of optics. At that time, many scientists believed that mixing light and darkness created color, an opinion that turned out to be erroneous. This error was proven by reflecting light onto concave lenses—"

Buzz! Buzz! Buzz! Lintang barked, "Newton's rings!"

The moderator gave a wide smile. She had been silently on our side. The guy calling out *one hundred* also smiled. He wailed, "One hundred!"

Our supporters roared and jumped for joy. We won! I couldn't believe it—our Muhammadiyah village school won! I hugged Lintang. He threw his hands up high. We jumped up and down. But it didn't last long. During our victory celebration, we heard someone shout from a bench in the back: "Your Honor! Your Honor! Your Honor, head of the jury! I believe that the question and answer are false!"

Everyone fell silent and looked to the back. It was Drs. Zulfikar, the model physics teacher from the PN School. Oh, no! This could mean trouble. Lintang remained calm. When the teacher got to the front, he took a cocky stance with his hands on his hips and began to speak in an academic fashion.

"The experiment with concave lenses has nothing to do with the critique of the earlier theory of color involving light and darkness. The understanding regarding the creation of color is not an optical matter—that is, unless the jury would like to disagree with Descartes. Optics and the color spectrum are two completely different matters. In this ambiguous situation, we are faced with three possibilities: the wrong question, the wrong answer, or a baseless question and answer—it's not contextual!"

Oh, man! This was way beyond my understanding. And he was so clever in making the judges waver by quoting Descartes's opinion. Who had the audacity to disagree with a scientific expert? Hopefully Lintang would have an argument.

I looked at Sahara. She hid her face, as if she'd never met me and Lintang in her whole life. The spectators and jury were baffled by this seemingly intelligent objection. Responding was out of the question, since most didn't know what he was talking about. But someone had to save us from this situation. The head of the jury stood up. Lintang remained calm and smiled a little; he was very relaxed.

"Thank you for your well-argued objection," the head of the jury said. "What can I say, my field is Pancasila moral education . . ."

Drs. Zulfikar grumbled. Because he felt he had already won, he was unable to resist the temptation to further belittle us. He went from arrogant to just plain rude.

"Perhaps these *Muhammadiyah* students or the jury could be so kind as to explain Descartes's theory on the phenomenon of color?"

What hurt the most was the way he said *Muhammadiyah*, emphasizing it to remind everyone that we were just an unimportant village school.

I didn't understand optical theories, but I did know a little about the history of the discovery of color. I knew that Descartes worked with prisms and sheets of paper to test color, not to manipulate optics. It was Newton who was the great guru of optics. Drs. Zulfikar was clearly being a smart aleck, a classic problem in Indonesia: smart people talking in circles with lofty terms and high-level theories, not for the sake of scientific progress but to trick the poor, who were silent and unable to find the words to argue.

I stared at Lintang, begging for his help later if I spoke up against Drs. Zulfikar. I really needed his support. But what if it turned out that I was the one who was wrong? Seeing my anger, Lintang gave me a little smile. It was a peaceful smile. I knew, as usual, he had read my mind. He answered my stare with a soft one that said: *Patience, little brother. Let your older brother take care of this.* He was still very calm. Sahara and I shrank back.

The head of the jury drew a deep breath. He looked around to his colleagues, the other members of the jury. They all shook their heads as a sign that they were unable to go head-to-head with Drs. Zulfikar.

"I'm sorry, young teacher. On behalf of the jury, I have to say that our knowledge is lacking in that area."

His words were humble, the poor old man. He was a senior teacher with a kind heart, respected for his dozens of years of dedication to education in Belitong. He appeared embarrassed and hopeless. He directed his gaze to Team F, our team. Lintang smiled and gave him a slight nod. Unexpectedly, the head of the jury said, "But maybe this Muhammadiyah student can help."

The room was very quiet and laced with discomfort, and it grew even more uncomfortable because Drs. Zulfikar filled the air with another unfeeling comment.

"I hope his argument is as accurate as their previous answer!"

He went *beyond* too far! He had deliberately provoked Lintang, and this time Lintang was hooked. He stood up to speak.

"Sir, if your objection was about the answer not being in line with the question, then maybe it would be an acceptable objection. But the jury asked a question and the answer was already written on the paper read by the woman asking the questions. I am certain that Newton's rings is written there, and our answer was Newton's rings. That means we have the right to one hundred points. Even if it wasn't contextual, well, that would only mean that the jury asked the right question in the wrong manner."

Drs. Zulfikar was not willing to accept this. "In other words, the question was erroneous because the other contestants expected a different answer!"

Lintang rebutted. "There's nothing erroneous except for you, sir, disregarding the substance of the theory of Newton's rings and wanting to bring down our score for the sake of triviality."

Drs. Zulfikar was offended. He became angry. The atmosphere grew even tenser. He lunged forward.

"Well, if that's the case, then you can explain to me the

substance of that theory! You all have gotten your points by lucky guesses, not really knowing anything at all!"

Oh, boy, that was really boorish. Sahara scowled. After drifting off into space, she had returned as a leopard, her eyebrows coming together. The audience and the jury were astonished, mouths open.

Lintang stared at his puzzled mother in the corner. His face swelled up, his chest heaved in and out. He looked like he was holding on to a heavy load. I soon understood his reaction. The issue of Newton's rings surely reminded him of the time he was forced to sell his mother's wedding ring so he could continue going to school. He was visibly infuriated. This matter with Drs. Zulfikar had become very personal for Lintang, and this was how a genius went berserk.

"The substance is that Newton clearly succeeded in pointing out the errors in the color theories of Descartes, Aristotle, and even the more contemporary Robert Hooke! Those three people thought that color has discrete spectrums. Through concave optic lenses, which later gave birth to the rings theorem, Newton proved that colors lie along a continuous spectrum and that spectrum is produced not by glass characteristics but by light's fundamental characteristics!"

Drs. Zulfikar was stunned. The audience was lost in optical physics theory, unable to nod even a little. I was delighted. My hunch had proved true! I wanted to jump up from my seat, stand on the mahogany table in front of me, and yell: *You guys know what? This is Lintang Samudera Basara, son of Syahbani Maulana Basara, a brilliant boy and my deskmate! So take that, everyone!*

Lintang wasn't yet satisfied.

"Newton said—unless you, sir, would like to question a five-hundred-year-old proof—that the density of transparent particles determines which particle they reflect. That's the relation between the thickness of the layer of air and optics according to the color rings theorem. All of this can be observed only through optics. How can you say, sir, that these matters are not inter-related?"

Drs. Zulfikar slumped into a chair, his face pallid. He was out of clever words. His glasses slid feebly down the bridge of his nose. Our supporters jumped around like dancing monkeys because Lintang's argument had secured our school's place as the winners of this year's Academic Challenge, something no one had imagined we could ever achieve.

Bu Mus snatched the Muhammadiyah flag from Flo's hands and waved it with all her energy. Her eyes were glassy. She said, "*Subhanallah, subhanallah*, Allah is most holy."

I hugged Lintang and congratulated him for fulfilling his promise to his mother—to win the Academic Challenge to repay the sacrifice of her wedding ring.

When Lintang held the victory trophy up high, our first hero, Harun, whistled like a cowboy calling the cows home. Harun was moved by pride of Lintang, but he congratulated Trapani. No matter how great Lintang was, he still idolized Trapani; that was who he wanted to be. In the meantime, Ibu Frischa, the PN School principal, sat on a big chair, fanning off the mugginess. She sat restlessly, her face giving off the impression that at that moment her mind was somewhere else altogether.

31 ❋ MAN WITH A HEART AS BIG AS THE SKY

The next day, we lined up in front of the glass display case. It was Lintang's turn to receive the honor of placing a trophy in the display case. The Academic Challenge trophy took its place next to Mahar's carnival trophy.

Those two trophies answered our question as to why God had given us these two gifted boys. Mahar gave us the courage to compete. Lintang gave us the courage to dream.

The trophies were truly marvelous. They stood united, inseparable, as if they were the property of brave warriors ready to face any difficulties. Before, everyone believed that our mentality, our system, and even our school would collapse within weeks. No one ever expected us to win these awards. But look at us, with our two glorious trophies. Look at how proudly we stood in front of our glass display case. We were stronger and sturdier than ever. Bu Mus's and Pak Harfan's perseverance and persistence in educating us were starting to show promising results. Those two fought hard to hold back tears as they gazed at the trophies because they knew that from this moment on, no one would ever insult our school again.

Even though his health was deteriorating, Pak Harfan was even more enthusiastic to teach after our victory in the Academic Challenge. He tirelessly prepared us to face our final exam.

He coached us for hours. He worked like he was chasing something. While our workload was heavy, we were extremely happy. Pak Harfan's teaching methods made memorizing material seem like a delicious treat. Complex problems became challenges, difficult arithmetic became entertainment.

On the weekends, Pak Harfan rode his bicycle one hundred kilometers to Tanjong Pandan with a basket of *palawijaya* crops from his garden: pineapples, bananas, galangal, and sweet potatoes. He sold the produce in order to buy us schoolbooks. On his way home he stopped by the municipal library. There, he borrowed books with sample final exam questions from years past.

But Pak Harfan's asthma was becoming more critical. He was coughing up blood, and we often had to remind him to rest.

"If I don't teach, I'll get sicker," he always answered. "And if I die, I want to die at this school," he joked.

Every evening for several months, after studying al-Qur'an, we rushed back to the school to get extra lessons from Pak Harfan.

But one evening, after we waited awhile inside the classroom, Pak Harfan didn't come in. We went to his office beside the school garden. We knocked on his door, but there was no answer. We opened the door and saw him sitting with his face down on his desk. I called his name, but he didn't answer. I got a bit closer, and he seemed to be fast asleep. I said his name again once I was close. He was silent. I touched his hand, and it was cold like ice. He wasn't breathing. Pak Harfan had passed away.

Pak Harfan had been teaching since he was a teenager, for more than fifty-one years. He himself had chopped the wood from the forest to build the Muhammadiyah School. He had carried the first—and heftiest—piece of wood on his own shoulders, and that was the main support beam in our classroom. We had measured our heights on that beam throughout the years, leaving it full of pocketknife scratches. For us, that beam was sacred.

They say that a long while back Pak Harfan had had many students and teachers. But slowly the community lost faith in the school and the teachers lost pride in their jobs. The educational discrimination applied by PN dampened the people's enthusiasm for school. That discrimination made native Belitong inhabitants believe that only the children of PN staff could be successful in school and get the chance to go on to university—and that the only teachers with a future were PN School teachers. This led village children to drop out of school one by one, and one by one the village teachers began to step down as well. They became either PN coolies or fishermen.

"What's the point of school?" village children asked accusingly. "We won't be able to continue anyway."

The situation actually worsened with the "success" of small village children not in school. They drew earnings from working as pepper pickers, shopkeepers, boat caulkers, coconut graters, and errand boys for fishing boats.

For them, school was relative—especially for those who found work with good compensation, like those courageous enough to go into the jungle to look for agar wood and yellow sandalwood. They could afford motorbikes, while Pak Harfan, a school principal, had to save up, rupiah by rupiah, just to be able to change his decrepit bicycle tire. Education soon became a bleak endeavor for children trapped in a devilish circle with little hope of schooling, striving for life's necessities in the face of discrimination.

But Pak Harfan never tired of trying to convince those children that knowledge was about self-respect, and education was an act of devotion to the Creator, that school hadn't always been tied to goals like getting a degree and becoming rich. School was dignified and prestigious, a celebration of humanity; it was the joy of studying and the light of civilization. That was Pak Harfan's glorious definition of education. But that enlightenment didn't get through to the young children who were marginalized by discrimination and blinded by enticing material goods.

Pak Harfan never gave up trying to convince them to go to school. He'd even bring them books in the middle of the sea. He'd search for them on the floodplains of the rivers where they caulked boats. He'd wait for them under pepper trees. But no one accepted his invitation. Sometimes their bosses, and even the children themselves, would chase Pak Harfan away.

On a silent evening, a poor man with a heart as big as the sky passed away. One of the wells of knowledge in the forsaken, dry field was gone forever. But he had left a pure well in the hearts of eleven students, a well of knowledge that would never dry up.

We wept in the classroom. The one who sobbed most was Harun. Pak Harfan had been like a father to him. He sobbed and sobbed; he couldn't be consoled. His heavy tears streamed down, soaking his shirt.

32 ❈ SECRETARY OF THE GHOST FAN CLUB

They called themselves the Societeit de Limpai or, more simply, the Limpai Group.

The Limpai is a legendary, terrifying, supernatural animal in Belitong's mythology. Its story is an interesting legend, since many folk stories give contradicting definitions of the mysterious creature. Coastal people think it's a fairy who lives in the mountains. Mountain people believe it is an enormous white mammothlike animal. Malays living in lowland plains know it as a wind—a wind that, if angry, could fell trees and rice stalks. In the backcountry, *limpai* means the same as "bogey," a big black ghost. The young generation has it all wrong. For them, Limpai is an urban legend, an incubus or a death omen able to disguise itself as anything.

The Limpai story has its roots in ancient Belitong teachings passed on from generation to generation so that people wouldn't exploit forest and water resources. Those teachings hold a persuasive power, making people afraid of bad luck because the forests and water are guarded by the Limpai ghost.

Truly educated adults see Limpai as nothing more than haze

wafting in the heads of stupid, feeble-faithed gossipers without enough work to do: that's Limpai.

The Societeit operated secretly. It was an underground organization. Outsiders never knew when and where they gathered or what they discussed. If they were caught by surprise, they'd quickly change their topic of conversation and pretend not to know one another. That was how they masked their actions. It wasn't because they were on a dangerous, anarchic, communistic, or lawbreaking mission. It was to avoid mockery. The Societeit was nothing more than a bunch of useless people with too much love for the mystical world.

There were nine members of the Societeit. The requirements to become a member were exceptionally strict. The oldest member of the group, a retired harbormaster, was fifty-seven years old. The youngest members were two adolescents. The other six consisted of a Bank Rakyat Indonesia local branch teller, a Chinese who worked with gold plating, an unemployed person, a lone Electone player, an electrical engineering dropout who had opened a bike shop, and Mujis, the mosquito sprayer.

The strangest thing was that the head of the Societeit was its youngest member. He was the founder of the organization, respected by its members for his wide knowledge of the dark world and his comprehensive collection of rumors and foolish news. He was Mahar. The other youngster, of course, was Flo.

The Societeit's activities were very hectic. They went on expeditions to eerie places, investigated mystical happenings, and mapped Malay mythology. One way of looking at them was as brave individuals eager to dig up the secrets of the realm with an uncompromising skepticism—they wouldn't believe it unless they saw and felt it for themselves.

Mahar and Flo brilliantly incorporated Limpai into the name of their gang. Because the creature was metaphoric, depending on who was looking at it, the Societeit could be seen as a group of scientific crazy people or of religious heretics. Its philosophy was just like the differing perspectives of the meaning of Limpai.

Under the supervision of the dropout, they assembled an electromagnetic field detector that could read waves in observation areas ranging from two to seven milligauss because they believed that was the range where spirit activities could be observed. They also made a frequency sensor that could detect extremely low frequencies, below sixty hertz. According to their thinking, those were the frequencies in which ghouls conversed. They also equipped themselves with incense, aloewood, monitor lizard egg charms, and a wild dwarf chicken, the use of which was considered the quickest way to detect the approach of devils.

One time, they went to the Genting Apit Forest, the most forbidding place in Belitong. That forest hid thousands of eerie tales, the most prominent being that of the *ectoplasmic mist* phenomenon. The mist talked to itself and naturally—perhaps satanically—transfigured itself into human figures, animals, or giants. It was no rarity to capture these shapes on ordinary camera film. Drivers passing through the Genting Apit area were strongly advised not to look in their rearview mirrors because valley ghosts would often hitchhike for a while in the backseat. This was the sort of spooky area where the Societeit did their research.

To make a long story short, this underground organization was very busy and demanded a schedule for administration, funds, and props—they needed a secretary.

When Mahar offered me the position, I immediately seized it. Even though there was no payment whatsoever, I felt honored to be appointed secretary by a bunch of people who were friends with ghosts. I was also happy because the offer showed I had enough integrity to hold on to the money. At the very least, it meant I could be trusted, even if it was only by people who couldn't think straight. Now, my friend, if the job mentioned could be called a career, then my chest would overflow with pride—so if I may, becoming the secretary of this invisible organization, the Societeit de Limpai, was my first career.

My task was simple and could be arranged through a register book. My responsibilities included recording member dues, keeping the money, and making note of personal items that members would sell or pawn to buy equipment and fund expeditions. Other duties, according to orders from my bosses—Flo and Mahar—were to arrange the secret meetings and to pour tea for the attending members at the secret meetings. In this capacity, it would be fair to call me a waiter.

Upon returning from their mystical journeys, Flo and Mahar would always bring exciting stories to school. One day they told us that in the middle of a dark forest, they had discovered some graves, measuring three by six meters with a distance between tombstones of at least five meters. Since Malays believed in placing tombstones at the head and tips of the toes, it could be inferred that the corpses buried beneath the tombstones belonged to exceptionally large human beings.

Mahar told us about the relationship between the gigantic ancient graves in Belitong and the theories of famous archaeologists like Barry Chamis and Harold T. Wilkins, who believed that at one point in time giant humans roamed the earth. Mahar linked the Belitong graves to the giant *pasnuta* human skull found in Omaha and the incomplete skeletons exhumed from an ancient grave site in the Golan Heights. When reconstructed, the skeletons formed a human almost six meters tall.

Mahar may have been an eccentric boy who straddled the gray area between reality and imagination, but he was undoubtedly bright, with both a vast knowledge of the paranormal world and a well-structured way of thinking.

Flo and Mahar sat casually on a low branch of the filicium, like storytelling priests from a Sikh temple, while we, Laskar Pelangi, squatted bright-eyed and astonished as we listened to their story about a cave on an isolated island.

"We investigated the cave. When we held up our oil lamp, we were surprised to see a Paleolithic painting depicting naked people eating raw cave bats," Flo recalled.

The amazing thing wasn't so much the discovery of the painting itself but rather, as Mahar recounted, the whisperings that came from the Paleolithic painting as he lay half sleeping, half awake.

"Lemuria, Lemuria," Mahar moaned. "The paintings hissed in my ear like a *manau* snake. Do you guys know the legend of Lemuria?" He trembled with fear. "The whispers entered me like a premonition. It was a scary prediction that a power in Belitong will soon fall!"

Mahar liked to exaggerate, but it was undeniable that his nonsense was sometimes, sooner or later, proved true—this had been demonstrated time and again.

So I took Mahar seriously. Would the people of Belitong disappear like those of Babylon and Lemuria? What made me apprehensive was Lemuria. Many people believed the tale of Lemuria to be nothing more than a fairy tale, just like Atlantis. However, if Mahar's premonition proved true, would the tale of Lemuria also be proved true? The scary word *lemures* haunted me. *Lemures*, the root of the name Lemuria, means "vanished spirits." What disaster lay ahead for Belitong Island?

In another world, Bu Mus was dizzy thinking about the direction of Mahar's development. He had plunged into the mystical world, not toward artistic achievement, as his plan A should have been. With the presence of Flo, his talent was further wasted.

And then Bu Mus really got a headache—she received a letter from PN advising her to halt studying activities at our school. Three dredges would soon come to dig up the tin beneath it.

33 ✻ BRUCE LEE FOR PRESIDENT

Construction workers began building barracks for coolies around our school. The sounds of roaring dredges drawing closer to our school rattled us.

Even though she had been warned, Bu Mus was still determined to teach. Sometimes she had to shout while explaining something just to compete with the noise of the machines.

Bu Mus had already responded to the warning letter with a plea to the highest PN authority not to knock down our school. She also asked for the chance to speak with him personally. Not one person paid heed to her letter.

Since the passing of Pak Harfan, it was Bu Mus's duty to teach all the lessons, overcome the school's financial difficulties, prepare for exams, and face Mister Samadikun's threats. Now came the biggest problem of them all: the menace of the dredges. She faced all of this alone.

Although we were in a critical situation, Bu Mus stood tall. If we were being pessimistic, she'd invite us to talk about our two trophies and would remind us that those were awards for people who weren't given to complaining. But our euphoria didn't last long. In the distance we heard the terrifying sputtering of a muffler. Mister Samadikun!

It was time for his final inspection. We scrambled about, preparing ourselves. Bu Mus hurried to make sure everything was in order. If we failed, we wouldn't have to wait to be pulverized by the dredges. Our fate was in Mister Samadikun's hands.

This time, however, we were more optimistic. Everything was complete: our first-aid kit, even though it contained only APC pills and worm-extract syrup, would pass muster. We'd used money from the carnival to buy a chalkboard and a new eraser. And while it wasn't that great, we had a bathroom. It consisted only of a sunken barrel, but it meant that we no longer had to answer nature's call in the bushes.

We had all of our shirt buttons. Our hair was neatly combed. Everyone had something on his feet, even if it was only *cunghai* sandals made from car tires. Not one of us wore a slingshot. Our clothes were still stained—that is, mine, Kucai's, and Syahdan's—but just vaguely, with some sap. Harun's report card had also been prepared. We had specifically taught Harun that the correct answer to two plus two is four. But every time we quizzed him, he still held up three fingers.

Bu Mus even fulfilled Mister Samadikun's trivial and finicky requirements: calculator, compasses, and crayons. She was able to buy a few compasses and some crayons with money from her sewing. And because calculators were expensive, she bought an abacus instead. The important thing, however, was that we now had two trophies that would certainly impress Mister Samadikun.

Bu Mus ordered us to move the glass display case from the corner and place it next to her desk so that Mister Samadikun would see the trophies right away. Sahara ran like crazy to the well and returned with a rag and bucket. She cleaned the glass so our trophies could be better seen.

Now we were ready to greet Mister Samadikun. Bu Mus lined us up on the left and right of the glass display case; she even instructed us to smile.

We were tense but ready. She looked around to see if anything was missing. Her neck stiffened as she saw the wall above the chalkboard. She looked as if she'd seen a ghost. Her once-bright face instantly turned pale. The rest of us followed her gaze. Oh, no! We immediately became aware that we had forgotten the pictures of the president, vice president, and the state symbol—Garuda Pancasila!

This had happened because we hadn't yet received them from Cahaya Abadi, the school supplies store in Tanjong Pandan. We often asked the shop owner about our order, and he said they were all out and awaiting a new shipment from Jakarta.

Those pictures were the most important requirements. Without them, everything else meant nothing. Mister Samadikun would not be willing to accept our excuse.

The sputtering of the muffler stopped. Mister Samadikun was already out front. Earlier we were ready to go, but now we were limp and hopeless. Bu Mus stood stupefied. Sahara sobbed. Kucai, as class president, let out a bleak sigh. Our exhausting efforts to fulfill the requirements and win the trophies were all in vain. Our school would surely be closed by Mister Samadikun.

We could hear him parking his motorbike. Suddenly, as our situation was getting critical, Mahar ran and leapt over the desks. Then, like a monkey, he balanced against the side wall. One of his hands clung to the wall; the other took down the Bruce Lee and John Lennon posters and the newlywed photo of Trapani's parents, and grabbed all the nails. We looked on, baffled. Mahar whirled around, jumped back over the desks, then swooped down and seized the eraser. While on his tiptoes on a desk he'd pushed up against the wall, he skillfully hung the pictures above the chalkboard. He drove in the nails with the eraser.

Mahar hung the posters triangularly in the fashion that our patriotic symbols are normally hung. Centered in the highest position, the normal spot for the Garuda Pancasila, he hung the newlywed photo of Trapani's parents. Below and to the right, a smiling Bruce Lee exuded presidential authority. Beside him, John Lennon filled the position of vice president.

Mahar returned to his place in line. Mister Samadikun suddenly stood before us.

No one made a peep. Bu Mus trembled.

Mister Samadikun took out his folder with his checklist. His gaze swept the room from corner to corner, and then he began taking notes. He didn't speak. His face was cruel, as usual. He placed the facility inspection form on the table in front of us; we could see what he wrote.

In the column for chalkboard and furniture, he raised his previous *(E) Bad* to *(C) Fair.* Our scores got even better in the columns for student conditions, toilet and lighting facilities, first-aid kit, and visual aids. At the basic level, there was no problem. But we were worried when he arrived at the national symbols column. He looked up above the chalkboard. It seemed like he had to try very hard to see up there. He squinted. He took off his thick glasses, pulled a handkerchief out of his bag, wiped them off, and put them back on. He rubbed his eyes, straining once again to inspect the pictures above the chalkboard. It was only then that the genius of Mahar's ruse dawned on us. He knew that Mister Samadikun suffered from severe nearsightedness and wouldn't be able to clearly see the pictures displayed high above the chalkboard.

Mister Samadikun returned to his form. In the column for

national symbols, our score was raised from *(F) Nonexistent* to an impressive *(A) Complete*. Mister Samadikun had no idea that the sovereign government of the Republic of Indonesia had been taken over by Bruce Lee and John Lennon.

Mister Samadikun put away his form and smiled. It was the first time I had ever seen him smile. His smile grew wider when he saw our trophies. He still didn't speak, but he nodded his head. Then he excused himself. The nod meant that he appreciated our continuous hard work to hold on to our school, and that we had succeeded in proving ourselves so much that he—or even the Indonesian minister of education—couldn't shut down our school.

After Mister Samadikun left, we stared at Mahar with admiration. As usual, he did his annoying but amusing signature gesture. He smiled at his idol Bruce Lee in *The dragon kung fu—fight to the death* poster. Bruce Lee smiled back at us. When Mahar had asked Bu Mus to hang the Bruce Lee poster, he had theorized that destiny is circular, and that one day the poster would be useful. Today his ridiculous theory had been proved correct.

34 ☼ PARALYZED RABBIT

A few days after Mister Samadikun's inspection, our order of state symbols arrived. We hung them in their honorable required positions. Bruce Lee and John Lennon did not put up a fight.

But the state symbols didn't last long. Three days later, a few PN foremen entered our classroom and asked Bu Mus's permission to take them down. Apparently they didn't want to be involved in any criminal proceedings later, in the event the symbols were run over by the dredges. They knew that the law protected the symbols, whereas to run over a hundred-year-old poor village school seemed to be no problem at all. There was no law to punish PN if they did that, and there was no law to protect us.

More and more tin exploration machines arrived, one after another. The dredges were getting closer. The giant machines, as big as football fields and as tall as coconut trees, pointed their snouts straight at our school. Our school sat like a paralyzed rabbit surrounded by a pack of hyenas.

We had been under pressure from Mister Samadikun for years. We had finally succeeded in subduing him. But PN wasn't something that could be opposed. Over hundreds of years, no one had ever stood in their way of exploiting the land for tin. If the case required compensation, their resources were limitless. It was common for dredges to roll over gardens, markets, villages, and even government offices. A poor school was petty, nothing more than a small speck of dirt under the tip of PN's fingernail.

Despite our strong desire to hold on, we finally became realistic. We were no match for PN. And with Pak Harfan's passing, Bu Mus's morale deteriorated. It had never happened before, but she began to ask us frequently if she could be excused from teaching.

Every rest period, we sat in a sad daze looking at the half of our schoolyard already crushed by land-leveling equipment. This was the biggest trial that had ever befallen us, and we grew more hopeless with every passing day. Bu Mus looked at us desperately. There was one thing that frightened her more than the school being destroyed by dredges, a fear shared by the late Pak Harfan. Ultimately, the thing they were most afraid of came to pass.

Following three days of not showing his big head at school, Kucai was absent once again. Our class was in chaos without the legendary class president. Bu Mus asked Kucai's father about it, and he informed her that Kucai had been leaving every morning for school. A scandal exploded.

After much investigation, it turned out Kucai had joined up with kids from the neighboring village to become a pepper picker.

Wednesday night, the night of payday, after studying al-Qur'an at al-Hikmah Mosque, Kucai pulled out a wad of money from behind his sarong. He licked the tip of his finger as he counted his money over and over again, just like a pawnshop cashier. He already knew the total. Not a word slid out of his tricky mouth. It was a truly dreadful solicitation. Soliciting, it turned out, was Kucai's hidden talent.

The next day, Samson went missing.

It was highly unusual for Samson to be absent on a Thursday—it was time for gym and health, his favorite class.

We didn't hear from him for a week. The following Wednesday night, he came to Koranic studies with a pitch-black body and even bigger muscles than before. He had become a copra coolie.

From behind his sarong he pulled out a bottle. "The newest hair-growing oil made in Pakistan!" he said proudly. "Expensive." He stroked a picture of a bearded man on the bottle. "It's made from lizard sweat! It's very strong! You could even smear it on your forehead and it would grow hair," he said as he rubbed my forehead.

Then he unbuttoned his shirt. My God, it was the real thing! Samson's chest was growing hair. He rebuttoned his shirt. In six years of school he hadn't been able to buy anything. Now, after just six days of carrying copra, he could buy a special tonic *made in Pakistan*!

The next day, Mahar disappeared.

Evidently he had added time to his job as a coconut grater. At first he had worked only part-time after school, but now he was a full timer. The upgrade in status meant only one thing: goodbye, school. Three days later, when our Koranic studies teacher wasn't looking, he pulled something out from behind his sarong: a double stick! Bruce Lee's ultimate weapon! Mahar was elated. He had wanted to buy a double stick his whole life, and now his dream had come true.

And whatever Mahar did would surely be followed by his

faithful disciple, A Kiong. One Monday morning, the tip of A Kiong's nose and his tin-can head went missing. He did not want to be far from his sensei, Mahar. He chose a career as a cake-seller. He carried the cakes in a washbasin on his head and sold them around the market where Mahar worked as a coconut grater at a Chinese produce shop.

A Kiong told me that carrying the moist cakes on his head actually seemed to be promising work.

"You make more doing this than you do diving for golf balls, Ikal. Selling cakes is little work for decent money, and you don't have to compete with crocodiles."

I thought about what we often did to make money, diving for the unreachable golf balls driven into the lake that the nouveau riche, PN staff, and beginning golfers were unable to retrieve themselves. We then sold the balls back to the caddies.

A Kiong patted the coins in his bulging pocket, and they jingled. The jingling enchanted me.

The next Monday, I abandoned school to sell cake at the market.

It was ironic: Kucai, the class president, the one who was supposed to raise our morale, had dropped out of school and, in doing so, had started a chain reaction that could bankrupt our school. Like I've always told you, friend, that is the opportunistic nature of a born politician.

That left Sahara, Flo, Trapani, Harun, Syahdan, and Lintang in the class. Syahdan was the next to go. He had wanted to persevere, but Bu Mus's endless grieving over the passing of Pak Harfan spread pessimism throughout the classroom. With just a little nudge from Kucai, Syahdan fled school to claim for himself the revered duty of boat caulker.

Someone was still enthusiastic, in spite of blown bicycle tires, a bicycle chain fastened together with plastic twine, and a commute rife with crocodile chases—Lintang. He didn't care that his friends had fled school and that it was under the threat of dredges. He still tried to arrive earliest and always went home last.

"I will keep on studying until the sacred beam supporting this school collapses," he said to me with conviction.

That sacred beam was a relic of Pak Harfan, and Lintang always saw it as a symbol of our school's struggle.

Because Bu Mus often didn't come to school anymore, Lintang took over her tasks. He taught everything, from math to Islamic history, just like Bu Mus. His students were Sahara, Flo, Trapani, and Harun. Together they were the five faithful students willing to hold on.

Bu Mus was incredibly surprised when Mujis told her that, from a distance, it looked like there were still people going to our school. She jumped on her bike and pedaled like crazy toward the schoolyard.

When she got there, she leaned her bike up against the filicium. She heard a jumble of voices coming from the classroom. She approached nervously and peeked through the cracks in the wall. Her body trembled when she saw Lintang explaining to Sahara, Flo, Trapani, and Harun the story of how Indonesia's first president—Sukarno—struggled to continue his studies for the sake of Indonesia's independence while he was imprisoned by the Dutch in Bandung.

Tears trickled down her face. She had once told us that story to ignite our spirits—it taught us to fight for our school, no matter what.

35 ❀ DON'T QUIT SCHOOL

I was hunched beneath the washbasin, so I didn't see the face of the person picking through the cakes.

She asked, "How much are these, young man?"

I recognized the voice from the first word. Bu Mus stood firmly in front of me.

"Ikal," she said, "come back to school."

I felt sorry for Bu Mus, but holding on to the school was about as possible as catching the wind in my hands.

"What else can we do, Ibunda Guru?"

"I have the ultimate plan," she said.

I brushed her off. I could see her disappointment. Then she approached A Kiong and Mahar. I saw them shake their heads, too.

"Don't give up hope. Come to school next Monday. We will talk about my plan," Bu Mus ordered us.

I later heard that, after visiting us, Bu Mus rode her bike for dozens of kilometers, deep into the pepper plantations in the forest, in order to find Kucai. She searched for her student among hundreds of underage boys and girls working as pepper pickers; not one among them had ever been to school.

Bu Mus asked anyone who would listen about Kucai, showing them his photo. After two days in the plantation, sleeping in the houses of the residents, Bu Mus succeeded in finding our class president. She was doing exactly what Pak Harfan used to do: persuading kids to go to school.

After giving an indifferent Kucai a long and thorough lecture, Bu Mus got into a boat with the Sarong people. She was sailing to Melidang Island on the east side of Belitong to find Samson, who was working there as a copra coolie.

Apparently Kucai and Samson held the same attitude as A Kiong, Mahar, and I. They had been poisoned by money and refused to return to school.

We didn't want to go back to school because we didn't want to get our hopes up. It would hurt Bu Mus even more if our school couldn't be saved, and it would also hurt us. If it were only a matter of financial difficulty, a nearly collapsed school building, people's insults, and threats from Mister Samadikun, we could still try, we would still be willing to hold on; but opposing PN was impossible. I tried to talk some sense into Bu Mus.

"It's over, Ibunda Guru. Maybe all those people are right. Just let go of the school."

Bu Mus's grip on the handlebars of her bicycle tightened visibly. She would never, for any reason, agree to watch the old Muhammadiyah School be destroyed.

"The head PN miner said that you would be given a job teaching at the PN School as compensation. Take the opportunity. The salary is huge!" Mahar said.

Bu Mus looked Mahar in the eye. "I would never trade you all for anything!"

When our discussion finished in the late afternoon, Bu Mus went to the floodplains of the Linggang River to search for Syahdan. She searched for him all evening. The tide was high, the wind was strong, and the fishermen were boarding their boats to repair them. Caulking boats held more promise for Syahdan than studying at a school that by tomorrow, or the day after, would be level with the ground. It was hard to blame him for thinking this way.

On Friday evening, one week after Bu Mus had come to see me at the market, I ran into Mujis. He told me the same thing he had told Bu Mus—that there were still students studying in our classroom. I wanted to see for myself.

The next day, when I finished selling my cakes, I went to the school. The schoolyard was already a mess. Amid the tin exploitation machines, our school looked like it had been backed into a corner. The machines gave off vibrations so powerful that they made the school more crooked and caused shingles to fall from the roof, rendering much of the school roofless. One gust of strong wind and the building would collapse.

Who knew where the yellow bamboo flagpole went? The bell had vanished, too. The Muhammadiyah name board had fallen down and lay pitifully sprawled out on the ground. Our beautiful flower garden had fallen apart. The planked wall at the back of our classroom was no more. The villagers figured our school couldn't be saved, so they'd pried off the planks in the dark of night.

Our classroom had become a half-open room. The beams that used to support the back wall were now being used by the neighbors to tie up their cattle. If one of the cows were to tug just a little bit, our school would surely fall down. The only things left were the chalkboard, the glass display case with the two grand trophies inside, Rhoma Irama's *Rain of Money*, Bruce Lee's *The dragon kung fu—fight to the death*, and John Lennon's *Life is what happens to you while you're busy making other plans.*

From between the gaps in one of the remaining walls I spotted Lintang explaining a math problem to Sahara, Flo, Trapani, and Harun. He was teaching under the intense sun because there was no roof above the chalkboard. He was pouring sweat, but his energy raged on and his bright eyes shone.

He spotted me out of the corner of his eye and came out of the classroom. "Hey, it's you, Ikal! Come on in, let's study! We're working on math. It's wonderful!"

It was touching; Lintang was not willing to accept our school's impending doom. I asked him, "Why do you hold on, Lintang?"

Lintang smiled. "Didn't I already tell you, Boi? I will keep on studying until the sacred beam supporting this school collapses."

Our school's main beam still stood strong. Dozens of other beams were connected to and depending on it. It was like someone holding a family afloat so they wouldn't drown.

"You see it yourself, right? Our school's sacred beam is still standing strong."

"But soon it will collapse," I said.

Lintang stared at me. He said slowly, "I will not disappoint my mother and father, Ikal. They want me to continue my schooling. We have to have dreams, high dreams, Boi, and school is the road we start on. Don't give up, Boi. Don't ever give up."

He had brought me to a halt.

"We have to continue our education so our children won't have to go to a school like this, so we won't be treated unfairly." His voice was bitter. "Don't quit school, Boi. Don't."

I hid my face behind the washbasin I was carrying. I couldn't bear to look at Lintang. I didn't have the guts to look at the face of such a great person. And I was ashamed, ashamed of my flowing tears.

On Monday morning, Bu Mus, Sahara, Flo, Trapani, Harun, Lintang, and I gathered under the filicium in front of the school. We were waiting for the other members of Laskar Pelangi, the deserters.

Like Mahar said, destiny is circular. Bu Mus was undergoing the same experience she'd had waiting for the tenth student back when we were beginning the first grade. She was staring beyond the edge of the schoolyard, her face showing both fear and hope.

It was almost ten o'clock and no one else had shown up. We were buried in silence. But suddenly I saw Bu Mus produce a smile. In the distance A Kiong appeared, riding his bicycle at a frightening speed. He was racing toward the school. His sensei, Mahar, sat on the back; he seemed to be barking orders at A Kiong. They arrived at the school and we cheered a greeting.

Soon another figure appeared in the distance, striding toward the school like King Kong. In his short time as a copra coolie, Samson's body had gotten much bigger. He strode calmly, strongly, and with authority while carrying a small black hairy thing on his shoulders. Only after they got close enough did we realize that the small hairy thing was Syahdan.

That left Kucai, our foul politician. By eleven o'clock he hadn't bothered to show his big head.

Finally Bu Mus ordered us to enter the classroom. She was sad that Kucai wasn't there and said we had to do whatever it took to get him back in school. Bu Mus's stance on this matter was extremely firm.

"For me," she said, "losing even one student is the same as losing half of my soul."

We thought to ourselves, *Why is one student so important?* But for Bu Mus, it wasn't that simple.

"As long as I can stand, this class will not lose a single student."

We knew from Samson that Kucai couldn't leave the pepper garden because he had been paid up front.

Bu Mus decided to take on as many sewing orders as she could handle. She sewed day and night to gather money so she could exchange it for Kucai. She turned the class over to Lintang for that whole week. We didn't mind that our class had turned into a roofless stable. We paid no attention to the tumult raised by PN project vehicles moving back and forth through our schoolyard as the threatening dredges drew nearer. Lintang was full of enthusiasm as he taught, and we were a diligent audience. We had a new outlook: the dredges could crush our school, but we would keep on studying, even if it meant standing in the open field.

After she had earned enough money, Bu Mus again rode her bike to the middle of the forest, to the faraway pepper plantation, to get Kucai back.

The school day was almost over when Bu Mus arrived with Kucai on the back of her bike. He was in wretched condition. Picking peppers was hard labor. We took turns hugging him as he sobbed.

Bu Mus gathered us in a circle. Her gaze falling on us one by one, she told us that Pak Harfan certainly would not want to see our school destroyed. "This is the time for us to stand strong," she said. "We will defend this school no matter what happens. We must defend Pak Harfan's honor!" Her hands were shaking. At the mention of Pak Harfan's name we were struck by sadness.

"Wipe away your tears," Bu Mus said with resolution as she attempted to hide her own. "Wipe them away immediately! Outside of this room, don't ever let anyone see you cry."

After saying that, Bu Mus suddenly walked out the door. We followed her. She moved quickly out into the schoolyard, straight into the roaring noise, and screamed to the heavy machinery operators, "Turn off those machines!"

They were stunned and looked around at one another.

"Turn off those machines! I said turn them off!"

The machines died at once. The operators, drivers, and coolies were stupefied.

"Destroy this school if you want, just destroy it. But you'll have to do it over my dead body!"

We formed a human barrier in front of Bu Mus. If PN wanted to knock down our school, they'd have to knock us down first.

37 ❀ A YOUNG GIRL CHALLENGES THE KING

From the beginning, everyone knew we were quietly challenging PN. Everyone also knew Bu Mus had sent a letter rebutting PN's warning. Yet in screaming at the operators to turn off the machines, Bu Mus had expressed outright her intent to oppose the PN kingdom. This was the first time PN was being challenged openly by an ordinary citizen, and she was only a young girl—a teacher at a poor village school.

In accordance with her letter, Bu Mus insisted on meeting with the head of PN. This was very brave. Never before had anyone acted this way—not even the head of the government establishment whose building had been trampled by the dredges.

Because of her behavior, many people thought Bu Mus had gone mad. Every morning she pedaled past the market as fast as possible because she couldn't take the jeers. But not everyone acted like that. She drew applause from the barbers' union, palm juice sellers, coffee stall visitors, and parking attendants.

"Keep it up, Bu Mus," they yelled. "We are behind you!"

A few narrow-minded people started intimidating Bu Mus. Pessimists tried to explain to her that her foolish behavior would get her nowhere. At that time, opposing those in power was taboo. The powerful were that strong. Many critical voices had mysteriously disappeared.

Bu Mus didn't back down. She stuck to her position: if we really couldn't stop the dredges from destroying our school and plundering the tin below it, we should at least be heard by the highest PN authority first, so we could tell him what our school meant to us.

But who was Bu Mus? Who were we? The head of PN was too high up for us. It would be beneath him to give us the time of day. He had far more important things to do than deal with an insignificant village school. PN delegated this task to the head of the survey team, the lowest managerial official they had.

The head of the survey team was a well-mannered middle-aged man. He was not an astute negotiator. He himself was not pleased with the assignment to meet with Bu Mus—perhaps he respected her courage or felt that condemning our school was morally wrong.

"I have been assigned by my office to speak with you about the matter of moving this school to another location so the dredges can operate here," he said, wasting no time with pleasantries.

Bu Mus smiled and didn't reply. He waited for her response, but our teacher remained silent. This team head was wise enough to know that by not answering, Bu Mus had already answered. He thanked her and excused himself.

"I will inform my boss of your decision, ma'am."

His boss, the lead foreman, was unhappy when he heard what had happened. Now he was on the warpath. His operation was impeded just because a village school was brave enough to stand in the way of the determined path of tin exploration. He sent his subordinate to summon Bu Mus to his office. Bu Mus furrowed her brow.

"Please tell the foreman that if he needs us, we'll be here. The discussion of this school's fate must be in front of my students, inside of this classroom. They are the ones with the most at stake here."

The foreman finally came. Without much fuss, he took out a calculator and showed Bu Mus a very large figure.

"This is a lot of rupiah, Bu Mus. You all can buy land ten times the size of this schoolyard; you can build a school ten times better than this one." He spoke in a condescending tone.

"Foreman, this is not my school, it is the people's school. Moreover, I have already said it again and again: we will not sell this school, however decrepit, or the land it stands on, no matter how high the offer."

Her reaction was calm, and from the way she spoke, anyone would know that for someone like Bu Mus, money was irrelevant. Although Bu Mus was dirt-poor, she had never been dazzled by money.

The foreman was offended and became spiteful. "Well, maybe that's because you all are not actually in the position to sell. As far as I know, this is the property of the religious community, not you."

The foreman's point of view was actually valid in the eyes of property law, but it was flawed as an argument in this case.

"Good sir, indeed this land is held by the religious community, so it cannot be sold. This land has been entrusted to us, and we will keep that trust. If you, foreman, are a Muslim, must I explain to you what trust means for a Muslim?"

The foreman's face turned beet-red with embarrassment.

The head miner, the foreman's boss, was furious. He was very temperamental, having begun his career as the head of PN's special security forces, the guys armed with AK-47s. He was angry with the foreman for not being able to take care of a simple task. Frustrated, and already preoccupied with negotiations with investors in Jakarta and Belitong, he had to come to our village school to take care of this seemingly trivial problem.

Though she knew she would be dealing with an infamously callous official, Bu Mus remained calm. But Mahar was not so relaxed. He assigned Syahdan, our intelligence agent, to do an investigation. Syahdan reported that the head miner had a dull brain and a thuggish nature—a dangerous combination. Mahar gathered the Laskar Pelangi members under the filicium tree. He said that the situation could become heated and even out of control. We deliberated. Finally, we reached a solution, but it was the kind we had been trying to avoid. The solution came from our politician, Kucai.

"I will invite my reporter friends from Tanjong Pandan," he said.

Kucai's idea was brilliant.

The head miner rushed to our school. It was clear from his body language that he had come with the intention of getting angry.

"Bu Mus," he began, "need I remind you that PN is owned by the state? There are government regulations that guarantee state businesses operational freedom for the sake of public benefit!"

Bu Mus had vast knowledge and remarkable self-control.

"Public benefit?" she asked. "Sir, need I remind you that there are laws that guarantee a citizen's right to education? That law is written in this country's Constitution. As far as I know, the Constitution is the supreme law of the land. Shall I cite the article for you?"

The head miner was stunned. He had underestimated Bu

Mus. And now it was as if he had been hit by a brick. He should have learned from the experiences of the head of the survey team and the lead foreman.

"If you insist, sir, we will tie ourselves to this school," she said.

The head miner wanted to let his anger boil over, but he was aware of the reporters off in the corner ready to snap a photo guaranteed to make the next day's front page. Printed above the photo, the headline would read, "PN Official Acts Cruelly Toward Small Community" or "Head Miner Doesn't Know Constitution!"

The head miner was in a tight spot. He had to admit that Bu Mus was correct. He was also afraid of becoming headline news. The reporters could read his intentions from his cursing and behaving without manners under the roof of an old Islamic school. We knew that there were two things in this world that couldn't be opposed: God and reporters.

The next day, news of our resistance appeared in the local papers. And just like that, our copra shed of a school became famous. All over the place people were raving about the young girl brave enough to challenge the king, and her eleven students who suddenly shot up in rank to "exemplary heroes." The articles brought out huge amounts of sympathy for us. They ferreted out all sorts of public judgments, already brewing at the coffee stalls.

Within no time at all, through the coffee stalls, of course, stories spread that Bu Mus was in fact a state governance lawyer who had graduated from a top university in Jakarta, disguised as a Muhammadiyah village schoolteacher. Purportedly, in order to perfect the disguise, she also pretended to be a seamstress. And it turned out, too, that Pak Harfan was a bicycle technician professor who for fifty-one years had disguised himself as a poor teacher. In order to perfect his disguise, he also pretended to plant cassava in his garden.

The students were actually the children of wealthy people. Our parents disguised us as poor children. We allegedly did all of this to reveal PN's unjust treatment of the people of Belitong.

Because of all the buzz, our school—never visited or given the time of day before—became rather crowded. Politicians, party members, and members of the legislative assembly took turns visiting, along with high government officials. They were suddenly very interested in our plight. All this time they had surely passed our schoolyard along the main road on the way to their luxurious offices and had never given it a second thought. The news, the large amount of tin beneath our school, and the opportunity to take on the image of caring for the little people had cured their blindness. As the old Malay saying goes: the noise of honey brings noisy bumblebees.

There were those who came ready to represent us and to speak on our behalf for free. And all of a sudden everyone became generous. Someone wanted to pay Bu Mus for her years of unrewarded service; organizations and institutions were ready to fix our school.

Because all of that was for personal gain, Bu Mus politely declined all the aid. One institution wanted to donate a water pump and was repeatedly turned down by Bu Mus. But they were determined, and late one night they installed it in our well without permission. After installing it, they took a photo near the pump with our school as the background.

Bu Mus had many interviews with reporters. I was even interviewed and photographed a few times. Each time I was questioned, I trembled. I didn't know what they were asking or how I should answer. The important thing was that we were photographed. The happiest to be photographed, of course, was

Harun. Each time he was photographed, he held up three fingers.

In the meantime, Kucai was laughing to himself. He was elated that his political career was running smoothly. He may have been sly, but this time we had to salute him. The attention had spread so far that it finally disturbed Taikong.

Taikong worked directly above the head miner. He was second only to the head of PN. Because it was such an esteemed rank, people often carried the title Taikong over into their retirement years—take, for example, our Koranic studies teacher, Taikong Razak.

Taikong spoke differently than those below him—the head of the survey team, the foreman, and the head miner—because he was very well educated. He did not carelessly mete out orders and threats.

"It is not PN that I am challenging. And it is not this school that I am fighting for, but thousands of Malay village children," said Bu Mus.

Taikong nodded.

"This building is not just a school, Taikong. It has become a symbol, a symbol of hope for poor people to study. If this school comes down, village children will be forever stuck in pepper gardens, copra factories, boats that need caulking, and Chinese produce shops. They'll believe even less in the usefulness of village schools and cease to believe in education itself."

Taikong stared at Bu Mus in amazement. He said that he supposed if the decision were in his hands, he would cancel the condemnation.

"But the power lies in the hands of the highest official, Bu Mus."

We cheered when Taikong said he would arrange a meeting between us and the head of PN. While the possibility that our school could be saved was slim, at the very least our persistence had made our request to meet with the head of PN come true.

38 ☼ HEAVEN, IT TURNS OUT, IS IN OUR VILLAGE

Finally, with the help of Taikong, Bu Mus's letter was answered by the PN secretary. It told us when the head of PN would be so kind as to receive us.

The village was rife with talk about the meeting—the first of its kind ever to take place. Many people contacted Bu Mus, offering to represent us. She turned them down.

We gained more supporters. Negative feelings toward PN, long buried, were now bubbling up to the surface. And though our efforts would surely fail, our pioneering had opened people's eyes, showing them that a corporation, even a state-owned one, couldn't treat people however it wished. Now those who had written off Bu Mus as insane were scrambling to take back the things they'd said. They'd never imagined she'd be received by the head of PN.

We focused on the meeting. Bu Mus, with the help of our politician, Kucai, put together a great speech. It was five pages long on HVS paper. We borrowed a typewriter from the village office. Sahara was the typist.

The speech began by quoting the preamble to the 1945 Constitution. It continued with the history of Islamic education in Belitong. It went on with the story of poor Malay children who no longer believed in school. And it didn't forget to mention the dramatic tale of the struggles for education by unknown heroes like Pak Harfan and the other pioneers. It was seasoned with the prestige from the two great trophies we'd won.

Before closing the speech, on Kucai's advice, Bu Mus quoted Article 33 of the Constitution, the one that says every citizen has the right to an education. After going on and on, the speech's conclusion was concise: *Therefore, sir, please don't close our school.*

As planned, we gathered in front of the main gate to the Estate. We wore the best clothes we owned. It seemed Syahdan's and Mahar's best clothes were still missing some buttons. Lintang's best clothes were speckled with rose-apple sap, and my best clothes were my religious clothes that I had gotten as a third-place prize in an *azan* contest the previous year. Before setting off to the PN central office in the Estate, we prayed together. It was both exhilarating and heartrending.

The security guards opened the gate and invited us in.

We stepped into the Estate, and what happened next would be hard to forget for years to come. We huddled closer together, feeling scared to go any farther because we were so stunned. Our mouths hung open at a sight that we had never imagined before, even in our wildest dreams.

It was the first time that any of us—except for Flo—had seen the Estate. We felt like we were no longer in Belitong.

The building closest to us was like a castle. From the castle came an odd music that I now know was classical music. Strange animals roamed about the yard. A few months later we found out the names of those strange creatures from a *Himpunan Pengetahuan Umum*—a general knowledge book. There were turkeys, peacocks, English pigeons, and poodles. They were left to wander freely; no one was watching them.

There were some cats that also appeared strange. We'd never seen cats like that. They were very different from the village cats, which always looked like they wanted to steal something. These cats were elegant, handsome, and not wanting for food. Their faces showed that they were always spoiled. My friend, if you want to know, those were Angora cats!

Being from the Estate, Flo tried to make herself more useful as a guide.

"Those homes were left behind by the colonial Dutch. Their architectural style is Victorian," explained Flo.

The curtains of the homes were wide and layered. Their gardens were the size of our schoolyard. The yard was carpeted with neat manila grass, like a golf course's. There was a park and a pond, at the edge of which grew beautiful lilies.

"Ibunda Guru," Sahara whispered shakily, "heaven, it turns out, is in our village."

Bu Mus was like someone lost in space and time. She was holding her breath, choking on her words.

"*Subhanallah*, my child, Allah is most holy . . . Look at this place."

Security escorted us to the PN central office in the middle of the Estate complex. We were then invited to enter the secretariat's room in the central office. There, Bu Mus met her old classmates, who had become PN secretaries and administrative workers. They appeared far wealthier than Bu Mus. They wore fine clothing, while Bu Mus's clothes were rather simple.

A man in a safari jacket approached and asked us to enter the meeting room. It was rather fancy. The furniture was large and tall. We were nervous just being there. Not much later, a man we immediately assumed was the head of PN entered, accompanied by three men wearing suits. He looked the most authoritative, and those around him bustled about as they vied to wait on him. One of the jacketed men was Taikong.

Our early prediction of what he would look like was quite wrong; we had assumed he would resemble the foreman, intimidating and out to win. But standing before us, the head of PN was very different. It turned out he was a small man. His face was clean and he appeared highly intelligent. His hair was already white and thinning. He looked friendly and willing to listen to others' opinions. He looked at Bu Mus for a moment and then smiled.

A woman got up, gave her general courtesies, good this, good that, then said to Bu Mus, "Please tell us why you and your students are here to see the director."

Bu Mus fixed her *jilbab* and stood up. Though Bu Mus had been through many ordeals, severely intimidated by Mister Samadikun and the head miner, this was the first time I saw her quiver. She opened her five-page speech.

We were ready to hear Bu Mus's voice shake with the opening of her speech, the preamble of the Constitution, the never-ending fight for education, our school as a symbol of education for marginalized people, the fate of poor Malay children, and education as a human right. We were ready to clap our hands to support each paragraph as it came. Bu Mus remained silent, staring at the paper before her. A few moments went by. But it seemed she couldn't read the manuscript of her speech.

"Go ahead, ma'am," said the woman.

Bu Mus did nothing. She looked like she wanted to say thousands of things that were not duly represented by those five pages. Not one word emerged from her mouth. Her ex-classmates looked on impatiently.

"Come on, Mus, this is your chance. Speak!" one of Bu Mus's old classmates hissed.

Bu Mus remained silent. The head of PN looked at Bu Mus with surprise. We looked on and whispered. What had gotten into our teacher? Did she have stage fright? The woman who opened the meeting tried to calm down Bu Mus's friends. Kucai looked impatient, as if he wanted to snatch the speech out of Bu Mus's hands. Maybe he wanted to deliver the speech himself in front of the head of PN.

"What is it, Ibunda Guru?" Sahara whispered.

Bu Mus kept quiet. The head of PN spoke. "Go ahead, Ibu Guru, don't be scared. Speak."

Instead of answering, Bu Mus just stared at the head of PN. Her eyes widened and her body shook. She gripped the papers she was holding even tighter. It was as if she were possessed by something. Because we'd been her students for many years, our instincts told us what was going on. She must have been reminded of Pak Harfan. She was haunted by the faces of the founders of the Muhammadiyah School in Belitong, who had been threatened, jailed, tortured, exiled, tossed aside, and killed by the colonial authorities for establishing the school. She couldn't bear the thought of having to defend the school on her own. In any case, she wasn't up against colonial authorities but her own countrymen. Tears welled up in her eyes, but she refused to cry. Bu Mus never wanted to look weak in front of us.

The room was silent. Bu Mus took something wrapped in a handkerchief out of her bag. She walked up to the head of PN and handed the bundle to him.

Bu Mus returned to her seat.

The head of PN opened the package. Inside was a box of chalk. He opened the box and took out a few small pieces of chalk that had been used by Bu Mus.

"Thank you, Ibu Guru," said the head of PN.

We excused ourselves.

39 ✺ POVERTY TRADER

We went home empty-handed. Our mission had failed. Bu Mus had been so emotional that she couldn't put on a professional front to defend our school. The grandeur of the Estate had brought us down. It was true what everyone had said before: the Estate and PN were too strong to be challenged.

We could only submit to our fate. Everything we had done to hold on to our school—facing the supervisor, working our butts off to win prestigious awards, challenging the king—had been done in vain.

We agreed to go to school the following Tuesday to salvage what was left—our two wonderful trophies. Those were the only valuable things we had, and they were valuable to us alone. We also agreed to say our goodbyes under the filicium tree.

But when we arrived on Tuesday morning, we were surprised—the din of machines that had terrorized us for months was nowhere to be heard. PN workers were tearing down the coolie barracks. The logistics team was packing things up like they were getting ready to move. The dredges that had been pointed due east to tear down our school were now facing north.

Bu Mus darted around the schoolyard to find out what was happening.

A luxury car rolled in. A man got out and approached Bu Mus. It was Taikong. Smiling, he said, "The head of PN has ordered the captain of the dredges to turn around."

Bu Mus was deeply moved. She pressed her hands against her heart. She said thank you to Taikong and hurried to the back of the school. We followed her. Bu Mus rescued our school's sign, which had fallen and was lying facedown in the dirt. She wiped the sign with the end of her *jilbab* until the writing could be seen again. The sign had a sun drawn on it, and that sun's white beams shone once again. Our old school had come back to life.

We were ecstatic to have our school back. Bu Mus raised the red and white flag in our schoolyard. It rippled magnificently, blown by the wind, dust, and the sound of the heavy machinery leaving our schoolyard. We danced around and around the pole.

Bu Mus gave out tasks to restore our school. We fixed the roof, rehung the board on the wall, put up an extra support beam so our school wouldn't collapse, and rebuilt our destroyed flower garden.

The strange thing was, after hearing that our school would not be struck down by the dredges, the politicians, party members, and representatives who had been visiting our school suddenly disappeared. Their blindness had returned. People returned to their indifference. Even the institution that had installed the water pump without permission took it back, again without permission.

The experience taught me something important about poverty: it is a commodity. PN canceled its tin-plundering plans for our school, and that didn't make us any less poor. Because we were not being wiped out, there was no more conflict with PN. No one could blackmail PN to take advantage of the situation or become famous for defending poor people. No one could become a faux-hero, no election votes could be gained from the incident. There would be no sad photos attached to fund-raising proposals. The receding dredges had caused the market value of our school's poverty to plummet.

The sky had been dark since morning, and then came a heavy rain. We splashed along the puddle-filled road toward school, covering our heads with whatever we could.

All eleven students were in the classroom, but Bu Mus had not yet arrived. The rain grew heavier. Thunder boomed. We stood on our tiptoes to peer between the gaps in the planks of the wall. We were worried, waiting for Bu Mus. Then she appeared in the distance, running with small steps under the downpour, crossing the schoolyard using a banana leaf as her umbrella, pausing intermittently under one of the *gayam* trees bordering the northern end of our schoolyard.

We watched her with concern. No one spoke, but I knew everyone else's hearts were full of commotion, like mine: a feeling of pity mixed with pride and admiration. Obstacle after obstacle had been conquered by a thin, seemingly powerless young woman. But just look how powerful she really was.

Bu Mus saw us lined up through the cracks in the walls. She was soaked but laughing lightheartedly, impatient to get to her students. We felt, as always, that for her we were the most valuable of Malay children. Bu Mus didn't want to lose even one of us, and she, too, was like half of our own souls. We were so lucky God had sent us a teacher like Bu Mus. Her service was truly indescribable. As she crossed the schoolyard using a banana leaf as an umbrella, I drew up a promise deep in my heart: when I grew up, I would write a book for this teacher of mine.

Bu Mus quickly restored our morale. Our school became itself again, calm in its actions, celebrating learning even in its limitations, being dignified in its humility, peaceful in its poverty.

Before we knew it, report card day had come once again. It was a fun day because our parents came to school. After the distribution of the report cards, we would enter our final examination month. Blue marks were for scores above five, red marks for five and under. If we got more than three red marks, we would not be allowed to move up a class.

First rank continued to belong to Lintang, and I returned to my second-place seat. Harun was not happy with any number other than three, and he asked Bu Mus to fill in threes for all subjects on his report card. He looked at the number threes lined up while laughing loudly. He was happy even though the request relegated him to the fourth-lowest rank in the class.

And it just so happened that Kucai, for the first time in his political career, admitted his mistake. It was true that we had been used to working part-time after school, but Kucai had incited the members of Laskar Pelangi to leave school and work full-time. In a very gentlemanly manner, he asked Bu Mus to reduce the grade he had received for Muhammadiyah ethics by two. His grades were never too good to begin with, so further reducing them made him plummet in the rankings, right below Harun.

Bu Mus wasn't too surprised about Harun and Kucai, but the lowest pair of names made her massage her temples. Those two dramatic creatures were, of course, Mahar and Flo. What was most bothersome to Bu Mus was that they had lost interest because they were crazy about the paranormal, a serious violation for Muhammadiyah and for Muslims generally. To make matters worse, the violation took place in an Islamic school. Red numbers lined their report cards like someone's back had been *dikerok*—scraped by a coin as part of a traditional massage. They got blue marks only for agricultural knowledge, craftsmanship, etiquette, and Indonesian—and that was just for talking. Flo's scores were the worst. In math, English, and science, she received a flock of swimming swans—three twos. Her scores were even worse than Harun's.

Mahar and Flo were in a critical situation, and it was very possible that they would be bumped down a class level. They had already received three warning letters. Flo's father secretly conspired with Bu Frischa, the PN School principal, to lure Flo back there, where Bu Frischa had promised that she would receive grades to be proud of. To tempt Flo, Bu Frischa sent a young, flashy PN teacher to approach her.

That evening we passed the market on our way home from watching a football match. Bu Frischa and the fun teacher were shopping. Flo walked up to Bu Frischa like a cowboy about to have a showdown.

"My name is Flo, Floriana," she greeted Bu Frischa. The flashy teacher nodded politely and gave Flo his sweetest smile.

"Please inform this man that I will never leave Bu Mus and the Muhammadiyah School."

And Flo left it at that. Bu Frischa and the flashy teacher were left scratching their heads, and the idea of luring Flo back to the PN School was never broached again.

Flo and Mahar racked their brains to figure out how to overcome the crisis they faced. They wanted to keep going to school, but they were addicted to the supernatural world.

Out of the blue, Mahar came up with a most absurd idea. They would try a shamanistic shortcut: unique, ridiculous, and high-risk.

Mahar and, later, Flo were convinced that supernatural power could give them a magical solution for their plummeting grades, and they knew someone capable of harnessing that sort of power. Of course, this all-powerful person, half man, half ghost, was none other than Tuk Bayan Tula, who had proved his power when he was able to show the way to finding Flo when she was lost on Selumar Mountain. This king of shamans could easily change a six to a nine, a four to an eight, and a red mark to a blue one.

All of the Societeit's members enthusiastically greeted the idea to visit Tuk Bayan Tula on Pirate Island, but the risk involved was not trivial. If Tuk Bayan Tula was unwilling to receive them, the visitors would never return home. But they were willing to take that risk as long as they got a chance to see Tuk Bayan Tula's face, even if it was only once.

Sailing to Pirate Island was the most important and the pinnacle of all the Societeit's paranormal activities. The expedition was extremely expensive. They had to rent a boat with at least a forty-horsepower engine and an experienced captain—one of the Sarong people. He charged a very high fee because he was experienced, knew Tuk Bayan Tula's reputation, and didn't want to die foolishly.

All of the Societeit's members tried to raise money. Mahar pawned the bike he had inherited from his grandfather. Flo sold the gold necklace and bracelet given to her by her mother. Mujis let go of his most valuable possession, a Philips two-band transistor radio. He also took on extra mosquito-spraying jobs that took him as far as Tanjong Pandan. He even extended his service to include not just mosquitoes but rats, lizards, even ants—he was ready for them all. The unemployed one collected garbage and sold it to make money. The dropout borrowed money from his father. The lone Electone player pawned his Electone, his source of livelihood. The Chinese gold plater broke open his piggy bank in front of his weeping children. The BRI teller worked overtime until midnight. The retired harbormaster pawned his glass display case—which had to be carried by four people—causing a big fight with his wife. I myself lent my services to the postmaster.

Our hearts thumped anticipating the day of departure. We had collected 1.5 million rupiah. Amazing! The money—most of it in piles of coins—jingled.

Never in my life had I seen that much money. Not to mention that, as secretary, I had to hold on to it. I touched it and was startled at the feeling of being rich. It turns out that for one who has been poor since before he was in his mother's womb, that is a slightly terrifying feeling. I kept the money carefully in my pocket and never let go of it. Suddenly everyone looked like a thief. Money, indeed, has a cruel influence.

We departed the next evening. Many fishermen warned us that storm season had already arrived and that going to Pirate Island was a dangerous idea. But we didn't back down. The draw to Tuk Bayan Tula's supernatural power was very strong, as was Flo and Mahar's determination to tackle their problem at school. We didn't realize that in the middle of the sea, death awaited us.

41 ☼ PIRATE ISLAND

At four o'clock on a Saturday afternoon, we set sail for Pirate Island.

At first it was fun. Dolphins chased the boat's bow. The sun shone brightly. But not much later, as the time for Maghrib prayer approached, our boat began being tossed around. The waves grew higher by the minute. The farther out we got, the harder the boat was to control. A cluster of dark clouds moved toward our boat. Lightning struck, one flash after another.

The captain tried to turn around, but the forty-horsepower engine wasn't powerful enough. He feared that if we tried to battle the waves, which were now in a frenzy, we would capsize. And the true storm had not even arrived. Gigantic waves rolled in. We gathered in a small circle around the mast and tried to hold on.

I regretted coming along on this expedition with the Societeit crazies to meet a shaman who didn't even care about his own life. I gazed at the dark surface of the sea, unable to imagine what lay beneath. I dreaded sinking into that dark foreign world.

Then the storm came and pummeled the boat without mercy. Whirlpools swirled and the boat spun around like a top. We fell along the deck. The captain killed the engine. He lowered the wind-torn sail, closed the hold, and got sharp objects out of the way. He ordered us to tie our bodies to the mast. We wrapped the rope around our waists a few times and bound ourselves so we wouldn't be thrown into the sea.

The captain showed no sign of hope. He, too, tied himself to the mast. If we drowned, our bodies would float from the ends of the ropes at the bottom of the sea, dangling like octopus tentacles.

The moment we feared had arrived. In the distance we saw a terribly tall wave. It crashed into the boat and broke the mast we were tied to, creating two large splinters. One of these pierced the body of the boat, allowing water to gush in.

Mujis, Mahar, and the Chinese man, who had been holding on to the sail, were hit by the other splinter and thrown to the deck. If the hold had not been closed, they would have been fodder for sea creatures. They screamed. I thought this was the end for us, that the sea would soon turn red as the sharks had their feast. At the most critical moment, I heard someone shouting. The retired harbormaster was crying out the *azan*—the call to prayer—over and over again, as we were being tossed around and water began filling the deck. But gradually the boat's thrashing calmed.

The harbormaster echoed the *azan* over and over again, and as the *azan* rang out, the swells of waves calmed more and more. The savage waves became tame, and a moment later the wind stopped, as if a fan had been turned off. The storm just vanished. I had often heard from the Sarong people that in a troubling situation at sea, when there is nothing else they can do to help themselves, their last resort is to ask Allah's help through the *azan*. That approach had proved true.

Night fell. We bailed out the boat under the almost full moon and the stars that shone. The captain started the engine. The boat sailed once again.

Not much later, the captain turned off the engine and looked out from the boat with expert eyes. We saw black shadows in front of us, unclear, covered by mist. He pointed and yelled something in his hoarse voice.

"Pirate Island!"

Pirate Island looked like it did not want any visitors. The long howls of wild dogs could be heard swearing at the ghosts that haunted the island.

The place exuded mysticism. It had the feel of a cemetery: apostasy, betrayal, and rebellion against God. There were screams of animals being sacrificed. One could smell the tang of blood, the stench of corpses left out in the open air, and the smoke of incense used to summon the devil.

The dogs howling in the still of the night were nowhere to be seen. Sometimes they sounded like crying babies or old grandmas begging for mercy, being licked by the flames of hell. These sounds broke our spirits. Tuk Bayan Tula's hypnotic power was great. At that moment I had to admit that, wherever he was, he was truly a powerful shaman.

We got off the boat and followed a path toward the opening of a cave. At its mouth we found palm leaves laid down for each of us. We had been greeted. We had to be ready to accept the risk of death.

Inside the cave we could see a thin cloth flapping around. Slowly, a tall figure appeared. I saw the figure moving without touching the ground. Everyone doubted the existence of magic, but with my own two eyes I saw a human float on air, moving back and forth like a weightless object. It was Tuk Bayan Tula.

He was two meters away from us. We stood respectfully around him. A black cloth was draped over his body. His hair, his mustache, and his beard were long and unkempt. His cheekbones were defined, implying an ability to perform unimaginably cruel deeds. His eyebrows were thick and high, showing that he feared nothing, not even God. His most prominent feature was his eyes, flashing like a bear's, completely black.

The ghostly shaman showed not the slightest sign of friendliness. Mahar stared at him, not brave enough to approach. Flo moved closer to Mahar and tugged his hand. This extraordinary girl pulled Mahar toward the shaman without hesitation.

Very carefully Mahar whispered to Tuk Bayan Tula. The shaman paid no heed. He gazed far off to the ocean shimmering under the moonlight. Mahar, in a voice that could scarcely be heard, told him of the deathly danger we had experienced on the way to meet him.

"Storm . . . strong winds . . . broken mast . . . *azan* . . ."

Tuk Bayan Tula listened without interest.

"Flo and I . . . are going to be kicked out of school . . . we've already gotten three warning letters for our red marks . . . we want to ask your help so we can pass our exams."

Unexpectedly, Tuk Bayan Tula turned toward Mahar and Flo. The two naughty children turned deathly pale. He patted Mahar's shoulder and shook his head. Mahar lit up. The members of the Societeit looked proud because their chief had been touched by the powerful shaman they held sacred in their hearts. Mahar knew what he had to do. He took out a piece of paper and a pen and respectfully handed them to Tuk Bayan Tula. The shaman took them and went back in the cave with unfathomable speed.

What happened next was rather strange. We heard loud

voices clamoring inside the cave, like ten people fighting. We gathered closely, on guard, fearful of the invisible animals' howls.

Tuk Bayan Tula was fighting vicious creatures in there. It seemed that in order to fulfill Mahar's request, he had to fight off thousands of ghosts. Traces of regret appeared on Mahar's face. He couldn't bear the thought of his beloved idol dying because of his request to pass an exam.

Dust billowed out of the cave. The battle remained intense until finally a scream of defeat was heard. Dozens of shadowy figures appeared like corpses covered in black cloth flying out of the cave, through the *santigi* treetops, before vanishing over the sea.

Tuk Bayan Tula returned to the entrance of the cave in tatters. The cloth encircling his body was torn, and his face was a mess. I was alarmed to see such a powerful person in shambles like this. He had put his soul on the line in order to fulfill Flo and Mahar's request.

Tuk Bayan Tula raised a roll of paper with his orders up high as if to say, *Look at this, you useless little worms. No one, in plain view or as phantoms, can stand against me. I have vanquished devils from the depths of hell for miracles that defy the laws of nature. Your exam scores will transform in the dark to save you at your old school. Take your prize because you are brave young children who have fought death to meet me.*

Tuk Bayan Tula surrendered the roll of paper, which Mahar seized with both hands. Flo, Mahar, and all the members of the Societeit bowed to Tuk Bayan Tula. I didn't want to bow, which made Mahar quite unhappy with me.

Mahar put the roll of paper in a used cylinder for holding badminton shuttlecocks. He put the container in his jacket.

Tuk Bayan Tula gave us conditions for opening the message

when we got home, and he pointed to our boat so we would get moving. As quick as lightning, like the wind, he vanished, disappearing as the darkness and incense smoke from the cave engulfed him.

We ran to the boat. The captain immediately started the engine and we fled. We made an agreement to open the message in three days, under the filicium tree, after school.

42 ✸ THE SHAMAN'S MESSAGE

It was unusual. It was the middle of the day and many people were gathered in the schoolyard. All of Laskar Pelangi was there. The entire Societeit de Limpai, too. The delegation sent to Pirate Island while searching for Flo was also there.

Mahar also invited the boat captain, coffee-shop gossipers, the postmaster, boat skippers, and a few amateur connoisseurs of the paranormal. Everyone was excited to witness the opening of the message from Pirate Island.

The Societeit's success story spread quickly throughout the village and immediately lifted the Societeit's reputation. They became a respectable group and not a collection of ridiculous time-wasters. That was why so many people were gathered in our schoolyard on the appointed afternoon, to congratulate Mahar on his shamanistic achievement, to satisfy their curiosity about the half man, half ghost, and to find out what kind of magical recipe the shaman provided the lousy students so they could pass their exams.

The funny thing was, because of the Societeit's success, people also came to express their interest in becoming new members of the ghost organization. They considered Mahar the next Tuk

Bayan Tula, and Flo a new inspirational shaman. They were willing to give up healthy thinking in exchange for Mahar's outlandish thinking. As secretary of the Societeit, I was busy writing all the names of wannabe members.

Flo and Mahar waited impatiently for Bu Mus to go home. If she were to find out about the message-opening ceremony, she would surely shut it down.

After she left the school, everyone followed Flo and Mahar toward the filicium tree. Their faces shone with delight. The burden of their lousy marks would soon vanish.

Mahar took his place standing on a protruding root of the tree, the highest one. It had been reserved for him by his followers. It was like he was at a podium. As usual, he gave a speech. He was addicted to giving speeches. He stroked the shuttlecock container that held his and Flo's educational insurance.

"Fortune favors the bold!" his voice thundered. Applause erupted. "We sold our valuables, took the risk of being banished from the face of the earth by Tuk Bayan Tula, but in the end we proved that Societeit de Limpai is not a bunch of morons!"

The Societeit members nodded proudly to themselves and especially to their leader, Mahar.

"We conquered the sea, almost drowned, and were saved by the *azan* of the harbormaster."

The harbormaster was delighted with this praise. He put his hands before his chest and bowed in the Japanese manner.

"We ourselves witnessed Tuk Bayan Tula fight a deathly battle with ghosts for the sake of this message! As head of the Societeit, I feel respected by him!"

Mahar did his amusing but annoying signature gesture.

"Parapsychology, metaphysics, and the paranormal—they

have been proven to be usable in any area!" He pointed to us, his classmates.

"Hey, you there! You can read books until your eyeballs fall out. You can study until you throw up, but Tuk Bayan Tula will make me and Flo smarter than you. We can move up through the classes until there are no higher classes to be reached!"

My stomach hurt from trying to hold back laughter, but I was amazed by how great an orator Mahar was. His speech was better than any speech given by our politician, Kucai, and even greater than those of the minister of education.

Finally, the moment of anticipation arrived. Mahar opened the sealed shuttlecock container. His expression was at once giddy and tense. He would soon read his and Flo's declaration of independence from their demanding educational colonization. With great care, he took the roll of paper out of the container.

He didn't open it right away. "This is the highest honor for the Societeit de Limpai," he said in a choked-up voice.

Everyone wanted to know the magical words written by the most powerful shaman in the world. Their hearts were pounding. Those who couldn't get close enough got up in the low branches of the filicium because they wanted to witness the reading of the message. Flo's face was red from holding back her excitement. She jumped up and down. Slowly, Mahar opened the roll, and there, written clearly on the paper, was:

These are Tuk Bayan Tula's instructions:
If you want to pass your exams,
Open your books and study!

Twice a month, we watched movies after Maghrib prayer at a barnlike building that was usually used as the PN coolies' meeting place. It was also known as the blue-collar cinema. The movies were provided by PN especially for children of non-PN staff. The cinema was of a low-end drive-in quality, and it had two TOA speakers to project the sound. Because the floor wasn't designed like that of a normal movie theater, the viewers farthest back were not able to see. The ten of us, along with Flo, filled the bench at the very back of the theater.

The PN staff children watched at a different place called Wisma Ria (House of Fun). Movies were played there every week. The moviegoers were picked up by a blue bus. And of course there was a strong warning outside of the theater: NO ENTRY FOR THOSE WITHOUT THE RIGHT.

We had no idea that the beautifully titled film—*Princess Island*—was actually a horror movie. From the title, we thought we'd see a few beautiful princesses smearing themselves with suntan lotion, running around and giggling on the beach.

"Cool," said a glowing Kucai.

But we were way off. Just a few moments after the film started, a witch arrived with her sinister cackle. Ghouls joined in the cackling. S. Bagyo, the star of the movie, ran for his life.

Sitting in the back, I could see the coolies' children shrinking into their seats every time the evil flying witch appeared. The girls cried. A few children who weren't strong enough to watch ran for their lives from the ramshackle theater and never came back.

From my seat, I saw Samson to the left of me. He wasn't watching at all. He hid under Syahdan's armpit. Syahdan hid under A Kiong's armpit. A Kiong under Kucai's armpit, and Kucai hid under my armpit. Trapani and I hid under Mahar's armpit. Trapani cried like a baby for his mother every time the witch destroyed a village. Mahar kept his head down like someone praying.

The only ones still sitting tall were Sahara, Flo, and Harun. They laughed loudly at the sight of S. Bagyo running like crazy from the witch. When he succeeded in getting away, they clapped their hands.

On the way home from the theater, we held hands. When we passed the graveyard, Trapani's hand was cold as ice.

The next day during our afternoon rest period, Samson insisted that the witch was being chased by S. Bagyo. Why he thought this, we had no idea. It was the opposite of what actually happened.

"Impossible," Kucai said.

"I saw you shaking under Syahdan," A Kiong said.

Samson tried to defend himself. "Did you watch? As far as I know, Sahara, Flo, and Harun were the only ones not hiding."

Sahara glared at us with disgust. "All boys are cowards!" she said. Harun nodded in agreement.

"Just because we only looked up every once in a while doesn't mean we don't know how the story went," Kucai said, cornering Samson.

"Ah! What do you know, anyway? Go fix your hair or something."

We giggled. Kucai took out a comb.

We were in a war of words, but Trapani stood in a daze. Lately, Trapani was quieter than usual and often in a stupor.

Samson was ashamed to admit he had hid under Syahdan's armpit. He didn't want his macho image to be destroyed.

We needed a mediator to end the debate, someone with broad knowledge and smart words. But Lintang, who always provided the solution, hadn't been seen in two days. There was no news of him.

The next day, Lintang was absent once again, and we started to get worried. In all our years together he had never been absent.

It was rainy season, not time for copra work. It wasn't clam-harvesting season, either. The rubber trees had been tapped last month. Something serious must have happened to make him miss school, but his house was too far to send for news.

Thursday came, and Lintang had not shown up in four days. The class felt empty without him. I stared longingly at the empty seat beside me. I gazed at the filicium's branch where he had perched to watch rainbows. He wasn't there.

Class wasn't the same without Lintang—our drive was gone. We missed his great answers, his intelligent words, and we missed watching him debate the teacher. We even missed his messy hair, his lousy sandals, and his rattan sack.

The following Monday, we hoped to see Lintang with his bright smile and his latest surprising story. But he didn't come. While we were talking about going to visit him, a thin, shoeless man came. He was from Lintang's village. He handed Bu Mus a letter.

Bu Mus read the letter. We had been through a lot of sad times with Bu Mus over the years. Endless trials fell upon her, but this was the very first time we saw her cry. Her tears fell on the letter. We were taken aback. I went up to her, and she gave me the letter to read. It was short.

> *Ibunda Guru,*
> *My father has passed away. I will come to the school tomorrow to say my goodbyes.*
> *Your student,*
> *Lintang*

As the oldest child of an impoverished fisherman's family, Lintang now had to support his mother, many siblings, grandparents, and unemployed uncles. He had no chance whatsoever to continue his education because he had to take on the obligation of making a living to support at least fourteen people. That large burden had to be shouldered by a boy that young because his thin, kind-faced father had died. The pine-tree man had fallen. His body was buried along with the great hopes of his only son.

We would say our goodbyes under the filicium tree. I was dying inside. My heart felt empty. The farewell had not yet begun and Trapani was already sobbing. Sahara and Harun sat holding hands, weeping. Samson, Mahar, Kucai, and Syahdan repeatedly washed their faces—for praying, they insisted, but it was really to get rid of their tears. A Kiong was in a daze and wanted to be left alone. Flo, who had just met Lintang and was not easily moved, was now melancholy. She stared at the ground with glassy eyes. It was the first time I had seen her sad.

We had to let go of a natural genius. Lintang was like a lighthouse. He emitted such great energy, joy, and vitality. Near him we were bathed in light, which clarified our thoughts, ignited our curiosity, and opened the way to understanding. From him we learned humility, determination, and friendship. When he had pressed the button on the mahogany table at the Academic Challenge, he dared us to dream.

A genius, a native of the richest island in Indonesia, had to leave school because of poverty. A little mouse died of starvation in a barn full of rice. We had laughed, cried, and danced around bonfires together. We never tired of his fresh and rebellious ideas. He hadn't left yet and I already missed his funny eyes, his innocent smile, and every intelligent word that came out of his mouth.

This wasn't fair. Lintang, who had fought to the death for education, now had to leave. When our school was going to be destroyed, he held on to raise our spirits. I hated those who lived in the lap of luxury at the Estate. I hated myself and my classmates for not being able to help Lintang because our families were too poor. Our parents had to fight every day to try to make a living.

When Lintang came, his face was empty. I knew his heart was crying, desperately fighting the feeling of not wanting to say goodbye. The school, his friends, his books and lessons meant the world to him. They were his life and love.

We hugged Lintang. His tears fell slowly, his hug tight like he didn't want to let go. I couldn't bear to see his miserable face, and no matter how hard I tried, my sadness won and emptied my eyes of their tears. I couldn't utter even a fragment of a word to say goodbye. We were all sobbing. Bu Mus's lips quivered, holding back tears, her eyes red. But not one tear fell from her eyes. She wanted us to be strong. My chest ached seeing her like that. This was the saddest afternoon in the history of Belitong, from the Linggang River delta to Pangkalan Punai Beach, from Marang Bridge to Tanjong Pandan.

At that moment, I realized that we all were the brothers of light and fire. We had pledged to be faithful through strikes of lightning and mountain-moving tornadoes. Our pledge was written in the seven layers of the sky, witnessed by the mysterious dragons that ruled the South China Sea. Together, we were the most beautiful rainbow ever created by God.

TWELVE YEARS LATER

A middle-aged woman walking with a man named Dahrodji approached me. Trouble—there must be some kind of trouble again!

"If you're going to get angry, ma'am, pour it out on this messy man," Dahrodji snapped.

The woman, who was quite attractive for her age, examined me closely. She whined for a moment. Her makeup, the strange way she said her r's and g's, her raised eyebrows, and the way she was looking at me gave me the impression that she had spent quite a long time overseas, and she had had enough of this country's inefficiencies.

It turned out that the tax refund letter for a painting she got overseas, sent by the customs office, had arrived in her hands late because I had erred in sorting the letter. It should have gone in the Ciawi box, but I had accidentally thrown it in the Gunung Sindur box. Human error.

I had already messed up three times this week. I blamed it on being overloaded with work. Dahrodji, the head of delivery, didn't want to hear about my problems. I couldn't handle the explosion of letters and the extensions of unfamiliar postal codes.

I looked hopelessly at the three letter sacks marked UNION POSTALE UNIVERSELE while the attractive woman complained. I hated my mess of a life. One of the signs of an unsuccessful life is being yelled at by a customer before you've even had a chance to eat breakfast. However, having worked at the post office for so long, I knew how to turn off my ears.

"Hoe vaak moet ik je dat nog zeggen!" She dumped her words on me and turned to leave. I was right, wasn't I? Her sentence meant, *I have complained many times and you are still making mistakes!*

I returned to absentmindedly staring at the three letter sacks.

Even though I was feeling down from being yelled at, I still had to sort all the letters, because at eight in the morning the first shift of postmen had to take the special-delivery letters. I was a postal worker, a sorter, in a time-sensitive dispatch department, on the morning shift, who started working at Subuh—at dawn.

I was in a deep funk over the irony of my life. My plan A from all those years ago, to become a writer and a badminton player, had disappeared, stuck in the bottom of the letter-sorting box. Even my plan B, to be the writer of a badminton book, had failed, although deep in my heart I still held the sweet endorsements from the former badminton champions and the minister of education.

The book had already been written. It was at least thirty-four chapters and more than a hundred thousand words. To write it, I had conducted intensive research on the badminton federation. I studied pop culture and trends of personal development to enrich my book. Even its title was impressive: *Badminton and Making Friends.* Indonesia had never seen a book like that. Unfortunately, based on commercial considerations, there were no publishers willing to print the book. They were more interested in pornographic books full of words like *condom, masturbation,* and *orgasm*. Those were more profitable.

Look at me now, nothing more than a man who tried to reassure himself every day. And no matter how hard I tried to reassure myself, to make myself strong, I was almost drowning under the stack of failures piling up on top of me. Long ago, Bu Mus and Pak Harfan had taught me not to back down from any difficulty, but at this point in my life destiny had created a technical knockout—a TKO.

Then, on one especially frustrating morning, under the pouring rain, I bundled together with plastic twine four master copies of my writing along with six floppy disks containing the files. I tied a half-kilogram tin paperweight, the kind usually tied to the postal sacks, to the bundle with an unbreakable knot. I ran toward Sempur Bridge, Bogor, West Java. Then I closed my eyes and threw my badminton book into the depths of the Ciliwung River. If it didn't get stuck in the river bottom stones, it would float along in floodwaters headed toward Jakarta, drifting away with my dreams.

Whenever faced with uncertainty, I ran to the most beautiful place I knew—the one I had discovered in childhood when an enormous love attacked me for the very first time. The place is a beautiful village with flower gardens surrounded by gray stone fences and trails in the woods shaded by plum tree branches. Oh, Edensor, the nirvana of my imagination.

That village was the cure for my broken heart. The more difficult my life became, the more frequently I reread Herriot's book. I often visited Edensor in my dreams. When I woke up, my chest ached because I was reminded of A Ling, and life became more unbearable.

One day, when I came home from sorting letters, I sat down alone under a random tree at the edge of Sempur Field near my boardinghouse, faced the Ciliwung's lapping water, and protested to God. "Allah, didn't I ask You long ago to make me anything besides a postal worker if I failed to be a writer and badminton player? And not to give me a job that starts at Subuh?"

Apparently God had answered my prayer with exactly the opposite of what I asked for. That's the way God works. If we consider prayers and their answers as variables in God's linear function, then they are no different than the rainy season. The most we can do is make a prediction. Let me tell you something, my friend, God's actions are strange. He doesn't comply with postulates or theorems.

So here I am now. Officials from the government statistics bureau would describe people like me as *those who work in the public service sector, consume fewer than 2,100 calories a day, and are near the poverty line.*

Poverty, my lifelong friend. I was a poor baby, a poor child, a poor teenager, and now a poor adult. I was as accustomed to poverty as I was to taking my daily bath.

My demographic: living life alone, ignored, working ten-hour days, and falling within the twenty- to thirty-year-old age range. But my psychographic identity was: a lonely man desperately starving for attention. Marketing people would consider me a part of their target audience for hair oil products, height pills, hair-loss-preventing products, girdles, stench-preventing deodorant, or any product related to boosting self-confidence. The world didn't care about me and the country knew me only through my nine-digit employment number at the postal company: 967275337.

There was no joy in the sorting job. This job had not been included in professions displayed by PN School students at the carnival. Every day I was swamped with dozens of postal sacks from nations whose names I didn't even know. Sweat mixed with dust. The future for me was retiring poor, regularly visiting the meager clinic provided by government insurance, and then miserably dying a nobody.

After work, I was too exhausted to socialize, and perhaps because of the frustrations of broken dreams, I began to suffer from a sickness typical of those under stress: insomnia. Every night, half asleep, half awake, I was hypnotized by *wayang* stories on the radio. After the *wayang* story finished, I still couldn't sleep, and I started to enjoy listening to the radio static until morning. The disease of insanity slowly but surely started to descend upon me.

After the tormenting night, very early in the morning, while the people of Bogor were still snuggled in their warm beds, I had to leave for work. I crawled out of my bed in the cold and wobbled on my bicycle toward the post office along the Ciliwung River, still covered in thick morning fog, to sort thousands of letters. When the people of Bogor woke up, yawned, and snuggled back into their beds like caterpillars or shook open their morning papers in front of their hot tea and toast, I was enjoying breakfast, too—the complaints of the Dutch madam.

That was my life now. My future was unclear, and I no longer had any notion of what it would hold. The one thing I knew for sure was that I was a failure. I cursed myself every time I had to stand in the post office's yard on the seventeenth day of every month for the Indonesian Government Employee Corps flag ceremony.

If there was still something that could be called exciting in my life, it would be Eryn Resvaldya Novella. She was smart, religious, beautiful, and good-hearted. She was twenty-one years old. I called her *awardee* because she had just been given an award as one of the most accomplished students at one of the most prestigious universities in Indonesia, where she studied psychology. Eryn's father was my brother, who had been laid off by PN. I took over the responsibility of financing her schooling.

The exhaustion from working all day would suddenly disappear whenever I saw Eryn and her enthusiasm for learning, her positive attitude, and the intelligence reflected in her eyes. I was willing to work overtime and extra odd jobs as an English translator, typist, or part-time photocopier. I would sacrifice anything, including pawning my tape recorder, my most valuable possession, to finance Eryn's studies.

My bitter experience with Lintang was traumatic. Sometimes I worked hard for Eryn to compensate for the guilt I felt at not being able to help Lintang. Eryn had brought out the feeling that no matter how miserable or failed my life was, I was still a bit useful to the world. There was nothing I could be proud of at the moment, but I wanted to dedicate my life to something important. Eryn was the only meaningful thing I had.

She was in a state of panic. She had finished her class requirements last semester and now she had spent the past five months looking for a good thesis topic. Her proposals had been declined over and over again by her advisor. Along with the latest rejection letters, the advisor had attached fifteen pages of thesis titles already written by other students. I took a look at the titles. It was true, almost thirty students had already written about topics Eryn had suggested: personality disorders, autism, work satisfaction, Down syndrome, and child counseling.

Eryn's advisor demanded that she write something new, something different, something that would make a scientific breakthrough, because she was an award-winning student. I agreed.

In fact, Eryn already had a concept of what that unique topic would be. She told me she would like to research a psychological condition in which an individual is totally dependent on another individual to the point where the dependent individual cannot do anything without the one they depend on. She told her advisor, and he approved.

The problem was, that sort of condition was a rarity. There were some existing cases of dependency, but their intensity was low, so no special treatment was needed for them. Eryn was looking for an acute dependence. In searching for her case, she corresponded with psychologists, psychiatrists, university professors, mental health institutions, and mental hospital doctors all over Indonesia. Eryn had been searching for a case for almost four months and hadn't found one. She was getting frustrated.

But today good fortune was on Eryn's side. She received a letter from the director of Sungailiat Mental Hospital in Bangka saying they had a case like the one she was looking for.

Bangka Island is Belitong Island's neighbor. The two islands are in the same province, Bangka-Belitong. So when Eryn asked me to accompany her, I didn't mind taking leave from my letter-sorting job. We also planned on visiting our hometown in Belitong.

Sungailiat Mental Hospital was very old. It had been built by the Dutch, and the people of Belitong called it Zaal Batu, or "Stone

Room," because the walls in the examination rooms were made of stone. Because there were no mental hospitals in Belitong—which holds true to this day—people there who suffered from serious mental illnesses were often sent across the sea to the mental hospital in Bangka. For that reason, the name Zaal Batu always meant something painful, desperate, and dark for people in Belitong.

When we arrived, the *azan* was ringing out from the mosques around Zaal Batu. We entered the old white building supported by tall pillars.

We saw steel doors with large locks, medicine rooms filled with short bottles, rolling examination tables, workers in white, and patients talking to themselves or staring strangely. It smelled like a hospital.

A male nurse approached us. He knew we were waiting, so he opened the door. We entered a long hallway with patient rooms lining each side. I stared at the faces of the patients behind the steel bars. The steel bars transformed into dozens of human legs, and between the gaps in the legs I could see a pockmarked, familiar face. The sadness of the mental hospital opened a dark place in my head—the place where Bodenga hid.

The nurse took us to the office of Professor Yan, the director of the hospital who had written Eryn the letter. The professor had a calm face, and his fingers were moving over a *tasbih*—a string of prayer beads—in his hand.

"This case is one of an extreme mother complex," he said in a heavy voice. "The young man cannot be torn away from his mother even for a minute. If he wakes up and doesn't see her, he screams hysterically. The chronic dependency has all but made the mother insane. They've been here together for almost six years."

Professor Yan led us to a small isolated room. I was afraid to imagine what I would see. Was I strong enough to witness such immense suffering? Would it be best if I just waited outside? But it was too late—Professor Yan had already opened the door.

We stood in the doorway. The room was big and dead-silent. The only light came from a low lamp that failed to project light up to the high ceiling. There was no furniture in the room except a long, skinny bench off in the corner.

And there on the long bench, approximately fifteen steps away from us, sat two poor creatures close to each other, a mother and her son. They looked anxious, almost as if they were pleading to be saved.

The son, very thin, sat with good posture, his long hair covering his face. His sideburns, eyebrows, and mustache were thick and wild. His skin was ashen.

His mother was fragile. Her eyes hid an enormous amount of pain. She wore flip-flops that were too big for her feet. Her face showed the unbearable mental stress she felt.

The two of them looked at us every once in a while but mostly kept their heads down. The son clutched his mother's arm. When we came in, he moved closer to her. I excused myself from the room.

Professor Yan helped Eryn to interview the two patients. An hour and a half later, the interview was over. Eryn signaled to me to say goodbye to the mother and son. I came back into the room and tried to smile even though my heart was broken from imagining their suffering.

The three of us left. I was the last one out and reached back to close the door behind me. At that moment, someone called my name.

"Ikal . . ."

Eryn and Professor Yan were as surprised as I was. We turned to look. There was no one else in the room besides the three of us and those two poor souls. I hesitated to open the door.

"Ikal," the voice called out once again.

It was clear that one of those two patients was calling me.

I turned the doorknob and approached cautiously. They both stood up. I observed them carefully. The mother's head hung low and the son was crying. His lips trembled as they uttered my name over and over again, as if he had been waiting for me for years. He waved for me to come closer. Still confused, I moved forward to look at them more closely. The young man pushed his hair away from his face, and I was flabbergasted. I wanted to scream. I knew that man—it was Trapani.

The bus that took us back to our village passed by the Sinar Harapan Shop. The store hadn't changed a bit—it was still a mess. Next to it was a new shop called Sinar Perkasa—Ray of Might. The coolie there caught my attention. He was big and tall, with shoulder-length hair tied back like a samurai's and his sleeves rolled up. I wouldn't be surprised if the new store's name had been inspired by the coolie's appearance.

I turned my gaze to Sinar Harapan and smiled to myself over nostalgic memories from the shop. They were still beautiful feelings, even for an adult. Apparently that love of mine ran deeper than the bottom of the old kerosene cans jammed in the shop. Inside this decrepit bus, under siege by longing, I suddenly felt lucky to be someone who had at least expressed his love. I knew not everyone has that chance, and not everyone has a thrilling first love experience. Even though I had lost my first love, I considered myself one of the lucky ones.

We can become skeptics, always suspicious because we have been deceived just one time by just one person. But one sincere love is apparently more than enough to change one's entire perception of love. At least that was the case for me. Although love frequently treated me unkindly in adulthood, I still believed in it, all because of a girl with magical-looking nails at Sinar Harapan Shop. Where might she be now? I didn't know, and for the time being, I didn't want to know. The picture of love was beautiful as a lotus pond, and I wanted it to stay that way. If I met A Ling again, that image might fade. She had been the Venus of the South China Sea, and I wanted to remember her that way.

I took from my bag *If Only They Could Talk*, the book given to me by A Ling as a token of our first love. Sitting there in the bus, I soon realized that my entire adult life had been inspired by that book, which was now tattered because I brought it everywhere with me. Herriot's example, the village of Edensor he described, and the book's connection with my emotional experience with A Ling, had inspired me to seize my future with optimism.

One week after I had thrown my *Badminton and Making Friends* manuscript into the Ciliwung River, I read an announcement for a scholarship to pursue a master's degree in the European Union.

I went home right away. I reached for a piece of paper, took a pen, sat my butt on a chair, placed the paper on the table before me, and began writing steps for a plan. This was my plan C: I wanted to continue my education!

I studied like crazy for the entrance exam at the university where Eryn studied. After being accepted, I began to live my life like a battle. I worked day and night sorting letters and doing any other odd jobs I could find in order to pay for school. I hadn't yet finished my undergraduate degree, but my mind was set on the graduate school scholarship from the European Union. Focus! Focus! That was my mantra.

I finished my undergraduate courses quickly, and without wasting any time at all, I grabbed the application for the European Union scholarship.

I didn't spend even a minute on anything other than studying for the scholarship test. I read as many books as I could.

I read while I sorted letters, while I ate, while I lay on my bed listening to *wayang* stories on the radio. I read books on the *angkot*, the public transportation minivan. I read them in *becak*s, little pedicabs. I read them while I was in the toilet, while I did laundry, while I walked, while I was being yelled at by customers, while my boss threw masked insults my way, and during the flag ceremony. If humans could read while sleeping, I definitely would have done that, too. There were times I read while playing football; I even read while I was reading. The walls in my boardinghouse room were covered in calculus formulas, GMAT test pages, and the rules of tenses.

One Saturday night, I went to Anyar Market in Bogor. At a *kaki lima*—mobile vendor—I met someone from Minang selling posters. A kind face with round glasses caught my eye. I knew that at this phase in my life I needed inspiration. I bought the poster. That night, John Lennon smiled on the wall of my room. At the bottom of the poster, I wrote the magical saying of his that always reminded me to be more effective. *Life is what happens to you while you're busy making other plans!*

I soon became a faithful visitor of LIPI (the Indonesian Institute of Sciences) Library in Bogor. I now requested the Subuh sorting shift I had once hated so I could go home earlier to study. When my workload was heavy, I made little summaries of my readings on small pieces of paper—a donkey-bridge method

Lintang once taught me. I read the small pieces of paper while I waited for the deliverymen to unload sacks of letters from the truck.

At home I studied late into the night. It turned out that my insomnia supported me. I was the most productive insomniac ever. Whenever I tired of studying, I opened *If Only They Could Talk*.

I have to get that scholarship. There is no other option. I have to get it! Those were the words that rang in my heart every time I stood in front of the mirror. That scholarship was a ticket out of a life I couldn't be proud of.

The nerve-racking test went on for months. It began with a preliminary elimination round in a football stadium filled with test-takers. Seven months later, I was in a phase called the final round, which consisted of an interview at a great institution in Jakarta. The final interview was conducted by a former minister with a handsome face, and he loved smoking. "A disgusting habit," I remembered Morgan Freeman saying in a movie.

I arrived at the institution, and for the first time in my life, I wore a tie. That thing truly did not want to be my friend.

A woman asked me to come into a room. The smoker was already settled inside with a cigarette hanging from his lips.

He asked me to sit down in front of him, and he examined me carefully. He must have thought this village boy would surely embarrass Indonesia overseas. He then read my letter of motivation—a letter written by each applicant about why we felt we deserved the scholarship.

The former minister took a deep drag of his cigarette, and afterward, like magic, no smoke came back out, as if he had swallowed the smoke and let it sit in his chest for a moment. His eyes seemed to relax, blinking slowly a few times as he enjoyed the poison of nicotine. Then, with a horribly satisfied smile, he blew the smoke back out and it wafted in front of my face.

My eyes stung and I battled coughing and nausea, but what could I do? The man in front of me held the much-needed ticket to my future. While the urge to vomit grew stronger, I held my position and answered his smile with a fake one like that of an airline stewardess.

"Hmm, I am interested in your letter of motivation. Your reasons and the way you delivered them in English are impressive," he said.

I smiled again, this time like an insurance salesman.

He doesn't know yet, Malay men are very good with words, I said in my heart.

Then the former minister opened my research proposal, which contained my field of concentration, research materials, and the thesis topic I would pursue if I received the scholarship. My proposal was to do further research on a model of transfer pricing. I designed the model especially for solving the pricing problems of telecommunications services, and it could also be used as a reference for solving interconnection disputes between telecommunications operators. I developed the model using multivariate equations, the principles of which Lintang taught me all those years ago.

"Ahh, this is also quite interesting!"

He wanted to continue speaking, but his beloved cigarette seemed more important. He went back to filling his lungs with smoke.

"Hmm, hmm . . . this is a topic that deserves further study, full of challenges. Who guided you in writing this?" He smiled wide as smoke billowed out of his mouth.

I knew it was a rhetorical question. I just smiled. *The Muhammadiyah School, Bu Mus, Pak Harfan, Lintang, and Laskar Pelangi,* I answered in my heart.

"I've been waiting a long time to see a research proposal like this. Finally it came, and from a postal worker! Where have you been all this time, young man?"

Also a rhetorical question. I smiled and thought, *Edensor.*

Not long after that, I began studying at a university in Europe. My new situation made me see my life from a different perspective. More than that, I felt relieved because I had repaid my moral debt to the Muhammadiyah School, Bu Mus, Pak Harfan, Lintang, and Laskar Pelangi.

45 ❖ HIS THIRD PROMISE

The decrepit bus rolled past the market. The Sinar Harapan Shop faded from sight. I soon got off the bus across the street from my mother's house.

From a neighbor's house, I heard the song "Rayuan Pulau Kelapa"—"Allure of Coconut Island." It was Radio Republik Indonesia's trademark song, which meant it was time for the noon news report. It was a hot and quiet day. But the quiet was broken by a long honk from a semi with a ten-ton load capacity. It had double axles and eighteen one-meter-wide wheels.

A small man bounced up and down in the driver's seat. He was too small for the oversize truck he was driving to transport glass sand.

"So you've finally come home, Ikal. It's a busy day! Come down to the barracks," he shouted. It was Lintang.

I released the four bags slung over my shoulders but got only the chance to wave my hand. I was left waving to dust as he drove away.

The next day, I visited the barracks. They stretched along the shore, and there was no door—like a cattle stall. This was where dozens of sand drivers rested as they took turns working twenty-four-hour shifts, always chasing a deadline to fill the barges. The barges were loaded with thousands of tons of Belitong's riches. Their destination was unknown.

I entered the barracks and looked around. In the middle was a large hearth where they could warm themselves against the cold winds of the sea. In the corner were piles of kerosene cans, cigarette packs, jacks, various keys, oil pumps, drums, and a jug of drinking water. Everything was disheveled. Black pots, tin plates, boxes of mosquito repellent, coffee, and empty packs of instant noodles were scattered about the dirt floor, where a prayer rug lay as well. A calendar featuring bikini-clad women hung crookedly on the wall. Even though it was already May, no one was interested in changing the page from March—apparently they all agreed that the March model was the most attractive.

Lintang sat facing me on a sofa near the hearth. He was dirty, poor, unmarried, and undernourished.

I said nothing. It was clear that he was exhausted from fighting fate. His arms were stiff from hard labor, but the rest of his body looked thin and frail. Despite his dry, greasy, oil-eaten skin, a sweet, humorous smile decorated his face. His hair had become redder and more tousled. Lintang and the entire building conjured up pity—pity because of the wasted intelligence.

I remained silent. My chest felt tight. The barracks were built on land that protruded into the sea. I heard a booming sound and, looking out the window to my right, I saw a tugboat sliding past, pulling a barge. The boom of the tugboat's engine caused the beams of the barracks to shake. Black smoke billowed. The tugboat broke the calm of the sea, leaving waves and shiny water in its wake, the floating oil making the water look like multicolored glass.

I kept watching the chugging tugboat, but at the moment I felt as though it weren't moving and, instead, the barracks and I were moving. Lintang, who had been inspecting me from the beginning, read my mind.

"Einstein's relativity of simultaneity," he said. He gave a bitter smile. His longing for school must have pained him.

Strictly speaking, Lintang hadn't experienced precisely what I had. Two people looking at the same object from different perspectives have separate perceptions. That was why Lintang had said simultaneity. It was a useful metaphor for examining our lives at the moment.

I heard the booms again. It was actually a second tugboat heading in the opposite direction of the first one. The first tugboat's stern hadn't yet completely disappeared from sight. I looked left and right, comparing the lengths of the passing tugboats.

Lintang observed me. He was reading my mind again.

"Paradox," I said.

Lintang smiled. "Relative," he replied. "The size of a moving object as seen by still and moving subjects is not the same. This is a proven hypothesis, that time and distance are not absolute but relative. Einstein defied Newton with this notion, and that's the first axiom of the theory of relativity that launched Einstein's fame."

Ugh, Lintang! Ever since we were little, I'd never had the slightest chance to stop admiring him. He was still very sharp, even if his lively eyes had become like dulled sanded marbles.

I stared at him deeply and felt overwhelmingly sad. I imagined him wearing long white pants and a snug polyester knit vest over a long-sleeved sea-blue shirt, as he took the stage to present a paper at an honorable scientific forum. The paper was probably about breakthroughs in the field of marine biology or nuclear physics.

Perhaps he was more deserving of a prestigious scholarship than those who claim they are intellectuals but are no more than phony scientists who contribute nothing to society other than their final projects and their marks. And those were only for themselves—they were just busy making their own fortunes. I wanted to read Lintang's name under an article in a scientific journal. I wanted to tell everyone that Lintang, the sole genetics specialist in Indonesia, someone who had mastered Pascal's triangle back in elementary school and understood differentials and integrals at a very young age, had been a student at the Muhammadiyah School in Belitong, my deskmate.

But today Lintang was only a thin man sitting on his heels waiting for his shift to begin. He worked day and night, surrendering his aspiration to become a mathematician to the sandglass bosses for a petty weekly wage. I remembered when he'd closed his eyes for no more than seven seconds to answer a difficult math problem. When he yelled, "Jeanne d'Arc!" When he'd reigned as king of the Academic Challenge, making our confidence soar.

I looked around the barracks. Lintang's parents' wedding picture was hanging on the wall. I remembered that photograph. He'd brought it with him to the Academic Challenge. His mother and father stood in front of a tacky background photo: a meadow, a sedan surrounded by a happy-looking family, and odd trees with red leaves. It was supposed to look like it had been taken somewhere in Europe. Until this day, I'd often fantasized about Lintang becoming the first Malay mathematician. But that fantasy evaporated because here, in these doorless barracks, was where my Isaac Newton had ended up.

"Don't be sad, Ikal. At least I fulfilled my promise to my father that I wouldn't become a fisherman."

Now I was angry. I was disappointed that so many intelligent children were forced to leave school for economic reasons. I cursed all the stupid, arrogant people who acted smart. I hated those children of the rich who threw away their educations.

46 ✺ ISLAND OF BELITONG, ISLAND OF IRONY

And this is the saddest part of the story. Because not a single leaf falls without God's knowledge, it isn't absurd to compare PN to the Tower of Babel. It's a fitting analogy: when our province, Bangka-Belitong, was created, its official abbreviation became *Babel*.

In the early nineties, the world tin price plummeted from $16,000 U.S. per metric ton to $5,000. PN was brought to its knees. Its production facilities were shut down; tens of thousands of employees were laid off. It was the biggest layoff Indonesia had ever seen.

Without warning, the Gulliver company that had reigned for hundreds of years collapsed in a matter of days. So Babel was an omen. God had destroyed arrogance in Belitong just as he had destroyed decadence in Babylon.

The plummet in tin prices was not just because of a global economic crisis but also because substitute materials had been discovered. On top of that, large supplies of tin had been discovered in other countries, like China. PN was left gasping for breath like a fish flung from its bowl onto the living room floor.

The central government, which for years had received royalties and dividends worth billions of rupiah, suddenly acted as if our small island didn't belong to it. It looked the other way when the people of Belitong screamed over unjust compensation for their mass dismissal. Belitong Island, once sparkling blue like millions of comb jellies, had become as dull as a drifting ghost ship—dark, abandoned, and alone.

The ones hit hardest were, of course, the staff living in the Estate. It wasn't just because they lost their positions and image but also because they had long been settled in an organized feudalistic mentality, and all of a sudden they were poor, unprotected by the system.

Luxurious PN guesthouses in Java now had to be traded for cultivating, climbing, fishing, digging, trapping, prospecting, and diving to support their families. Mahar's story about the whispering Paleolithic Lemurian paintings in the cave that warned a large power would fall in Belitong had finally come true. That large power was PN Timah. *Lemures*: the banished spirits that rise again. An anachronism befell the residents of the Estate. They searched for food in the forests and down in the river, living as primitively as the ancient Malays had.

Because they were unused to hardships—not to mention the burden of their uncompromising children, who were unwilling to lower their standard of living while they studied at expensive private universities in Jakarta—the staff were under a lot of stress. It wasn't uncommon for them to end up suffering strokes, heart conditions, or sudden death. They had dropout children and mountains of debt. They were choking on their silver spoons.

Those incapable of accepting reality lived lives marred by self-deception. They walked tall with false pride, showing off power and wealth that had been taken from them. They became the butt of coffee-stall jokes. They didn't last long. They soon checked in to Zaal Batu, the mental hospital on Bangka Island.

The greatness of the PN School vanished into the earth's stomach. A large number of students left the school or left Belitong Island altogether with their families, returning to their places of origin. Besides, what did they care? Belitong was not their homeland. Let it become a ghost island. Let the natives bear the consequences. What remained of the PN School students was handed over to the state schools in Tanjong Pandan.

The Estate was abandoned. At night its Victorian-style homes, its fairy-tale wonderland, were pitch-black. The dense foliage of the banyan trees umbrellaed the main road as if they were breeding grounds for evil spirits, poised to prey on all that passed beneath. Artificial lakes became homes to monitor lizards.

In 1998, the people of Indonesia demanded reformation. Brave students brought down President Suharto, who had been in power for thirty-two years. His New Order regime had come to an end.

The people of Belitong felt the Estate had been protected by the New Order regime and immediately assumed it to be ownerless. One night, inspired by the chaos in Jakarta, thousands of people attacked the Estate.

The natives—whose property had been destroyed, whose land had been seized, who had withheld their resentment for dozens of years—looted the luxurious homes in the residential area. The PN Special Police ran for their lives. People tore down walls, pulled off roof tiles, caught geese, knocked down fences, stole doors, ripped off window frames, broke anything made of glass they came across, pried up flooring, took curtains and ran with them.

The NO ENTRY FOR THOSE WITHOUT THE RIGHT signs were taken down and brought home like souvenir chunks of the Berlin Wall. Some angry plunderers took a break to sit on a large chesterfield sofa and eat at the expensive terra-cotta table, pretending to be the staff before they went back to plundering.

The home of the highest PN official, which stood gloriously like a castle at the peak of Samak Mountain with a spectacular view of the South China Sea, was ransacked until it collapsed. The biggest power generator in Asia—called the IC—was burned until nothing was left of it.

The great PN Hospital also was smashed to smithereens. Medicine lay scattered on the street. Wheelchairs and examination tables were taken home. At the time, I could smell something putrid; it was trays of Revenol. It was the stench of riches and neglect of the poor.

The looting lasted for days. Telephone wires were rolled up. Live high-voltage electric cables were cut with axes, resulting in mini-fireworks like a meteor shower. The dredges were sawed to pieces and sold by the kilogram. A strong and arrogant dynasty had fallen.

The strange thing was that the native inhabitants were now free to mine tin wherever they pleased. They dug up tin in their own backyards and sold it like sweet potatoes at a tin market they set up. In the past, that action would have been considered *subversive* by PN.

The natives sifted tin with their bare hands. They even opened new schools, and more children like Lintang were saved. In Belitong Island, it wasn't a giant corporation or the government that succeeded in restoring education as a basic human right for every citizen. It was the poor people themselves.

47 ✿ DON'T GIVE UP

Our school stood firm for a few years after we left it. It proved that old cliché, *What doesn't kill you will only make you stronger.*

Look at us again: We survived the fierce Mister Samadikun's threats, we withstood the dredges that wanted to wipe away our school, and we survived the economic difficulties that strangled us on a daily basis. But above all, we survived the most immediate of threats: the threat of ourselves, our disbelief in the power of education.

Our low self-esteem was acute, a consequence of being systematically discriminated against and marginalized for years by a corporation that had penetrated every aspect of our lives. That pressure made us terrified of competing and afraid to dream. But our two special friends—Mahar and Lintang—gave us courage, and our two teachers—Bu Mus and Pak Harfan—were the guardians who helped us prevail in whatever difficulties came our way.

But in the end, our school finally lost. We were brought to our knees by education's strongest, cruelest, most merciless and hardest-to-fight invisible enemy. It gnawed away at the students, teachers, and even the education system itself. That enemy was materialism.

The current world no longer saw school as Pak Harfan had seen it. To him, knowledge was about self-value, and education was a celebration of the Creator, a celebration of humanity, one that stood for dignity, the joy of learning, and the light of civilization. He knew that school didn't have to be a means toward getting to the next level, making money, getting rich. School nowadays was part of a capitalistic plan to get power and fame.

Because of that, there were no longer any parents who wanted to send their children to a Muhammadiyah village school. The building leaned farther toward the ground. The sacred beam that Pak Harfan himself had carried back when he first built the school—the beam we had carved our heights on—was leaning to the point where it was beyond help.

One sad evening, after the rain fell, a seven-layer rainbow formed a half circle in the sky, beginning at the headwaters of the Marang River, then dropping itself into the mangrove forest near the Linggang Bridge. The moment that rainbow appeared, the sacred beam leaned a bit farther and then fell. Unbeknownst to anyone, a legendary school, almost 120 years old, collapsed. Along with it collapsed the stage where our childhood drama, Laskar Pelangi, had been performed.

After our school collapsed, Bu Mus stopped teaching in order to be a full-time seamstress. But teaching was her true calling. I have never seen anyone who loves the profession as much as Bu Mus, and consequently I have never seen anyone as happy with her job as she was. She later decided to go back to teaching and was hired as a state employee at a state elementary school. But she admits that she has never met students as phenomenal as Lintang and Mahar.

My stomach hurt from holding back laughter when I saw the coolie forcing himself to carry so many goods outside of Sinar Perkasa. Many years had passed, but I immediately recognized Samson. He never wanted his macho image to deteriorate. He tried very hard to make it all the way to the pickup truck and put all of the goods in the back. He walked like a gorilla, just as he had when I'd kicked him in the groin those many years ago: when he'd enlarged his chest muscles with a halved tennis ball.

Samson received some money from the chubby woman who owned the pickup truck. He said thank you, nodded politely, then returned to the store. He handed the money over to the shop owner, who then fanned the money over the merchandise for luck. The wife of the shop owner shook her head. I recognized the shop owner from the shape of his head: it was A Kiong, his head still like a tin can.

But his fate was much better than mine. At least he had a wife. In fact, his wife was his former archrival, Sahara.

Whenever they had free time, Samson, A Kiong, and Sahara would visit Harun. Harun still told the same story about his three-striped cat giving birth to three kittens—also with three stripes—on the third day of the month. Just as before, Sahara listened faithfully and wholeheartedly. If, before, Harun had been a child trapped in an adult's body, he was now an adult trapped in a child's mind.

Harun routinely visited Trapani, who had returned from Zaal Batu. He'd leave for Trapani's house, which was forty kilometers away, every Friday afternoon on his bicycle. He always departed at three o'clock.

Harun's aspirations hadn't changed a bit—he still wanted to be Trapani when he grew up. A lot of times Harun got sad about his unfulfilled dream, I think because Trapani was an adult and Harun was already old.

If you were to judge our situations now, the shattered aspirations were everywhere. There were mine and Harun's; Trapani's, to be a teacher; and Lintang's, to be a mathematician. Clearly, A Kiong had forgotten about his hope to hide his tin-can head under a captain's hat, and his wife, Sahara, had failed to become a women's rights activist.

The saddest, in my opinion, was Samson. He hadn't even been able to achieve his simple goal of becoming a ticket ripper at the cinema. He had always been the most pessimistic among us. I have seen it everywhere: the most unfortunate in this world are the pessimistic.

Meanwhile, Syahdan was still chasing his dream to be an actor, but he was barely scraping by in Jakarta. He had joined a theater group, but the problem was, in Indonesia people rarely watch theater. Syahdan was like a lost boy in Jakarta. We never heard anything about him.

As for Mahar, he never let go of his dream to be a white-magic shaman. But just as before, he didn't take a problem like this to heart. He remained convinced that the future belongs to God and he would faithfully await his circular fate. Moreover, he was busy arranging a patent for a traditional children's toy: the *pinang hantu* leaf that we used to play with during the rainy season.

Flo, Laskar Pelangi's last addition, had never disclosed her aspiration. We later found out she married the BRI teller, her fellow member of the now-defunct Societeit de Limpai. (After the Pirate Island expedition yielded a ridiculous message from Tuk Bayan Tula, Mahar, as the leader of the Societeit, had suspended all Societeit activities.)

During our school days, Kucai always was the underdog

when it came to grades. He was always the victim of our insults for his low marks. He subscribed to the swan-shaped number two for math. The bat-shaped number three permanently occupied his slot for natural sciences. He and Harun were the lowest-ranked in the class. But look at him now—he, who we had assumed was the stupidest—was the only follower of the Prophet Muhammad from our class who had reached his aspirations.

Kucai was a social creature who, from an early age, understood our culture and how the value system in our society worked. If a populist is skilled enough to represent himself as a defender, he has a chance to be politically successful. So from the very beginning Kucai maintained his most prominent qualities: he was a populist, a compulsive debater, a shameless know-it-all. Eventually he became a candidate for a political party and then successfully realized his plan A, to have a position in the House of Representatives. So who was the real genius, then? Lintang or Kucai? Lintang, always number one, or Kucai, always at the bottom?

When Kucai was elected as a representative, he invited us to celebrate at a coffee stall. He expressed his gratitude to us, especially to Lintang, who Kucai said actually had been his inspiration.

"Lintang, my friend, thank you for making me the way I am," Kucai said in his third-class politician style.

His eyes were glassy. He looked at Lintang sadly, but Lintang's eyes seemed to be fixated on Harun.

From a materialistic aspect, we couldn't say that the futures of the Laskar Pelangi members were secure. But we felt very lucky to have had the opportunity to study at the poor school with the extraordinary teachers who made us appreciate education, fall in love with school, and celebrate the joy of learning.

Who we are today was shaped at that school long ago. But

the most valuable lesson from those magical years was one that Pak Harfan had taught us, and I could see it on every member of Laskar Pelangi's face. We had learned the spirit of giving as much as possible, not taking as much as possible. That mentality made us always grateful, even in poverty. The poor Pak Harfan and Bu Mus had given me the most beautiful childhood, friendships, and rich souls, something priceless. Perhaps I am mistaken, but in my opinion, this is actually the breath of education and the soul of an institution called a school.

I felt lucky to have the opportunity to continue my education in a foreign country far from my own, and I later traveled to many places as a backpacker. Wherever I went, I was always interested in seeing how people interacted with each other in a particular social system and how they saw their lives. I enjoyed my unofficial profession as a life observer.

I met leaders of various religions. I asked them about the wisdom of life. I saw people search for peace in their lives. I also saw people depart for Mecca, India, Bethlehem, and the Himalayas, looking for peace of mind by dedicating themselves completely to a belief. I even frequently met people desperately searching for themselves, adventurers sometimes ending up with the police looking for them.

I tried to draw a conclusion from all my experiences. But apparently I didn't have to travel far; I didn't have to conquer the world or meet a variety of people. The final conclusion, the wisdom I believed, was the simple philosophy I drew from my years of learning in the Laskar Pelangi school, the school eventually blown down by the wind.

The wisdom was as simple as the humble school itself. Fate, effort, and destiny are like three blue mountains cradling humanity. Those mountains conspire with each other to create the future, and it's difficult to understand how they work together. Those who fail in some aspect of life blame it on God. They say if they are poor, it is because God made poverty their destiny. Those who are tired of trying stand still, waiting for destiny to change their fate. Those who don't want to work hard accept their fate because they believe it is unchangeable—after all, everything has already been preordained, or so they believe. So the devil's circle hems in the lazy. But what I know for sure from my experience at the poor school is that a hardworking life is like picking up fruit from a basket with a blindfold on. Whatever fruit we end up getting, at least we have fruit.

I always want to learn and to work hard. I am convinced that this is what made me finish my studies in Europe. I came back to Indonesia and worked for a telecommunications company.

When I was working at the company in 2004, a tsunami struck Aceh. Hundreds of thousands of people died. I signed up to be a volunteer and was in Aceh for three weeks.

On my way to the Aceh airport after my volunteer work, I saw a young girl wearing a *jilbab*. She stood on the side of the road holding a banner. Behind her lay a school that had been destroyed by the tsunami. Her banner read: COME ON, DON'T GIVE UP ON SCHOOL.

I was stunned. That young girl may have been a teacher, a teacher trying to collect what was left of her students in the wake of the disaster. I found myself struggling to hold back tears at the sight of her. I was moved by her strength, and at that moment I was reminded of a teacher who once told me losing a student was like losing half a soul.

Then I remembered my old promise—the promise I made back in the sixth grade when I saw Bu Mus crossing the schoolyard, protecting herself from the rain with a banana leaf as her umbrella. Deep in my little heart, I promised I would write a book for Bu Mus. The book would be my gift to her, proof that I truly appreciated and valued all she had done for us.

Two days later, in Bandung, I came home from work and began writing the book. In the following days, I smiled to myself, giggled, was touched, felt annoyed, and found myself sobbing late into the night, alone. Before I knew it, I had written hundreds of pages.

As a final touch, I felt relieved to write on the front page: *I dedicate this book to my teachers, Ibu Muslimah Hafsari and Bapak Harfan Effendy Noor, and my ten childhood best friends, the members of Laskar Pelangi.* I called it *Laskar Pelangi—The Rainbow Troops.*

Setiap warga negara
berhak mendapat pendidikan
(Undang-Undang Dasar Republik Indonesia, Pasal 33)

Every citizen has the right to an education
(Constitution of the Republic of Indonesia, Article 33)

ACKNOWLEDGMENTS

I would like to express my heartfelt thanks to Kathleen Anderson and Sarah Crichton; to Daniel Piepenbring and the rest of the team at Farrar, Straus and Giroux; to Claire Anderson-Wheeler and the team at Anderson Literary Management; and to Angie Kilbane and James Alan McPherson.

A Note About the Author

Andrea Hirata is an Indonesian writer. He was a participant in the International Writing Program at the University of Iowa in 2010. His first novel, *The Rainbow Troops* (*Laskar Pelangi*), sold more than five million copies in Indonesia, making him the country's bestselling writer of all time, as well as its first to enjoy truly international success: *The Rainbow Troops* has been published or is forthcoming in twenty-three countries and counting. An Indonesian film adaptation of *The Rainbow Troops*, released in 2008, went on to become the highest ever grossing film in the country. Hirata's work has been adapted and performed by the CityDance Ensemble in Washington, D.C., and his short story "Dry Season" has appeared in New York University's *Washington Square Review*. Hirata has written three sequels to *The Rainbow Troops*: *Sang Pemimpi* (The Dreamer), *Edensor*, and *Maryama Karpov*. He lives in Indonesia.